Autumn Violets

ˈkræk,dʒə:

Crackjaw Publishing
Guelph, ON
www.crackjawpublishing.com

Library and Archives Canada Cataloguing in Publication

Reilly, Nuala, 1975-
    Autumn violets / Nuala Reilly.

ISBN 978-0-9782026-9-9

    I. Title.

PS8635.E455A87 2009   C813'.6   C2009-904276-2

Acknowledgements/Dedication

As every good writer knows, to find the time to bring your story to the page, there are many people who must be willing to share in the experience with donations of their time, their expertise and their patience.

I would like to thank Deb Herald and Cindy Hutchins for their unerring support and editing assistance. For them to take a chance on working with a relative unknown was appreciated more than I could ever express.

I would also like to thank Kelley Armstrong and Piers Anthony for taking time from their busy schedules with their own work to talk to an up-and-comer who was looking for some mentoring.

To Jolene, Kelly, Kathy and Suzy; your enthusiasm over the first draft was invaluable, and your friendship and laughter made it easy for me to keep going even when frustrations set in. To Sarah, I want to thank you for years and years of conversation about sisters, weddings and men. Without you Jaye would not have had much of a voice at all.

To my own sisters, Niamh, Roisin and Bridget; thank you for all the years of good ol' sisterly fights (and make ups). You are each an inspiration to me in your own ways, and I can't imagine not having you in my life to keep me grounded and to be my sounding boards.

I would also like to thank Hags, Craig and certain other writer friends I've met through the years for inspiring me to keep on writing, and for practically daring me to do something more with my work than the newspaper articles I became so comfortable with.

Last but definitely not least, I am forever indebted to my wonderful husband Shawn and my children. You put up with the late night writing sessions, the elation of a good day, the emotional upheaval of a bad day, and never lost faith in my abilities. I am but a product of the support you gave to me, and I wholeheartedly thank you for giving me the room to find this part of myself.

This book is dedicated, with great love and admiration, to the memory of Bill "Papa Smurf" Moffat. You may have lost your battle, but your valiant fight was an inspiration. Rest in Peace.

Chapter One

Monday morning, Moira's alarm went off early, as usual. She forced her arm out of the warm blankets and tapped the snooze button with her finger before defiantly turning back over. The ringing of the buzzer sounded in her head even after the noise had abated, though in her head it sounded like *crap crap crap crap* over and over again. There was no question about it, the natural chipper mood she had in the morning at the thought of heading downstairs to her beloved bakery was gone, replaced with the sour feeling of dread at knowing what the day had in store—another dress fitting for her sister's wedding, the fifth one in as many weeks. She was expected at the house before nine in order to be there before the dressmaker, Lara. Moira hated the thought of pulling that dreadful dress onto her body yet again, but she steeled herself into getting out of bed with the knowledge that this would be the second to last time she would ever wear it before burning the shit out of it in triumph the day after the wedding was over. Smirking at that, she headed into her bathroom, stubbing her toe in the process.

"Shit!" She yowled, and grabbed her foot. She hopped into the room and leaned on the counter for support. Wincing, she picked off the piece of skin that had come loose from the collision and flicked it into the garbage in disgust. She turned to the sink to brush her teeth. So frustrated was she that no sooner had she begun to scrub away that she stabbed herself in the cheek with her toothbrush.

Moira closed her eyes in fury. Was nothing going to go right today? Ignoring the pain in her toe and now in her mouth she leaned over the sink and spit out the toothpaste, rinsing her mouth and tapping the excess water from the bristles.

She leaned over the tub to turn on the tap for a shower. No way in hell would she show up looking anything less than perfectly groomed, not if her stunning sister and those two twig-like friends were going to be there. Already, at five foot nine, Moira felt like a large clumsy ox next to the pixie-like features of Sloane and her friends. To arrive looking less than put together was just like asking for a paper cut between the fingers with a little salt thrown on for effect.

Ten minutes later she was back in her bedroom, trying to figure out what to wear that would look nice and put together but not like she was trying too hard. The mere process was making her even angrier, since she realized that there was no way that a smart, successful woman such like herself should even give a shit anyway. It wasn't like she and Sloane were the type of sisters who'd ooh and ahh over each other's outfits.

She moved a pile of laundry off of a chair and stopped dead in the middle of the room. It was a sock—a man's sock. Fucking Mark must have left it here when he moved out. Moira grabbed it and threw it into the garbage, wondering what the hell else could possibly go wrong this morning. Fucking Mark had moved out a month and a half ago, after she had caught him in her own bed with some other girl, and she was still finding little things of his everywhere. She wondered how the hell he had thought he was going to get away with screwing around on her, when the apartment was right above her bakery. *Men really are stupid*, Moira thought. Let their dicks do all the thinking, so that sleeping with someone one floor away from your supposed girlfriend seemed both plausible and possible. She shook her head to abandon that futile line of thought before she once again started to wonder just how long and how many women had been there before she had caught him and thrown him out. It was her best friend Jaye who that very day had started calling him Fucking Mark, and to Moira that couldn't be more appropriate.

Finally she found some nice jeans and a clean pretty top that weren't too casual and put them on. Moira gathered her keys, her coat and her purse and let herself out the door and down the stairs into the morning sunlight.

While she made her way up the hill from the downtown area, Moira paid little attention to the various store windows of this trendy part of town where she lived and worked. The quaint older buildings did nothing to capture her attention today, nor did the unseasonably warm autumn weather. She was cranky, her toe hurt, her mouth was sore, and she was feeling bruised from the sight of that sock on the chair. All she wanted to do was get to the house, put on the horrible dress and go back to her shop so she could lose herself in her kitchen, where she was in control of everything. Moira kicked an errant stone that had loosed itself from the side of one of the buildings, forgetting until she made contact that this was the same foot with the sore toe. Gritting her teeth, she started to walk a little faster.

"Stupid rock ... stupid foot ... *fucking mark!* This is the worst morning in the history of bad mornings and *I do not* want to go to this stupid *fucking* dress fitting again."

The barrage of obscenities flowed from her freely, startling two older women in matching track suits who were out walking their dogs down the hill towards her. Moira didn't even care. She didn't bother to look at them as they passed her. Hearing them mutter something about rude youth, she pushed past them and kept her head down as she headed farther up the hill.

***

In another part of town, in another apartment, Jack Wallace was also having a bad Monday morning. He had gotten right up with his alarm today, determined not to be late, and gone straight into the bathroom to shave. Jack loaded his face up with foam, filled his sink with hot water and began drawing the razor across his stubble. His jaw was clenched as he went through the motions. The weekend's activities had done nothing to alleviate the stress he had been feeling.

Sure, it had been fun to go out to the bar and meet the cute blonde who had been working there. Of course he had not minded walking her to her car after the bar had closed. He had damn near been relieved for her to shyly offer him to join her at her place for the proverbial night cap, which meant sex. The only problem was that these one night stands didn't ease his tension as they used to, and getting back to his apartment after two in the morning was doing nothing to help his arrival time at work. One of these days his boss was going to say something about it. Jack grinned at the memory of the girl; she had been very enthusiastic.

"Dammit," he swore to his reflection as he nicked his cheek. He stared at himself for a moment, watching the blood droplet from the cut slide down his face and turn the foam beneath it pink. This was no way to start a day. He carefully finished his shave, rinsed out the razor and the sink and attached a small piece of toilet paper to the cut. Jack went back to his room to dress and then into his kitchen, where he grabbed a muffin from his fridge. He didn't really want to eat, though, so he brought it into his living room and set it on the small table by the couch before sitting down and picking up the phone. He punched in the numbers for his father's room at the hospice. Jack found himself picking at the paper around the muffin while the phone rang on and on. His eyes flickered to the clock on the wall, then back at the phone. No answer. His father, Kevin, always picked up the phone in the morning. It was pretty unusual to let it ring like this. After the ninth ring, Jack hung up and dialed the number for the switchboard, secretly hoping that he had just caught his father while he was in the bathroom and that there was nothing further wrong with him today. After only three rings, someone picked up.

"Good morning, River Bend Centre. How may I help you?" Jack recognized Grace's voice right away. She was one of the main nurses on the day shift, and over the last few months he had become familiar with the light breathy tone of her voice.

"Good morning, Grace. It's Jack Wallace here. I was trying to get a hold of my dad, only he's not answering the phone this morning. Is everything okay with him there?" Jack seemed unaware that he was twisting the phone cord around his finger, until a slight twinge made him look. The end of his finger was turning a deep red. He untwisted it while he listened to Grace shuffling what sounded like papers in front of her.

"Hold on for a moment, would you?" she requested, and then music filled the lines, annoying Jack still further.

Less than two minutes later she was back.

"Jack? Your dad is doing just fine. He's just a little tired out from the weekend. It looks like he turned the ringer on his phone off, probably just to get a little more sleep. There's no change reported in his notes here since you were in Saturday, so there's nothing to worry about."

"Great, thanks. Tell him I'll come see him later," Jack said, not without sarcasm.

She must not have detected his tone because her answer was so cheerful.

"Okay. Ask him to show you the notes we've been getting." She chuckled.

"What kind of notes?" Jack asked her.

"Oh, he leaves us food orders for the tube—steak and lobster, chocolate mousse, things like that. Or he leaves notes from the tube, like 'my host and I do not get along, kindly reassign me elsewhere'. Your Dad's a character." She chuckled.

"I know ... thanks Grace."

"Sure thing, have a good day," Grace told him before she hung up the phone.

Jack clunked his own receiver back into its cradle and tried to smile at the thought of his father teasing the staff. Over the weekend the team had hooked his father Kevin up to a feeding tube, since he wasn't keeping down much food, and the ensuing arguments with staff over the very presence of it and the recent change in pain medications had left Kevin worn out and tired. The continuous dealings and fall-outs from managing end stage pancreatic cancer were not easy, and Jack knew that his father didn't care much for being "handled".

He was running late now, since he had called twice and waited to get an actual person on the phone. Though he was pleased to hear that his Dad was managing okay and that his sense of humour was still intact, he wasn't much in the mood for Grace's stories this morning. Jack grabbed his briefcase and keys from the hall table. He grabbed his jacket from the closet, picked off the corner of tissue from his face and flicked it into the garbage by his door before locking up.

Jack left the building and got into his car, thinking that he was going to need coffee before getting to work today, whether he was running late or not. He crossed town without paying much attention and pulled in to a spot in front of The Bean Post, his favourite local coffee shop at the top of the hill to the downtown area. He went inside, grimaced at the line and took up his spot at the back, shoving his hands into his pockets. There was a piece of paper in the right one, which he pulled out.

"Sarah Roberts ... call me," it read, with a number and a lipstick kiss underneath the line of writing. Jack crumpled it up and threw it into the garbage when he finally got to the front of the line. He ordered his coffee, not noticing the pretty young girl smiling at him from behind the counter. Sarah had been fun on the weekend, but he had no intentions of calling her again. With all the shit going on with his father, the last thing Jack wanted was a girlfriend. Of course his father would be disappointed; he thought that a girlfriend, or one day even a wife, was the precise thing his son lacked, but Jack hadn't needed a woman in his life for a long time now and wasn't about to change that. He had no trouble meeting women when he wanted to, so why fix what wasn't broken. Jack left the shop still lost in thought and didn't even see the woman barreling around the corner towards him.

They crashed together hard, with Jack's coffee taking the brunt of the force and covering them both with hot, dark, angry looking splotches.

"Shit, sorry," she said when Jack jumped back with a yelp.

"What the hell are you doing?" he yelled. "I'm going to be late for work now." No need to tell this woman that he was already running late.

"Hey! I said sorry. It was an accident, jeez," she shouted at him.

Jack took a closer look at the woman he had collided with. She was tall, almost as tall as he was and looked both angry and upset. It occurred to him that she was attractive, but he was not really in the mood for flirting when covered in hot beverage.

"Wait here, I'll get napkins," she instructed.

Jack watched her dash off into the shop and then saw her in the big picture window grabbing a bunch of napkins from the holder on one of the tables. Running around like that she looked even prettier, if not a little crazy. She must have been totally preoccupied. While he couldn't fault her for that, he wondered what a nice-looking girl like that would have to worry about. *And anyway,* he thought, *who walks with their head down?*

"No, no, don't worry," he said when she came back out to him and tried to pat him down with the dry, useless napkins. He noticed that she smelled of vanilla.

"I really am sorry," she told him.

"It's okay. It was my fault, my mind is somewhere else." His voice was softer now than it had been moments ago. It was hard to stay annoyed when she was trying so hard to dry him off and apologize.

11

"Must be going around," she muttered. They locked gazes for a moment. Jack found himself a little flustered as he looked into the dark pools of her emerald eyes. For the briefest of moments, the world stopped as the two regarded each other. Still thinking that she must have been little nuts, Jack kept his gaze still and unbroken. Those emerald eyes seemed to take in Jack's features, and he almost felt that he was being transported to somewhere safe and calm, the morning rush of people fading into a blur of colours and random faces. They were standing in such a close proximity to one another that their breathing seemed in sync, and darts of electricity almost danced between them. Then, just as quick as it had come on, the moment ended, and the two said quick further apologies and turned in opposite directions to get on with their days.

***

Moira headed off once again towards her mother's house. Her bad mood had lifted somewhat from the collision. It had startled her that she had felt a bolt of attraction to the handsome stranger whose morning drink she had wasted with her single-mindedness. She brushed thoughts of him out of her head, however, when she stood before her childhood home.

It was a tall, two-and-a-half story red brick century home with pale yellow embellishments in wood to mark out the contours to their greatest advantage. She knew it had been a miracle for her mother to have kept the house after dad left. Angela had picked up another job baking birthday cakes in addition to her teaching job, and she had taken in her mother, Siobhan to help with the large mortgage. If it had been tough, Angela had never let on, and Moira's memories of this time were joyful, with none of the bitterness she may have felt from losing a parent.

Shaking out of her reverie, Moira glanced at the cars in the driveway. *Great,* she thought. Katie and Michelle were already here. She didn't know how she was going to stand another couple of hours with her sister's friends. She groaned and went into the house.

"Moira's here!" The shout emanated from the kitchen.

Sloane stuck her blonde head around the corner of the door frame.

"You're la—" she started to say, but stopped and stared instead at Moira's clothes.

"What the hell happened?" she shrieked. "You're covered in ... what is that?"

"Coffee, and I don't want to talk about it. Do you have something I can wear?"

"Ask Mom, my stuff is too small," She said and disappeared off back into the kitchen.

Great, another reason to not want to be here! She hated how a simple comment like that from her sister could throw her into a panic over her looks. Wasn't it bad enough that Sloane always looked fantastic? It was just like her to make such a statement and not see how she was being hurtful with it, which of course made it something that Moira never discussed with her. How do you tell your sister she's upsetting you, when none of it was ever contrived? Sloane wasn't mean on purpose, just a little self involved.

Moira poked her head into the kitchen and took in the tableau with amusement. It seemed her Grandmother, Siobhan, was holding court from her wheelchair in the corner. The loss of her abilities never seemed to have an effect on her manner of overseeing with authority all major functions in the house. Her mother bustled about, laying down mugs, spoons, plates of biscuits and little treats, and engaging in conversation. Sloane and her two friends, Katie and Michelle, were sitting at the other end of the table from Siobhan and giggling over something. Stepping all the way into the room, Moira watched the conversations grind to a halt when they all turned and looked at her.

"Ma," Moira said.

"What, dear?" Angela replied, the only one who wasn't staring at her.

13

"Can I borrow a shirt?"

"Sure love, top drawer of my dresser." She looked up and gasped at Moira's appearance. "You better set that to soak before it stains."

"Put some salt in the water," her grandmother piped from the corner.

Moira ran up the stairs to her mother's room and changed her shirt to one of her mother's pale blouses. She stole a moment to regard herself in the mirror. She didn't think she looked so bad with her shoulder length brown hair in a ponytail. Sure, she wasn't willowy like Sloane, but she wasn't fat either. She shrugged at her reflection; no wonder that guy didn't look twice. But then again, she did dump coffee all over him. No time to think about that now; there were hideous dresses to try on. Moira grabbed her soiled shirt in a bunch and walked back down the stairs. She bypassed the kitchen and went into the laundry room, where she filled the sink with warm water and rubbed some soap into the stain, and then went back into the kitchen to meet with the demanding faces of her family.

"What happened?" her mother asked.

"Nothing much, I just bumped into someone and spilled coffee all over us both."

"I'll bet it was a guy," Sloane said. "You would have said if it was a woman. Was he cute?"

"Put the kettle on," Siobhan muttered from her chair in the corner.

"Does it matter?" Moira asked.

"Cute always matters," Sloane stated.

"Cute doesn't figure in when you pour hot coffee on a guy's chest. I wouldn't call that a prime opportunity to look for a date."

"Who's putting on that kettle?" Siobhan wondered from her post.

"Oh, don't be so pissy. You're still upset about Mark." Sloane stared at Moira.

"Shut up."

Angela stood up and held her arms out between the

14

two girls. "Peace, peace."

Moira sat down on a chair in a huff. Trust Sloane to find some way to bring up Mark. She didn't want to think about him again this morning. It was bad enough that she had let him move in with her so fast, to the chagrin of her family, but to let herself be sucked in so well to his world of deceit and duplicity ... it was not her finest moment, and Sloane liked reminding her perfect sister of this one lapse in judgment in her otherwise well thought out life.

Moira, making up her mind to devote no more time to relationships past, sat back in her chair and watched the activity of the ladies around her. Katie was threading little bits of satin ribbon through the tiny pouches that she and Michelle had filled with silver wrapped candy. Angela was talking to Siobhan non-stop in a chipper tone that made Moira giggle when she caught her grandma rolling her eyes from across the room. Sloane was pouring tea into the tea-cups, and Katie was fidgeting in her chair with the deep pockets of her long skirt in between pouches. It was just about nine-thirty in the morning. The seamstress would be here soon.

***

By the time Jack pulled into the parking lot at work it was just before nine. He hadn't even gone home to change. The coffee that covered his front had dried in the car to a pale beige splotch that he didn't care to mask. He noticed Evan looking up from his office when he passed by his door. Evan pointed to the clock. Jack pointed to his shirt. He knew that his boss wouldn't press him on the lateness just yet; there was already enough on his plate. Further down the hall various employees averted meeting his eyes after letting theirs lie on his clothing for a fraction of a moment. He heard a few snickers, though, and knew that people were wondering what had happened. When you work in a small office, everyone soon came to know everyone else's business. Most days Jack would have been the first to make a loud

15

joke about his attire, but today his heart wasn't in it. All he really wanted to do was get in his office and get to work. He walked past one desk, and the new young man seated there didn't even try to look down or ignore it like everyone else. Jack attempted to smile back at his loud laughter, even though he thought it probably made him look weird. Forced smiles made him look a bit like a deranged clown.

Jack let himself into his office and sat down to turn on his computer. He was a graphic artist for an advertising company that dealt in internet ads and computerized campaigns. It wasn't a bad job, but it required a lot of attention to detail and, with his father's failing health, that aspect had been lacking a bit. Even so, he was one of the most talented in his field. On his good days, Jack had an eye for detail and a way of presenting his work with subtlety and panache.

The hours slid by while he punched at the keys and glanced at the work still to be done in his inbox. At 10:45 Evan poked his head in the door.

"Got a second?"

"Sure, boss."

Evan came in and sat down in the other chair, opposite Jack.

"How's your dad?"

"He's pretty much the same," Jack replied.

"Sorry to hear that." He paused for a moment, and his gaze fell to Jack's shirt. He raised a quizzical eyebrow. Jack shrugged.

"I had a talk with the CEO yesterday. We're going to go ahead and hire a creative director here."

Jack looked up. That had his attention. This was the kind of opportunity he was hoping for when he had started here four years ago.

"I want to put you down for it Jack, but I'm worried about you. Look, Jack, I know that your father is taking most of your attention right now, but you're letting it get to you here. You've got to find some way to turn it off when you're at work. That last design you did had a lot of flaws in it. We caught them before they went out to the client, but Jack, we can't cover for you. I know you can do this."

"I don't know what to say. I'll try not to let you down. Oh, and about this morning ... "

"No need. I saw your shirt. Did you at least get her number?" Evan grinned.

"Ha ha," Jack retorted. A momentary image of the woman from that morning passed through his thoughts.

Evan left the office, and Jack buckled back down to work, pondering his words. A promotion—now there was something to get excited over, but not if his work was slipping.

It was almost alien to be excited over ... anything. The last six months of his life had been nearly consumed with the health of his father, to the exclusion of everything else.

Jack's father Kevin had been diagnosed with pancreatic cancer almost six months ago. It began with persistent problems in his back and abdomen. At first, Kevin had shrugged it off, saying that it was due to the physical labor that was part and parcel of running the gas station. Besides, he wasn't young like he used to be, so filling cars and propane tanks was a little trickier than it used to be. Sure, he had young men working for him that could afford him the pleasure of standing proud in his doorway and chatting with the regulars, but Kevin was never one to leave work to someone else. Though he had always encouraged Jack to do more with his life than run the station, he never intimated that his honest job was anything but satisfying and a pleasure to him.

The first few appointments had left doctors bewildered. They checked his yellowed complexion for jaundice or kidney problems and sent him to a chiropractor for his back pain. Then they sent him to a specialist for the upper GI series, an endoscopic ultrasound and the biopsy to confirm what they suspected; advanced pancreatic cancer.

The crippling blow of the diagnosis was handled with remarkable poise by Kevin, and brute defiance and

17

crushing emotion by Jack. Kevin just seemed to accept that he would not survive this, while Jack blustered and asked hundreds of questions.

The surgery had been scheduled right away, and the chemo and radiation treatments followed. Kevin fast became a favourite with the nurses and the staff at the hospital.

He often made jokes, laughing and cajoling his way through a process that must have been both painful and frustrating. He never complained, even when two months later a PET scan showed that the cancer had spread to include his lymph nodes and several other organs. Jack cried in the cold doctor's chair while Kevin just asked to be recommended to a local hospice where he could end his days close to his son, with a minimum of pain and discomfort. He was given four months to live. The move was made as fast as the changes to his physique. The beloved gas station was quietly sold to a large company that signed an agreement to keep the current employees on staff out of respect for Kevin. His hair fell out, eyebrows, eyelashes and all. He became a shell of the grand man that he once had been, but for the twinkle still shining in his eyes.

Jack spent most of his time doing one of three things: working, visiting his father or finding a brief temporary release from the stressors of his waking hours in the arms of a woman. Never anyone specific, never anyone special—he didn't have time for relationships. If Kevin noticed this disturbing behavior of his son, he didn't always comment on it. He chose instead to fill their hours together with plans for Jack's future. The advancements he would make at work, the house he would buy when he tired of that little apartment, the wife he would meet and the children he would have. Jack knew that his father sensed that he was never really listening. His father's eyes always held such vacant pain, and he could imagine him seeing far beyond the here and now, witnessing some exquisite moment of heartache too delicate for this world. Still, their time passed easy enough, and they talked about everything from politics to music. Considering that it had just been the two of them since Jack's mother had died in a car accident years ago, the relationship between them was strong like that between the oldest of friends.

The loud beep of the intercom on his phone snapped Jack back into the present. He was needed in the conference room for an update meeting on the Brisk account. "I'm on my way," he reported to Rebecca, the office administrator.

"No rush," she said. "You still have five minutes."

"Thanks," he replied.

He groped around his desk for the papers and disks he would need for the demonstration of the campaign so far and fumbled for his jacket from the hook behind the door to hide his blemished shirt. Leaving his office in a rush, he spared a quick glance at the fading photo of his parents that was displayed beside his computer screen. His mother had beautiful green eyes. The realization struck him and caused him to pause in the doorway to the office. It was the eyes. That was what had taken away his anger and frustration at the collision this morning. That was the one thing about the crazy girl on the sidewalk. When she had looked up at him, her eyes were almost the exact same shade as those of his mother. He smiled to himself as he headed down the hall.

What a relief! he thought. It wasn't that he had found her attractive when their eyes had locked. It was just that she had those same eyes. Rebecca winked at Jack as he walked past her. Maybe he had better lay off the women for a while. With the late night last night, cutting his cheek thinking about it this morning, dealing with feet-staring crazy girls who ran into him and flirty nurses at the River Bend Centre, he was just as well to stick to what he knew and avoid women all together. *Well, maybe not all together,* he thought as one of the very cute girls from research handed him a Styrofoam cup with a flirtatious smile. He was still a man after all. But even in a town as small as

19

Fayette, the chances of running into the girl with the green eyes again had to be slim to none ... didn't it?

Chapter Two

At 9:30am sharp, Moira was just finishing her cup of tea while the ladies of the kitchen continued chatting, when Lara the seamstress poked her nose in the front door.

"Anyone home?" she hollered.

"In the kitchen Lara, need a hand?" Angela replied.

"If you don't mind," she said.

Moira looked at her sister, who was making no motions to show that she had even heard, let alone cared to help lift in the three heavy garment bags in Lara's trunk.

"Oh, let me," she said. Sloane barely looked up.

Angela gave her daughter a smile, and the two of them headed out to assist Lara in her task. They followed her out to her beat up old pick-up, and each hoisted one of the bags from the behind the driver's seat. The three ladies lumbered toward the house and, once inside, laid the bags horizontally over the various sofas and armchairs in the living room. Laughter came streaming from the kitchen, where Sloane could be heard teasing her friends over a second pot of tea.

Moira watched Sloane bounce out of the kitchen, through the dining room and into the living room to join her mother and herself.

"Well, are they done?" Sloane asked Lara.

"You bet. Did you want to see them on the ladies one more time?" Lara barely disguised the laughter from her voice.

"Of course." Sloane looked at the girls, now all assembled with her. "Well … gettem on, girls!"

Katie, Michelle and Moira each picked up a bag and unsheathed a dark turquoise creation that was breathtaking in the worst sense of the word. They shuffled off to various rooms of the house, with Moira staking claim to the downstairs bathroom. Once she had the door closed behind her, she again took the opportunity to drink in the monstrosity. It was a full skirted, empire waisted, bow and lace covered sateen nightmare. She couldn't tell if she hated the color or the design more. As she tugged the dress over her shoulders, she decided it was the design.

"Oh hell!" she exclaimed when she turned to face the mirror. The dress managed to rob her of her boobs while making her hips and bum appear larger than ever.

She headed back to the living room for the final inspection.

Siobhan was now sitting in the doorway between the living room and the dining room.

"That looks like gangrene," she commented as the ladies entered from three different directions.

"Oh, Nana, it's fantastic!" Sloane howled. "I have never seen anything more perfect. I only wish I had been bold enough to go for it in metallic melon. Now *that* would have been memorable."

Katie and Michelle collapsed in a fit of laughter and tulle. They actually agreed that this whole idea of the purposeful tacky gown was genius.

"They look diseased. That's not clever, Sloane dear, that's contagious," Siobhan quipped.

"Mum," Angela intoned. "It's her day, give her a break."

"Oh, whistch! Sloane knows I'm teasing her."

"You're going to upset Lara."

"Don't mind me," Lara piped from the armchair. "It's not my job to judge, just give the bride what she orders. Sloane, the last of the hemming is done, so the dresses can be kept at my shop, and I'll steam them and bring them back the night before the wedding, unless you wanted anything changed, of course."

22

"No, no they're perfect, Lara. Thank you," Sloane told her with a smile while Moira rolled her eyes behind her sister's back.

When the girls had all changed back to their normal clothes and Lara had departed, the company of women made their way back to the kitchen for more tea and some sandwiches. Angela's eyes began to mist over.

"Here we go," muttered Siobhan under her breath.

"I just can't believe my baby is getting married in under a month! I'm so proud of you, honey."

"Thanks, Mum. Stop getting so misty eyed. It's not like I'm going to the dark side of the moon. We'll just be seven streets away," Sloane reminded her. "Besides, you have Moira to keep you company."

Moira looked up. She managed to smile at her sister, though she really wanted to spit at her. *Ooh, there's an idea. Hock up a real good loogie and spit it right into her perfect, perfect blonde hair.* She chuckled to herself and then jerked her head slightly to the left. Katie had been fidgeting with her pocket all morning. Moira watched in shock as she lifted a small, airline sized bottle of vodka from her pocket and quietly used her long sleeves to disguise the fact that she was lacing her tea. Another sharp look around was all Moira needed to know that this had not gone unnoticed by her grandmother either, though no one else seemed to be aware.

"Sloane, how's that man of yours, still *up* for the wedding?" asked Michelle, twinkling.

"I don't know," Katie joined in. "He looks like he'll *rise* to the occasion."

"Sure he will," Siobhan chuckled. "*Big* man that he is." "I just hope your mother thinks he *measures* up."

"Mom, really!" But Angela was laughing too. Even Moira had to join in the mirth of the occasion. Martin was a good man. Already he had Siobhan eating out of the palm of his hand, a feat not attempted easily and seldom won.

Martin and Sloane had enjoyed a whirlwind romance. They met a little over a year ago at a softball game

23

held by Martin's law firm. Sloane had been along to help Michelle catch the eye of another of the young men, but found that she couldn't keep her eyes off Martin the whole time, and he in turn seemed to be truly entranced by her attention. When the game ended, she walked straight over to him and asked how he'd like to take her to dinner. That was Sloane for you, right to the point, and no use in dallying around the issue when a few simple words would do. Martin was charmed with her straightforward approach for one so young looking and so tiny. She was like a little firecracker, and he delighted in making her throw her head back in unabashed laughter. The ring was bought by Christmas, the date set for early fall, and the plans entered into with the same youthful exuberance that governed their very union.

Martin was ingratiated into the family with the maximum of fuss and the minimum of persuasion. He had an easy charm about him and was able to transition from trading wise cracks with Siobhan to waxing poetic with Angela with a slow charm that held all of the family women transfixed, including Moira. She never tired of chatting with her soon-to-be brother-in-law while Sloane flitted around spreading her attention between her friends and strangers. Martin never seemed to mind either. He would laugh with Moira while letting his gaze wander to his beloved, a bemused and admirable look on his handsome face. It was peaceful to see that there was a man out there so obviously destined to be Sloane's one true match. Maybe that's why it had hurt so much when things had turned sour with Mark. Moira really had thought that he would be the one for her.

Maybe this was also why she was so surprised to have had such a strong physical reaction to the man she banged into this morning. After Mark, she thought that part of her brain had been turned off. Even soaking wet and a little angry, he was gorgeous, and his face had flashed before her eyes several times that morning already.

"Someone get me to the toilet," demanded Siobhan,

snapping Moira from her daydream.

"I will," Katie volunteered.

"No thanks, dear. You shouldn't be driving my chair right now. Michelle, grab the back here and wheel me to the can."

Michelle stood, bewildered but willing, and wheeled her out of the room while Katie sat in her seat and pouted.

"What was that about?" Sloane wondered, looking at her friend.

"I really don't know. Maybe your grandmother doesn't like me."

"Whatever. Katie, did you get those ribbons I gave you over to the florist in time?"

"Yeah, don't worry. She said the bouquets would be ready in loads of time and she'll have them delivered the morning of the wedding to the house."

"Okay." Sloane studied her friend's face for a moment. "You alright, Katie?"

"M'fine, just a little sleepy," Katie told her. Moira studied her face. There were already two red dots of color on her cheeks, and her eyes appeared to be bloodshot. "I had a late night at the club last night. Don't worry about me, though. I'll just go home and have a nap later."

"Must be nice, trust fund baby," Sloane laughed at her friend.

"Hey, don't tease! Some of that trust fund is gonna get you a really nice wedding gift."

"I never tease friends that spoil me. By the way, aren't you taking me out to lunch today?"

"Right, did you want to go to that new place down on Main St?"

"You mean La Cantina?"

"Sure."

"Love to. I hear the waiters there are really cute. Maybe we can get you a date for the wedding," Sloane suggested.

"Ha ha, I can get my own dates, lady," Katie informed her, though she shot a look at Moira as she said

25

this.

Michelle and Siobhan returned from the bathroom and, as Michelle sat to join her friends in the debate over lunch and men, Siobhan motioned to Moira.

"Come take me for a walk outside."

"Sure, Nana," Moira reserved that name for her grandmother for times when she was feeling particularly tender towards her.

She grabbed the handles at the back of the chair and wheeled her out through the kitchen door and into the backyard.

"Why your mother wastes so much time with plants out here is beyond me. She should've just left it grass so we could pitch a tent for that wedding and save the ridiculous amount of money your sister spent on the hall," Siobhan grumbled.

"Ah leave her, Nana, Mom likes to garden. It relaxes her after spending her whole day with those teenagers. I can't imagine where she finds the patience to deal with them."

"Well, it attracts bees. I don't care for bees."

Moira laughed. She knew her grandmother loved this garden just as much as her mother did.

"Now what about this boy you met today?" Siobhan asked her.

"There's not much to it, Nana, I banged into him ... "

"I know that part. What did he look like?"

"He looked nice, really nice, and he had lovely eyes." Moira smiled at the memory of standing so close to the man on the sidewalk.

"It's always in the eyes. Look at that bum you dated before. He had those wishy-washy bedroom eyes. I never trusted him," Siobhan told her, not for the first time.

"I know."

They were quiet for a few moments, enjoying the atmosphere and the mid-morning peace of the air. Moira had much on her own mind, but she found herself wondering what it was that her Grandmother was thinking about.

Watching her face, she decided that she would save it for later. It had been a pretty good morning so far, all things considered, and she didn't want to break the mood by asking what was going on in her Grandmother's head.

"I just want you to be happy," Siobhan said after a spell.

"I am," Moira told her, and in all honesty, she realized that she was. Things were going well at the bakery and, apart from dwelling on the recent break up from time to time, she was happy to be on her own and in control of her own life. It was time to keep reminding herself that she needed no man to define her and that she could get along just fine on her own, thank you very much. She had her family, she would soon have Martin in her family, and she had Jaye. Looking down at her Nana staring out over the garden, Moira thought about how neither she nor her mother had remarried or dated much again after their own marriages had fallen apart. Perhaps there was a lesson there. The Ryan women seemed to do much better alone. Moira hoped that Sloane would be the exception to this rule, as her fiancé was the only man all the women had truly come to trust in a very long time. She gritted her teeth. *He better not let any of us down,* she thought.

Chapter Three

At the end of the work day, Jack finally turned off the
monitor to his computer, stacked his papers neatly and filed
his work discs away for the day. He dropped his mail on
Rebecca's desk and quietly made his way out of the office.
Once outside, he adjusted his jacket to once again hide the
now faded stain on his shirt, climbed into his car and made
his way to the hospice for an evening visit with his Dad. He
pulled his car out of the parking lot and let it find its way
around the bend and to the riverfront where the hospice
was, an eight-minute drive from work.

Due to the hour, there were a lot of cars in the visitor's spots tonight. Jack found a vacant one down at the end
near a cluster of trees and a seldom-used bench and climbed
out of the car, chewing on a hot rod that he had found in the
glove box as dinner. He locked the doors and made his way
to the entrance. The night guard was just coming on duty at
the front security desk.

"Evening Jack, how's things?"

"Things are fine, thanks. How's life treating you
these days?" Jack said the same reply to that same question
every time he saw this particular guard. If he had wanted
to, he could have spoken the response right along with him.

"Can't complain," the guard said.

They waved each other goodbye, and Jack wound his
way down the corridor towards room 19, hiding his chuckle
over the predictable banter. The door was slightly ajar, and
a soft light from the bedside table lamp cast a listless glow
over the room. He pushed the door open slightly and walked

in to greet his father.

Kevin was propped by pillows into a semi-sitting position. There was an open copy of *The Collected Works of Yeats* on his legs; he had obviously dozed while reading. His glasses sat on the end of his nose, as if in refusal to fall off completely. Jack stole a quick look around the room. It was pretty generic, like the dozens of other rooms at the hospice. The difference in here was that almost every available surface was covered with either books or pictures. Kevin had insisted. He had said that he wanted to be surrounded by the things he loved: Yeats, Browning, Dickens and endless photos of his wife and Jack. He gulped. Just looking around the room here made him sad. For despite the pictures of family, there was no real warmth to it. You knew, as one knows it's raining or snowing, that there had been no love in this room. No new lives, no genuine laughter, no food or wine. It had finality to it that he felt he would never grow accustomed to.

"Dad," he said quietly.

Kevin's eyes fluttered a moment, and he sucked air in through his mouth.

"Jack. You're later that I thought. How was work?" His face crinkled into a smile.

"Work was fine, Dad. How're you doing today? I called this morning and you were still asleep. Is the morphine wearing you out?"

"I don't want to talk about drugs; they're such a nuisance. I don't see why I need them anyway." Kevin made a motion with his hand as if he were swatting a fly. "Hey, what happened to your clothes?"

"Some woman knocked into me this morning and spilled my coffee on me. I didn't have time to go home to change."

Kevin chuckled.

"Ohh, a new lady. Is this one going to vanish in a few days too?"

"Don't start, Dad. I don't need a girlfriend, especially not a clumsy one."

"Of course you don't, you need a wife. You can't keep on living alone Jack."

"I like living alone."

It was a common argument. Kevin had been trying to convince Jack of this for ages now, since he was about 24 and had finished grad school.

"You only think that because you've never lived any other way. Share your life, Jack. Share it with someone soon. Besides, I need someone cheerful to keep me company. You can't expect me to just look at your puss every day. Some of my nurses are single. I could fix you up."

"No thanks, Dad. I've met them, they're not my type."

"Vicky liked you," Kevin told him. "So does Grace, she mentions you sometimes."

"Vicky is nice. We had a few dates. It just wouldn't work long term."

"So you slept with her."

Jack sighed. "I really don't want to talk about it."

"Okay, son."

Jack knew exactly what it was that his father had an issue with. Since leaving high school, Jack had had an unsettling habit with women; he was a love 'em and leave 'em kind of guy, and his father knew it. He was never callous with the ladies, but neither was he looking for or making any kind of real connection. Sometimes, when his life was a little on the tense side, Jack would make a rare effort to meet women. Usually in a bar, in a movie theatre, somewhere people go when they're feeling lonely or looking for attention. A conversation would be struck, a flirtation established and with his absolute charm, within days of their meeting or sometimes even less, Jack would have sex with them. Oh, he was never mean or conquest-ish about it, never boastful with the "boys". It was not for sake of bragging rights or racking up notches as some Casanova might do, it was simply borne out of a desire for physical contact without emotional involvement. The women were never left feeling used; to the contrary, some of them remained quite

31

friendly with the charismatic man. Jack was quite schooled in the art of careful flattery and attention ... so long as it suited him; but as Kevin's health had declined, so had Jack's conquests, and he didn't know whether his father was glad for his son that he was no longer substituting sex for relationships or worried that he now had little contact at all with any people outside of work and the hospice.

Jack remained quiet for a moment or two, watching the lines of tubes coming out of his father's blanket and trying not to stare too hard at the new one that was now attached to his belly. Finally Kevin spoke up again.

"I want to go off the morphine and get this feeding tube out. The morphine is making me too tired, and it doesn't matter if I eat the food or if they put it in me, I still get nauseous from it. Even being on Gemzar was better than this thing. Not that this is the greatest food I've ever had, but come on, not being able to even stomach the sight of food some days! This isn't how I want to go, Jack. I need to be awake and alert, and I want to enjoy a meal again."

"We can talk about this later, Dad. It's been a long day." Jack was weary of his father's attempts to slough off any treatments.

"I'm not waiting too much longer. My doctor is coming in to see me on Wednesday. I want to tell him then."

"Fine, we can discuss this tomorrow then." He was dying to change the subject. Jack decided to pick up the book on his father's lap. "What are you reading?"

"Yeats. He makes me feel alive. Why don't you read to me a while?"

Jack opened the book at one of the page markers that were sticking out. He scanned the page and saw that a title had been underlined in pencil. Clearing his throat, he began to read.

Pale brows, still hands and dim hair,
I had a beautiful friend
And dreamed that the old despair
Would end in love in the end:

She took my heart away one day
And saw your image was there;
She has gone weeping away.

Kevin had a tear in his eye as Jack read. "It reminds me of your mother." He said simply.

Just at that moment, one of the orderlies bustled into the room and began fussing around, removing a medication tray, replacing bathroom supplies. He barely seemed to notice that there were any other people present. They watched him go through the motions of his job, oblivious to the life seeping in and out of every space of this room, this very building. Maybe that was how you kept your sanity working at a place like this—brute denial of the exchange of life force within its walls. It made Jack upset that someone could be so close to his great father and yet still not see him.

"Don't you want to get out of here, Dad? I can put another bed in my place. It wouldn't be hard," he told him as the orderly left the room again. It was a question he had asked his father before, and although he knew what the answer would probably be, he couldn't help himself in asking one more time.

"What, and lose my playboy status? I like having all these young ladies fussing around me all day. At your place I'd just be a sad old man living with his son and waiting for the reaper. Not to mention, it would put a bit of a halt to your giddy up," Kevin chuckled.

"I just thought, you know, you might not want to stay here with all these ... strangers." He nodded towards the door that the orderly had shut behind him.

Kevin leaned over and put his hand over Jack's.

"It won't be long, Jack. Let me be here where I am calm and only have to worry about you some of the time, instead of all the time." His voice was gentle, but firm. "Go on, go home, put on a clean shirt and search this city for your mystery clumsy lady."

"Okay, Dad. See you tomorrow?" Jack leaned over

and kissed his father on the head. Kevin reached up and placed his hands on either side of his face. They regarded each other, and then Jack walked out the door and headed down the corridor to the main entrance once again.

As Jack climbed back into his car he checked his clock. Only a few minutes after seven, a little over an hour and already ushered out. The drugs must indeed be tiring him out.

Jack drove home in silence. No radio, windows up to keep out the sound of the migrating birds and other cars. He wondered about what could be going through his father's head. Some days it seemed like he just wanted to be alone, and yet Jack couldn't imagine being in that position and not wanting someone to talk to. Some nights he stayed for hours and played cards with his dad or wheeled him out to the sun room at the back of the building to watch television, but those nights were no easier. Eventually his dad would talk to him about women and about how much he thought Jack needed one. It made no sense. He remembered well the years after his mother had died and how shut off his dad was. They had barely talked and, when Jack was in his twenties and had tried to get his father to date again, he wouldn't hear of it. Why then was it so important to him now? As for combing the city for some woman that he would probably barely recognize, well, that was out of the question. All Jack wanted to do now was to go home and catch up on some sleep.

He pulled into the lot at his building, trying to remember as he got out of the car and headed towards his apartment if he had anything for dinner inside. Cooking for one was sometimes more of a chore than he liked, but it meant that if he had nothing but a bottle of wine and some chips, no one would be there to tell him what a bad choice that was. Jack comforted himself with this thought and brushed aside the tiny little feeling in the back of his mind that it would be nice to have someone to come home to again.

Chapter Four

The next morning Moira woke early and set to work in the bakery long before Jaye was due to come in. It was a peaceful time when she could toss flour and sugar together with abandon and lift tray after beautiful tray of her golden creations out of the ovens. The large kitchen quickly filled with the smells of smooth vanilla, biting cinnamon and tangy lemon. She hummed while she went through the motions letting go of thoughts of weddings, men, and all other sources of stress in her life. Two full hours passed before she sat down and set her coffee maker on to keep her energy level at its fullest. When she had finished her first cup, she looked up at the clock at the same time as Jaye burst through the door.

"Good morning, sunshine!" Jaye's singsong cut into the tranquil air with authority.

"Hi Jaye! Grab an apron, I feel creative today."

"No kidding, you've got more than half the work done already. Just what I am supposed to be doing? You've got the cookies, three of the cinnamon cakes, the lemon tarts, the *strawberry* tarts ... what's left?"

"Well, we still have orders for birthday cakes, and we have the flowers to start for Sloane's cake, not to mention whatever new orders are on the machine and in the computer. Take your pick."

The two women worked in comfortable silence borne of years of being able to complete tasks and anticipate each other's moves and needs. At ten o'clock they opened the doors and Jaye took up her spot behind the counter, where she would remain for the day as Moira filled and refilled the colourful trays of sumptuous treats. The giddiness of the pace made Moira feel like she was in a sped-up old film. It was good to have so much to do, since she didn't much feel like talking to anyone. Jaye must have sensed this, because around lunchtime she came back into the kitchen.

"How's it going back here?"

"Great. Except I ran out of icing sugar and our supplier is tied up again. I'm going to have to go up to the bulk food store. Do you want anything?"

"Yeah, some sesame snaps and a diet cola."

"Okay, back in a few."

Moira hung her flour-covered apron on the back of the door in the kitchen and scooped up her purse. She made her way out the back door of the bakery and out onto Main St. to head up the hill. It wasn't a very busy day downtown, just the usual women of the area checking out the ever-changing shop windows and a few tourists dotted here and there. Moira smiled to herself. She felt exuberant today. There was a slight fever to her steps and, as she walked, she planned in her head the cake to be designed that afternoon for a little boy's birthday. She passed The Bean Post, where she had bumped into the attractive man with the sad eyes, and crossed the street to the Bulk Food store, where each bin of goodies made her feel more and more comfortable.

Moira dallied in front of the jars of brightly-coloured candies and jellybeans. The urge to stick her hand in the jar and let the cool texture of the confectionary slip through her fingers and against her skin was almost overwhelming, but she resisted and moved on to make her purchases. She bought a ten-pound bag of icing sugar and two smaller bags of candy dots and sprinkles. This cake would be a lot of fun; it had a fireworks theme, and the top of the cake was going to resemble the starbursts of color that accompanied the bang. Then she scoured the shelves for Jaye's sesame snaps and drink.

***

Jack sat at his desk for yet another long day of watching his clock and trying to make a dent in the account he was working on. He had not slept well the night before, his dreams haunted by thoughts of his mother's car accident, his father's illness and random tragedies occurring all over the world that had nothing specifically to do with him, but whose pain and suffering felt as solid as if they were resting on his shoulders alone. Jack felt bleak, heavy and unable to bounce out of this stupor. It was one of the more unfortunate side effects of the dealings of such a solitary man with so many taxing issues on his mind.

Jack never really was one to talk about his feelings, with anyone. Even as a child, his parents had often gazed softly at their small boy, wondering why he had no loud crowd of rowdy friends to busy himself with. Once his mother had died, Jack had withdrawn even further, eventually losing the interest of the few friends that he had to the excitements of football games and high school dances. The folks he worked with were well used to him coming into work and sequestering himself in his office until he went home on one of his bad days. It was on his good days that they really enjoyed having him there in the office. Jack had a smile for everyone, especially the women, but he was always courteous and sometimes even playful. Today was not one of those days, though, with thoughts swimming through his head at alarming speed, wreaking havoc on his concentration. By mid-day, Evan strode into his office and once again took the seat opposite him with a serious look on his face.

"Nice job at the meeting yesterday. I'm glad you listened to what I told you about being truly present in your job."

"Thanks. I hope the clients are pleased."

"So far, so good; but that's not why I came in here today. I need you to run into the town and pick up the new quarterly reports from the printers."

37

One of the reasons Jack loved his job so much was just because of this; Evan believed in utilizing as much of the local business as possible.

"Sure, but why me? Isn't that usually the kind of thing Rebecca or one of the young guys does?"

"Just thought you could use a break. Every time I have walked by your office this morning you have looked so serious and frustrated. If you'd rather not, I can get someone else."

"No, no. I can do it. You're right, I would like to get out for a minute. Should I bring you a real coffee?"

"Thanks, but I can make do with the stuff we have here. Besides, I wouldn't want you to get in another collision." He laughed, and Jack joined in quickly, finding humour in this escapade, which had by now made the rounds of the office staff. A bit of the weight lifted off of his shoulders as he joined in making fun of himself. It felt good to laugh.

Jack left the building with a lighter step than he had possessed all day. As he reached his car, he realized he was still holding the pen that he had been using when Evan came in. He jammed it into his pocket and fished for his car keys. The metal clip of the pen stuck on the material and hung on the outside of his pants. Jack climbed into the drivers' seat, gunned the car and drove off into the town. He passed the turnoff for the Hospice without even turning his gaze. This was not the time to dwell on his father; there would be plenty of time for it later. Besides, he was trying to follow Kevin's advice about living in the now and Evan's advice on being an active participant in life as opposed to watching it pass by through his pain. As he drove, he let his eyes wander instead to the multi-coloured hues of the trees, the glorious persistence of the river and the exceptional golden light suffusing the city. Fayette really was a beautiful place. Though it had grown and developed over the years, it still had a lot of the small town charm that kept most of its residents feeling as though they all knew each other. He turned his car to traverse the bridge that sepa-

38

rated the more industrial sector of town, where he worked, to the more intimate, touristy part of the area. Small shops and restaurants dotted the sides of the road near the river, and people strolled lazily down the sidewalks with their children or pets, holding hands and smiling at the Dickensian romance of it all.

As Jack made his way uptown, he noticed a spot available near the coffee shop and swung his car into it. He hopped out and crossed the street, passed the bulk food store and went into the printers.

The man behind the counter was jovial and made small talk with Jack as they loaded him up with a box of neatly printed papers and an invoice to take back to Evan. Jack backed out of the door, his hands full, and turned to make sure it had closed all the way.

Once he was sure it had shut securely, he turned again and walked straight into the woman from the day before, causing the metal pen clip in his pocket to get snagged on the fragile plastic of her purchases. They both watched as the entire contents of her bag floated in slow motion and coated both of their feet in a layer of snowy white sugar. In her surprise and effort to catch and recoup as much as possible, she spilled another bag of some kind of candy and dropped a can of soda, causing them to jump slightly out of the line of foamy spray and enabling the can's pressured contents to propel it down the sidewalk. They stood staring at the mess—a mound of white sugar peppered by candy and with a small river of soda leading away from them—and not even meeting eyes. To his chagrin, Jack found that he was suffering a small reaction.

He is at the hospital. It's a bad day for Kevin, and he has just knocked the entire contents of his medication and vitamin bottles onto the white surface of his hospital bed. He is crying and Jack just stares, unsure of what to do. It is the first time he has really seen Kevin lose his equanimity.

The woman finally regained her composure and looked like she was about to yell when she looked up at

Jack and noticed just who the buffoon is and that he looks very bothered about the whole thing indeed.

"You," she stammered as a slight flush began creeping about her face.

Jack looked up to see her watching his face with those deep green eyes.

"You?" Couldn't he meet her and be smooth and suave?

They begin to shake their feet in an effort to rid them of the confectionary when Jack asked her, "What it is we are covered in?"

"Icing sugar, candy dots and jimmies," she replied.

"Oh." He paused and looked down at the jumble of white powder and candy once again. Suddenly he burst out laughing. The idea that their feet now looked like they had been covered in snow, and the fact that they had met yet again by managing to slam into each other and spill the contents of what one of them was carrying, were just too much. Jack laughed louder, and the girl soon joined in. In seconds, both of them were in hysterics.

She reached out and put her hand on Jack's shoulder for physical support. The connection caused their mirth to slow, but the smiles that spread across each of their faces were real.

"I didn't mean to bang into you, sorry about this mess," he said.

"I know, anymore than I meant to yesterday. Thank God this time it's not hot." She appeared flustered by the effect he had on her when he smiled. *Interesting*, Jack thought.

"I didn't mean to be rude yesterday," Jack said. "It was a bad day for me."

"Well, it wasn't my best day either. Call it even?"

"Call it dinner?" Jack blurted out before he could change his mind. Dinner ... a date! It had been a while.

She looked Jack up and down again.

"Umm, okay. I'm Moira, by the way. Moira Ryan."

"Jack Wallace. It's a pleasure to meet you." He ex-

Nuala Reilly

tended his hand and they shook, tiny sparks of energy once
more jumped and played about their fingers at the contact
and, although they both noticed, neither said anything ...
for now.

"Where should I pick you up?"

"Do you know The Cakery on Main St.?"

"Sure."

"That's my store, well, I own it. You could meet me
there, say around seven?"

"I'll be there."

Jack reached into his shirt pocket and pulled out his
business card. "Just in case you need to reach me before
that," he said.

"You'd better get that stuff off of your feet soon."
Moira chuckled. "It'll make them horribly sticky."

"Thanks. It's nice to meet you, Moira. I should get
back to work, though, for now. I'll see you tonight."

"Okay. I promise to try not to drop anything on you."

Jack laughed and shifted the weight of the box as he
made his way back to the car. He could already imagine
Evan's face as he came into the office covered yet again in
some edible substance. *They must really think I'm losing it,*
he thought. He glanced back once and noticed that Moira
was watching him with a small smile playing about her
lips. Even covered in icing sugar, she was one of the most
beautiful women he had seen in a long time. Jack opened
the back door to his car, tossed the box inside and climbed
into the drivers' seat. He gave Moira a small wave as he
drove away.

***

Moira watched bemused as Jack drove away across the
street. Then she turned on her heel and walked once again
into the Bulk Food Store to repurchase the supplies she
needed for this afternoon, ignoring their bewildered looks.
Finally, after almost an hour, she made her way back
through the doors of her beloved shop and, after laying her

41

purchases down on the counter; she peeled off her shoes and socks, sat up on the counter next to the industrial-sized sink and proceeded to wash off her feet. Jaye came in to check in with her and found her partner sitting with her pants rolled over her knees hosing off her feet with the long spray nozzle of the sink.

"What the *HELL* happened to you?" she demanded, trying not to laugh out loud. Moira quickly filled her in on the story and, when she came to the part when Jack invited her on a dinner date, Jaye's eyes lit up with pleasure.

"You have a DATE? You have a *DATE?!*"

"It's no big deal. I think he just felt sorry for me. I must seem like the world's biggest klutz to him. Maybe I should just call him and cancel."

"You'll do no such thing!" Jaye yelped. "You need a date. You've been doing nothing but work and talk to your family since that dickhead moved out."

Jaye grabbed some paper towel from the roll and wet it in the sink, where Moira's feet and legs were making their way back to normal. She squeezed out the water and picked Moira's shoes off the floor to wipe away the sugar. Moira watched her friend carefully. She was slightly flushed from the excursion, but there was more than that. She looked happy and knew that Jaye was happy for her. The smile on her face may have been small, but it was the most genuine one that she had had seen in ages.

"Here's what we're going to do. We are going to finish making this amazing cake for the little Ellis boy, and then I am going to deliver it while you go upstairs and have a shower. By the time you're done, I'll be back, we'll finish up work and then I am going to help you get ready. You're not wearing jeans on this date," Jaye told her, looked satisfied.

"There's no need to make such a fuss." Moira retorted, now drying off her feet with a tea towel. "I'll wear what I like. Stop making such a big deal about it."

"I will not; this is a big deal. You're going to let me help you with your hair. You're going to wear makeup and a

42

dress," Jaye said.

Moira had to laugh. Jaye was the best of friends, but looking at her spiky hair with the cobalt blue streaks made her want to clarify one thing:

"I'm doing my own hair."

Jaye laughed as she left the room and headed back out front to man the counters again, and Moira put her shoes and socks back on and bustled around making the icing for the cake and generally tidying up. She thought about Jack and what he would be like on a date. It had been such a long time; Mark had never really taken her out for dinner. In fact, she thought the last time she had been on a bona fide dinner date was back in her college days. It wasn't that she didn't like dating and men; there just always seemed to be something more important to get done.

There was her training, her apprenticeship in the hotel with the long late hours, the weeks and weeks spent planning for and raising the finances for her own business. And of course once she had gotten The Cakery up and running, there were the consuming day-to-day routines that running a business had with it. She had meetings with her accountant, planning sessions with Jaye, phone calls and deals with suppliers—it was endless. She wouldn't have traded it for the world. Looking back, even when she was involved with Mark, work always came first. It just hadn't seemed to matter with him since he had no real job.

Moira picked Jack's business card out of her pocket and ran her fingers over the slightly raised type on it. A real date. She glanced at the clock. Almost an hour had passed since their bump on the street; surely he would be back at work by now? On an inspiration, she picked up the phone from the kitchen and dialed his work number.

"Jack Wallace."

"Hi Jack, it's umm Moira … from earlier."

"Hello, you're not calling to cancel already, are you?"

"No." Moira twisted the phone cord between her fingers and dashed a nervous glance to the doorway between the kitchen and the shop. She didn't want Jaye walking in right now. "I was just hoping that we could meet at the restaurant, instead of here." She was quiet for a moment, waiting for his response, but he didn't respond immediately.

"Umm, Jack? Is that okay?"

"Sure … sorry, I'm just trying to exit what I'm doing so that my attention is not split." He chuckled a little. "I guess that kind of backfired. You have my attention now, I promise."

"Well that was it, really. I just wanted to know if that was okay with you."

"Yeah, I don't mind at all," he said.

"So, did you get any raised eyebrows over your shoes?"

"Hmm, eyebrows … yes, I believe so. My boss seems to think the whole thing is kind of droll."

At this point, Jaye poked her head around the door to inquire about the next batch of cookies that should have been on its way out to the front by now.

"Gotta go, see you tonight," Moira said in a rush and hung up the phone. Jaye just nodded, and a soft *Mmmm hmm* could be heard under her breath.

Moira smiled to herself as she got back to work. *This is going to be good,* she thought.

Chapter Five

When Jack had arrived back at the office, he just couldn't keep the smile from his face. He walked in through the main doors and jauntily up to Evan's office, where he deposited the box on a nearby chair and the invoice to Evan's hands. Jack stood there in front of his boss, waiting for the moment when he would notice the state of his shoes and make comment. And of course, Evan did look up, but the first thing he noticed was Jack's face, not his shoes.

"Everything okay, Jack?" he politely inquired.

"Fine, everything's fine. Here are the reports, and that's the invoice." He was nearly twitching in his anticipation.

"I met her, Evan."

"Who ... oh, your clumsy girl," Evan smiled and scanned his eyes up and down Jack's clothing. He let his gaze pause at Jack's feet before returning to his face again. "Have you forgotten how to have a simple encounter with this poor woman without one of you covering the other in something?"

"It's just icing sugar, it will rub off." Jack smiled.

"So now what? Tomorrow should you run into each other in the grocery store and pour potato salad on each other?"

"I'm seeing her tonight," Jack stated and, on that note, he whistled to himself as he left the room. Evan let him go, happy to see his colleague finally smiling again and acting like his old self.

Jack settled himself down in the chair behind his

desk and went back to work on the series of complicated graphics that he had been working on when Evan had first come in that morning. When Moira called to change the date, he was a little surprised, but found that their banter came quite easily, even if she did hang up in a hurry. *Oh well,* he thought to himself, *she does run her own bakery, maybe something was burning.* The work and the hours blended together until most of the day had passed by. In fact, Jack had barely left his desk since returning to the office, so when the phone rang, it jarred him a little. His first thoughts were of his father. He didn't want to hear bad news. Jack gingerly picked up the receiver.

"Good Afternoon, Jack Wallace."

"Jack, its Rebecca. I didn't want to come in and interrupt you, you looked so engrossed."

"That's fine, anything important?"

"Nope, just heading home for the day and wanted to let you know that there were a few things on my desk for you on your way out."

"Okay, thanks. Have a good night."

He hung up the phone and sank back in his chair for a moment, then checked his clock. It was already nearly five o'clock. He saved his work and began the process of getting ready to leave for the day. The slight high that had bathed him all afternoon from his brush with Moira and the ensuing date was beginning to wear off as he contemplated the two tasks now in front of him: a real honest to goodness date, and telling his father about it. Telling his father wouldn't be too hard, but it would mean cutting short their time tonight. The prospect of spending more than just token time in a loud or crowded bar actually carrying on a conversation with a woman was a little more daunting.

Jack threw on his jacket and headed out for the night. He went out to the parking lot and climbed into his car, snaking around the streets, and finally parked at the hospice in the little spot near the bench. Making his way inside and down the long hallway to his father's room, he found Kevin sitting up in his bed reading through another book. His right hand held the tome as if it were a podium, with the deep rivulets of his veins standing through the pale skin from strain. His left hand was absently fiddling with the feeding tube protruding from underneath his shirt. A second tube connected his hand to his IV and further wires kept track of his heart and lung functions. He resembled a rumpled marionette.

"Jack," Kevin said jovially. "You're here! I wasn't expecting you for another half an hour."

He set his book down on the bedside table and laboriously shifted on his bed to make room for his son. Kevin patted the mattress, motioning for Jack to sit down. As Jack took up his place, Kevin reached out to take hold of his left hand. His eyes were shining.

"Hi Dad, how're you feeling today? You look better, you know. Happy."

"I am happy, Jack. It's a good day today. They cut back the supplements on this thing," he said, indicating the tube from under his shirt, "and I am having soup tonight. Care to join me? It's cream of asparagus."

"I would, Dad, and that's great news, really. I can't tell you how good it is to see you happy. They should run more tests on you; maybe that last round of chemo did more good than we thought. Anyway, I would join you, but I made plans. Would you rather I canceled?" Jack's eyes searched his father's.

"Cancel, are you kidding? You mean, I assume, that you have a date tonight? Is it Vicky, did you change your mind about her?"

"No, her name is Moira. Remember that woman that ran into me yesterday? I bumped into her today, and actually, I spilled some sugar on us, but I asked her out to dinner and we're going tonight."

Kevin smiled broadly.

"What are you doing here, then? Go! Go home and change and shower. Put on something nice and wear a tie for God's sake!" Kevin was laughing now. "Take it easy this time would-ya, Jack, talk to her. Or better yet, bring her in to meet me. I'll tell you, I could use some new female faces around here."

"Maybe Dad, let me get through tonight first. There's something ... different about this girl."

With that, Jack left the room to the delightful sound of his father's laughter and further shouted advice following him down the hall.

Once he reached home, the high spirits of his visit had fallen once again as the prospect of what lay before him began to make him nervous. *What's the matter with me?* He wondered. *I have never been nervous about women before.* Perhaps this was why it took so long for Jack to prepare. He showered, shaved and chose clothes with much more care than was normal for him for a night out. All the while reminding himself that dating was what he did best. He had never had trouble with women.

It was just those eyes ...

He remembers being about ten years old and standing in the living room in front of his mother. He is practicing a speech for class, one that he will have to present tomorrow. Jack's mother sat on the couch and watched him intently, her eyes focused and strong as she gave her son all the attention she had. What gave him the confidence to do so well was remembering looking up over his gnarled pages of handwritten work to see that vibrant green staring back at him, encouraging him to go on.

***

Moira stood at the sink in her bathroom, shaving her legs in her bra and underwear, while Jaye unceremoniously went through the contents of her closet, rejecting item after item. At one point, Jaye poked her head into the bathroom and ordered her friend to change into a matched set of underwear.

"Why? It can't be that important. I'm *not* going to sleep with him, Jaye, not on the first date for crying out loud!"

"Of course you're not, you twit, but you'll feel more confident if you know you're wearing the sexy stuff."

"Yes, boss," Moira said mockingly. Jaye guffawed and stuck her nose back into the closet.

"Good lord woman, you need to go shopping. Don't you own anything hot?"

"Yeah, my ski suit is in the back."

"Haw haw. I might have to resort to that; at least it has some color," Jaye said.

It was amusing that her wardrobe, which had never inspired any conversation between the two of them, was now the subject of such debate and recrimination. Finally, Jaye emerged from the depths of the closet holding up a dark blue dress with a delicate silver thread embellishment and a pair of strappy silver sandals. The dress was from a semi-formal occasion that she had attended at her college about seven years before. It had not been worn since.

"Perfect," Jaye said, twirling the dress from the hanger.

"Where did you find that?" Moira mused. "It must have moths in it by now. Besides, it's far too dressy. Let's find something else."

"Absolutely not! This is what you're wearing tonight. Time to dust off this dress and your social life. Now get your butt back into that bathroom and dry your hair. Here," she tossed the dress to Moira, "be wearing this when you come back out."

Moira caught the dress and headed back into her bathroom. *I'm too old for this,* she thought as she shrugged her shoulders into the dress and twisted to do up the zipper. The soft fabric floated around her knees, and the loose and lovely sleeves fell to just above her elbows. There was a subtle shimmer of silver around the neckline, the edge of the sleeves, and at the waist and hemline of the dress, making little fragments of light bounce from her periodically and casting a romantic glow on her skin.

Moira leaned in to the mirror over the sink and applied her mascara carefully. She smoothed some gloss over

49

her lips and fluffed her hair before heading back out into the bedroom. Just as she was turning to leave, she paused once more and grabbed a seldom-used bottle from the top shelf of her cabinet. A quick dab behind the ears and one on each of her wrists and she opened the door once more to her bedroom and stepped out to seek Jaye's approval.

"Why are you so quiet?" she demanded a moment later. "Is it bad? I knew wearing this old thing would be a mistake."

"Moira, you're stunning."

"Shut up, I'm going to put on pants."

"No, Moira. Don't change. I've never seen you look so lovely."

Moira was taken aback. She had never seen Jaye look so serious before. She sat down on the bed and put on the shoes. It was 6:35. Without speaking another word to her, Jaye stood up, hugged her friend and left the apartment. Moira gathered up her purse and her keys and followed her friend down the stairs and out the door. She watched Jaye continue on her way to whatever plans she had that night and locked the door to her apartment before walking across the street to La Cantina, the new Italian restaurant right on the river bank, just across the street and four doors down from her own shop. She walked in, was seated by one of the immaculate waiters, and ordered a martini while she waited.

The restaurant was amazing. Moira's table was at the back of the room, nestled against the large picture window that offered a lovely view of the river. She could, however, still see the front door. Candles and tiny white lights illuminated the room with their gentle brilliance, and the air smelled warm and comforting.

There were only four other couples in the room, and they all looked serious about each other, huddled together at their tables and booths, as if any physical distance between them would be too much to bear. Moira sucked pensively on the olive from her cocktail. She kept watching the door every time it opened. Two more couples came and were seated, quickly falling into the pattern of their dining comrades, a hand-holding, gaze-locking example of lovers. Moira shifted uncomfortably. Maybe they should have gone for pizza. It was a lot of pressure to have a first date surrounded by established intimacy.

Finally, at 7:13, the door opened once again, and there stood Jack. He was wearing dark blue pants, a red shirt with the top two buttons open and a nice dark jacket. Moira watched as he spoke to the host, who motioned him towards her. Jack crossed the room in a few easy steps and then stopped at the table and broke into a slow smile.

"Sorry I'm late. You look beautiful. Have you been waiting long?" He tilted his head to the side, waiting for her reply, and took a seat opposite her.

"Thank you. No, I haven't been waiting too long."

They regarded each other in silence for a while, glancing at the menus and each other. When the waiter came back, Jack ordered a martini as well and appetizers for them both. The silence between them was not awkward, to Moira's surprise. After a few minutes of reading menus and sipping drinks, Jack once again cocked his head to the side as he looked at her.

"Have you always lived in Fayette?" he asked.

"With a few small exceptions, yes, have you?"

"No, my father and I moved here when I was a teenager. He owned that gas station on Fountain St. I'm surprised that we have never run into each other before."

"Well," Moira sipped at her drink, "I don't really go out a whole lot. Running the bakery takes up most of my time. My family seems to take up the rest." She was quiet again for a moment, at a loss for what else to say. "I hope I don't bore you, I'm not really great date material."

"Nobody is, really. It just depends on how you are with the small talk portion of the evening." Jack smiled.

"Small talk?"

"Sure. You know, 'what do you do?', 'who's your family?', that kind of thing."

Moira giggled slightly. Jack looked great when he

51

was smiling.

"We must be ahead of the game, then. You already know what I do, and that my family is from town. My sister Sloane is getting married in about three weeks, so that is taking a lot of my time right now. What else do you want to know, favourite colours?"

Now it was Jack's turn to snicker. "Sure, favourite colours, food, flower … hmm, what else can you tell me?"

"Books, movies, music?"

"Oh yes. I think I am going to need all your stats."

The waiter arrived just then and placed an appetizing plate of antipasto in front of them.

"Are you ready to order?" he inquired. Jack folded his menu and placed it in front of him. "I have an idea."

"Shoot."

"You must know quite a bit about food, with your profession and all, but I am woefully ignorant of Italian cuisine. What I do know is wine. So you order for both of us, and I'll order wine. How does that sound?"

"Wow, I don't know whether to be flattered or feel tremendous pressure. Okay, we'll have … the Schiaffi, for Jack and I will have the Pollo alla Griglia, with the side of courgettes and portobello mushrooms." She handed the menu back to the waiter, who then turned to Jack to hear his choice for wine.

"I'm impressed! You'll have to explain to me what we're having." He turned to the waiter. "This wine list is amazing. I imagine that your import list is a treat to make up. We would love a bottle of the 2001 Marsilliana, thank you."

The waiter bowed flawlessly and hurried off to place their order.

"Now, you tell me what we're eating, and I'll tell you what we're drinking," Jack said to her.

Moira looked at his eager face.

"I ordered you a special kind of ravioli. They're very large; in fact, the loose translation means 'slaps'. But they are very good; I think you'll like them. For myself, grilled chicken with vegetables. Boring, I know, but it always sounds so romantic in Italian. What are we having for wine?"

"It's from Tuscany. You'll like it, I hope. This is a very serious wine though, one to sip thoughtfully, since it's rather heavy. There are a lot of layers to it. How is it that you are so immersed in cooking and not so with wine? I would have thought that the one would go with the other."

"When I was in school, there were some students who were very serious about the wine aspect of cooking, but since my passion has always been pastry and desserts, the only wines that I use are sweet ones. More often than not, I use liqueurs."

"Tell me more about your work."

Moira talked about her job and her shop from the antipasto to half way through the main course. She found Jack's genuine interest in her flattering, and a little disconcerting; normally people didn't bother themselves with her thoughts and feelings for such a long stretch of time.

"There isn't much else to tell you about. The cookies, tarts, bread and you know, finger treats, that stuff pays the bills and keeps a steady business coming in, but what I really love is doing the cakes. That's when I can get really creative."

"I can tell. You light up when you talk about it."

"I do? I hadn't realized. So, what about you? What is it you do again?"

"Nothing as interesting as cake making, I'm afraid. I'm a graphic designer for a computer advertising firm. Basically, I do the design for the paid advertisements on different sites on the internet. So if, for example, Pepsi wanted to have an ad on a website for a new movie about to come out, I would design the aspects of the ad. Not that I've ever worked with a company as large as Pepsi ... at least not yet. I'm working up to it." He winked at her.

"What about your family? You mentioned your father; do you have brothers and sisters? What about your mother?" Moira asked him with genuine interest.

53

"Nope, just my Dad and me." Jack dropped his gaze for a moment. When he looked back up, he was smiling again. "What about *your* family? It must be big if they take up a lot of your time."

"Actually, it's not really a big family, but it feels big. My mother, Angela, and my grandmother, Siobhan, live over on Marksam Rd., and my sister Sloane is there as well for another few weeks, and then she is getting married and moving over to Delhi St. It's this wedding right now that's taking up so much time. Sloane's a bit of a perfectionist."

"Interesting names in your family, Sloane, Shi-vohn, what background is that?"

"It's Irish. My grandmother and mother were born there. They came here when my mother was a teenager."

They talked on through the rest of the meal. Neither of them brought up the subject of family again, and neither of them brought up the subject of past lovers either. Instead, they found that they had a surprising amount in common. Both lived somewhat solitary lives immersed in work and, in their spare time, immersed in movies and books. Moira loved to read biographies and deeply involved fiction; the bigger the book and the more intricate, the better. Jack like autobiographies and historical accounts. He also had a weakness for murder mysteries and Stephen King. They enjoyed all kinds of similar music and movies too, and had soon made a date to go together and see the newest comic book turned movies series when it came to town on the weekend.

By the end of dinner, they were laughing together like the oldest of friends.

"See, you are a good date," Jack told her.

"You're not too shabby yourself. I had fun tonight, Jack. Thank you. So we're on for the movie on Friday?"

"Absolutely," he replied, staring into her eyes.

Jack paid the bill before Moira had a chance to reach out for it and then guided her through the restaurant and outside. It was a lovely clear sapphire night.

Jack turned to face her, marveling at how perfectly

the rays of the streetlight were hitting her hair.

"Do you want me to walk you home?" he asked, indicating her store across the street with his head.

"No, I'll be fine."

Moira wondered if he was going to kiss her. She locked her eyes onto his and leaned in to him slowly, as if granting her permission with her caution. Moira leisurely closed her eyes and met his lips briefly with her own. The kiss was perfect, gentle and shy. They stepped back from each other and let their fingertips caress for a moment before Moira turned and walked back across the street towards her home.

Moira walked through the little alley beside her store to the back door that led to her apartment entrance. She was surprised to see Sloane sitting on the step waiting for her. As she got closer, Sloane looked up and shrugged, a cool smile playing on her lips.

"Where have *you* been?" she inquired in a smooth tone.

"Out, what are you doing here?"

"Oh, I just came from Martin's. I thought I would come here before going home. There's some stuff I want to talk to you about. You know, for the wedding. Can I come in?"

"Sure."

Moira slid her key into the lock and opened the door. Inside was a small landing of a room with a few boxes. Directly in front of her was the back door to the bakery, and to the left were the stairs to her apartment. Once inside the rooms, Moira headed into the small kitchen and put the kettle on the stove.

"Tea?" she asked her sister.

"Sure."

Sloane had already walked past the little opening to the kitchen and was busy settling herself on the comfortable sofa in the great room. She ran her fingers lightly over the many books that Moira had stacked on the table in front of her. Moira watched as her sister looked around the

Autumn Violets

apartment carefully. Little had changed since Moira had
first moved here almost three years ago. Nothing that
showed a life full of energy; there was a small television on
the far wall, but books and candles took up almost every
available space. Sloane sat and fluffed a pillow in her lap.
She tapped her foot while she waited for Moira to stop put-
tering around in the kitchen.

Moira was taking mugs and teabags from her cupboard, trying desperately to ignore the lingering feeling of
Jack's soft lips on hers and get into the right frame of mind
for talking to Sloane.

"Here you go," Moira said when she came into the
room and placed a mug of tea in front of Sloane. She sank
into her own favourite comfy seat to the right of the sofa
and sipped at her drink.

"That's a blast from the past," Sloane observed, just
noticing Moira's attire. "And you're wearing makeup! You
were up to something. I can't believe you still have that old
dress. Were you at some kind of retro party?"

"Nope, just out." Moira had no time for Sloane's
weird obsession with her clothes. "What did you want to
talk about?"

"Well, Martin and I were finalizing the seating plan
tonight and we had some concerns. You don't have a date. It
throws everything off. I need to have an even number of
people at the tables; odd numbers just don't fit properly. I
talked to Katie and she says she has a friend, if you need
someone." Sloane looked at her hopefully.

Moira tinkled with laughter, slightly caught off
guard.

"Is that it!? I'm not worried about not having a date,
and I certainly don't want one of Katie's spoiled shallow
friends to feel bound to me all night, nor would I want to
spend my time at your wedding trying to entertain some
rich fool who thinks that I might sleep with him afterwards.
Better just to invite another person and let me do my own
thing."

Sloane pouted. Clearly, this was not the answer she

56

wanted to hear.

"You can't do this. I want this wedding to be all couples. No one else is going stag, not Martin's grandmother, not even Mom or Nana. It just won't look right if the only single person at this wedding is my own sister. What am I going to say to Martin's mother?"

"I don't know. Tell her I'm a lesbian."

"That's not funny. Besides, it wouldn't work; she'd want to know where your partner was. Hey, why don't you bring Jaye? We could say you are a couple." Sloane warmed to the idea.

"No way! I was just kidding. I'm not going to ask her to put on some charade just for your numbers to be square."

"Why are you being so difficult? This is my *wedding* we're talking about. I want it to be perfect. I can't have a head table without the right centre piece, I can't have a caterer who doesn't understand about the importance of a sit down dinner instead of a buffet, and I can't have my own sister go alone!" Sloane looked as though she were getting ready to cry.

"Oh no you don't! You can pull that pouty bullshit on Mom or Martin, but I'm not falling for it." Moira crossed her arms as Sloane's eyes instantly dried up. "This may be your day, but it's my life and I won't take some pity date of Katie's or pretend that Jaye is something she's not just to make you happy."

"You never want to make me happy. You've been rolling your eyes about this wedding since I first announced my engagement. When did you stop loving me?" Sloane sniffled.

Moira let out her breath in one long sigh.

"I've never stopped loving you, Sloane, but you have got to stop expecting everyone to jump when you say just because you're getting married."

Sloane rose to her feet. Clearly, this was not a subject on which she felt ready to compromise.

"They should so jump when I say! This is my *WEDDING,* Moira! This is important. Everyone knows that the wedding is all about what the bride wants. You're the only one that seems to have a problem with this. Even Martin doesn't care if I make all the plans."

"Martin knows that the *marriage* is more important than the perfect looking wedding. You don't even know how lucky you are to have him."

"What are you saying? That he's too good for me? I think you're just jealous that no one wants to marry you!" Sloane was crying real tears now. She headed for the door. "No wonder Mark slept with that other girl. You're cold, Moira. And you're jealous that for once I'm the one getting everything I want."

"For once, that's a laugh! You've always gotten what you wanted, Sloane." Moira was on her feet now too and, as Sloane headed down the stairs and jammed her feet into her shoes, she shouted after her. "You've just been too selfish to see it!" Her only answer was the slam of the door as Sloane left.

Moira went down the stairs and locked the door. She ran back up to her apartment and closed the door behind her. As she went through the room, picking up the barely touched cups of tea, taking them into the kitchen to dump them out, she thought about how the night had turned from wonderful to horrifying.

Moira put her head into her hands, sank down onto the cold tiles of the floor and cried.

Chapter Six

Jack watched as Moira walked across the street and around to the back of the building that she owned. He waited until he saw the lights go on upstairs before he turned the engine over in the car and wound his way through the streets and back to his own apartment uptown.

Jack lived in a non-descript building in the residential part of town. He was within two blocks of the grocery store and about three blocks of the upper part of Main St. It was a cozy but not swanky place, far from the trendy lofts on the river bank, but safe and somewhat comforting in its complacency.

Jack swung his car into its designated place and hummed to himself as he entered the building and made his way to his ground floor apartment. He tossed his keys into the small dish he kept on the table near the door and sank into the squashy armchair in his living room. Jack couldn't seem to sit still. His mind was buzzing. It had been a great night, but something still felt a little ... funny. It had been a long time since he had taken a woman out for a whole meal instead of just a few drinks. It had been even longer since an encounter had ended with a kiss, instead of a frantic night of tumbling through the sheets and the inevitable guilt that followed. He glanced at the clock on his cable box under the television; 10:23. Hmmm, long date.

Jack reached for the phone, and his fingers automatically punched in the numbers for the hospice. He waited for the automatic greeting and entered the number of his father's room. As the phone rang, he kicked off his shoes and stared at a painting hanging near the bathroom door. It was an abstract that always reminded him of a cluster of trees in mid-blossom.

"Hello?" Kevin sounded raspy, but alert.

"Hi Dad, how'd your night go?"

"Jack?!" Kevin couldn't disguise the surprise in his voice. "You never call me after a date. Did something go wrong? I thought by now you'd be undoing all the gentlemanly qualities I tried to raise you with." He chuckled.

"Very funny. Nothing went wrong. Actually, it was quite a nice date. We went to La Cantina, that new Italian place I told you about downtown. Great food, very good wine."

"That's nice. Great food, good wine, how was the *date*, Jack. You know, that other person sitting there having great food and good wine. Did she enjoy herself, or did you sit there soaking up that entire atmosphere while she twiddled her thumbs?" Kevin must have been enjoying this; Jack could practically hear him smiling through the phone.

"Moira, Dad. She was really good company. In fact, she knows a lot about food, so she ordered for us." On the other end, Kevin was wheezing slightly, trying to suppress a cough. "Are you alright?"

Kevin gave in to the cough and then wheezed a little more before answering.

"I'm fine, I don't want to talk about me tonight. I want to talk about you. I'm glad you had a good time, son. Tell me about Moira."

"She's very pretty, although she doesn't seem to know it. She's got this lovely dark hair and green eyes. And she lives in a family of only women, all of them Irish." He paused for a moment, reflecting on their conversation. "It was really easy to talk to her."

"When do I get to meet her?"

"Easy Dad, it's only been one date. I don't really know what she thinks about us meeting again, let alone bringing her to meet a playboy like you," Jack teased.

"Don't leave it too long."

"Sure, sure. Now, how about you? You don't sound as good as you did earlier tonight. Is everything alright?"

"Everything's fine. I told you, I feel better than I have in ages, weeks even. I always cough a little at night. Did you kiss her?"

Jack didn't answer right away. His mind immediately transported back to the street outside the restaurant. The look of the streetlight in her hair, their lips touching briefly ...

"Earth to Jack ... oohh, musta been some kiss." Kevin laughed again heartily, punctuated by more coughing and a small groan.

"Yes. We kissed. And then she went home and so did I. You sound like you need to get some sleep. Can I still come and see you tomorrow after work?"

"Of course, I want to hear more about Moira. Goodnight Jack."

"Goodnight Dad."

As Jack hung up the phone, he smiled. He looked around his apartment for a moment and then got himself ready for bed, feeling no stress at all.

***

Thursday morning Jack awoke feeling a little happy, yet a little unsure of himself. The old Jack would just shake off the night before and slip somehow back into his old, safe habits. And yet there was a part of him that wanted to run right out and see Moira again straight away.

As he made the motions through his morning routines—shower, shave and a muffin from the fridge for breakfast—Jack's thoughts alternated between Moira and his father. After he dressed, he picked up the phone and dialed the hospice main phone line. He spoke with Grace at the desk and learned that although his father's breathing was indeed becoming more difficult, on all other fronts he really did seem to be in the upswing that had him in such good spirits the night before. He had managed to eat and keep his food down for dinner and was planning to do the same, having solid food for breakfast. At the moment he was still asleep, and so Jack passed on his good morning wishes and the message that he would, as usual, stop in to see him after work that day. He hung up the phone, headed out the door and off to grab coffee before work.

Jack wound his car through the streets and pulled up by The Bean Post, where he parked and jumped out to get his morning beverage.

The lineup was not too long this morning, and Jack once again found himself tapping his foot, although not with total impatience, more so to go along with the flood of thoughts rolling through his head. After he had placed his order and was once again seated in his car, he rolled down Main St.'s small hill and slowed the car to have a look at the window of Moira's shop. The lights were still off, but the brightness of the morning sun caught the elegant cake in the centre of the display. It was really lovely. He smiled again and sped off across the bridge to the business sector of town and around the streets to his office.

As he passed Evan's office, he smiled while his boss gave a thumb up. There would be plenty of time to let him know how well the night went later; right now he felt ready to work. By mid-day, Jack had finished two of the rough proposals that he had been working on and was ready to begin to tackle a third. He sent the files to Evan's computer for his boss to proof what he had.

If the others in the office noticed the subtle shifts in Jack's usually sullen and withdrawn mannerisms, they kept the changes to themselves. Most of them knew of Jack's dying father, and provoking a swift mood change by asking the wrong question at the wrong time was something they tried to avoid. Even so, smiles were being exchanged with unusual regularity as Jack bustled through the office every so often for a drink of water or trip to the supply room. As the afternoon wore on, the overall feeling in the office was a good one, and Jack felt his mood continually elevating until it was finally time for him to leave and pay a visit to his father.

As Jack swung his car into the lot, he found his now favourite parking place under the tree at the corner was empty. Smiling, he pulled in and then hopped out, locking the car behind him.

Kevin was sitting in a more upright position today, nose buried deep in his book of Yeats' poetry and toes tapping under the covers to some melody that was only playing in his head. He looked up at Jack as he entered the room and smiled.

"Hiya kiddo, how did work go today?"

"Great, I finished two of the projects that I had on the go and am making some real progress on a new one we're working on. This one will get national coverage if we make the client happy enough; it will be on the official website for the Juno's. Enough about work though, you seem to be doing well."

"I am. They have cut back on the pain meds, and I have been eating on my own, without using this tube, so I have asked my doctor to remove it."

Jack frowned slightly for a moment. Although it was great that his dad was feeling better, the doctor had warned him that he might have a small upsurge in health before the disease finally claimed him. He knew that Kevin was aware of this fact as well, so chose not to dampen his mood by cautioning or questioning him.

"That's great news, Dad. I'm glad to hear you're feeling so much better."

Kevin studied his son's handsome face for a moment, trying to read him as he read the words of so many long-dead poets.

"It's okay, you know. The tube is staying in for now, the monitors are all still working, and I am just enjoying feeling more normal than I have in a long while. You worry too much."

"I know. Now, how about a game of cards?"

Kevin smiled as Jack wheeled the portable bed-top

table over and set up a game of gin rummy. The two men played comfortably for a while, tossing trash back and forth and catching up on the finer details of Jack's job and possible promotion. As the evening wore on, an orderly brought dinner for Kevin in on a tray. There was tomato soup and crackers, tea and Jell-o. Although the meal itself was fairly small, Kevin's triumph of being able to keep food down and eat unassisted was enormous. Jack remained for the meal, though he did not join in, and regaled his father with more details of his date with Moira. When Kevin finally finished eating, he regarded Jack levelly.

"I would like to meet this young lady, but I'll wait until after your next date. Have you decided what movie you're going to see?"

"Yeah, it's one of those comic books turned film, Mr. Marvel or something, but why do you want to meet her so much?" Jack was uncomfortable about bringing Moira here; under the circumstances he didn't see the point.

"Because Jack, this is the first time I am hearing actual information about a woman you see. Normally I hear scant details at best, and listening between the lines, I'd say you really don't see any of them as anything more than short-lived diversions. It's not the best way to treat women, Jack, and it's not going to help you, building no real relationships. If this Moira girl garnered enough of your attention to warrant a second real date and you haven't taken her racing to the bedroom, well, I want to meet the woman who did that."

"Maybe I'll bring her in next week. We'll see. I don't really want to subject her to a charming yet sick man until I know how she feels about it."

"You mean you don't want her to meet a dying man."

"It's a little weird, don't you think? Here we have only just met, and already I'm bringing this woman in to meet my father who, by the way, is dying. Oh no, that's not too heavy." Jack was trying to be light hearted but was starting to get flustered. Dealing with the imminent demise of his father and only living family was not something he felt like bringing someone else into. He was barely dealing with it himself yet.

"Don't get mad, Jack. I don't have a lot of time left; weeks maybe, months perhaps, but not likely. I just want to know that you're going to be okay when I'm gone and not buried with your nose in your work and a roster of anonymous women to call on when you're lonely. Is that too much for a father to want for his son?" Kevin looked quizzically at Jack.

"I don't know. Nothing really seems to make sense anymore." Jack stood up. "I'm going to go. I'll see you tomorrow night."

He bent over and awkwardly hugged Kevin's fragile frame and then made his way down the hall, out the doors and to his car by the bench under the tree. Jack sat for a moment on the bench, pondering the conversation of the night. He just got so frustrated with his father when he tried to convince him of the whole love thing. It couldn't be that great. Look at where love had gotten his parents, one of them dead and the other so heartbroken that, when he wasn't busy being consumed by grief, he was burying his head in the work at that shop to avoid it, not that that had gotten him anywhere either, and now that he was dying he suddenly wanted Jack to be this enlightened man who believed that love could conquer all. *No thanks,* he thought, *nothing I have ever seen supports this theory. Better just have a good time with Moira, and see where it takes us.*

Jack drove home feeling that on one level he had kept his head, but on the other, scenes of Moira in the restaurant and visions of their brief kiss danced before his eyes for the rest of the night.

Chapter Seven

Moira awoke early Thursday morning with a slight headache, the events of the previous night as jumbled as her hair from a restless nights' sleep. She shuffled into the kitchen of her apartment and turned on the coffee maker, then headed for the shower.

The hot water felt good, and she stood still for several minutes while the cascades bathed her face and watched the rivulets run down her body. Finally she got out and, as she was about to wrap a large towel around herself, she paused and stood naked in front of the mirror. Moira never seemed to feel any kind of connection to what her body physically felt like and what it looked like. Staring at her naked self didn't really seem to bring her any sense of knowledge about who she was. Perhaps that explained why her relationships had been so few and far between, and why she had been so hurt when each and every one of them had ended with the man in question having sex with someone else. Moira wrapped the towel around her and went to dress in frustration.

Sex was supposed to be some amazing way to connect with a person, and she had never felt that that was the case. For her, the five lovers she had had in her life all seemed to be disappointments. Especially Mark, but she didn't want to waste any more of her time dwelling on him.

Moira finished dressing and followed the heavenly aroma of fresh coffee into her kitchen, where she filled her large lidded mug and finally headed down to her shop.

The kitchen of The Cakery had been, as it always

was, left in immaculate condition the night before. Jaye had left a note on the counter next to one of the large mixers used for making icing. It read:

> *Moira,*
> *Hope you had a fabulous time,*
> *I expect details ... and not about the food!*
> *See you at 10:00.*
> *Jaye*

She smiled and tossed the note into the garbage. Moira loved these early morning hours alone in her shop. She could get into her head and completely tune out everything that was going on around her, any stress that she had or any problems with her family, and get lost in the swirls of the batter, the texture of the icing, the complexities of the pastries. It was truly her passion, and the success of the business made her feel like one of the luckiest people in the world, for few can claim that they get paid to engage in what is their calling and their joy for a living. She found herself humming as she went through the motions of filling trays and piping pastry dough.

Finally, at about ten to ten, she brought her piping bag of royal icing out to the small work station in the front and set up her space to work on the roses for Sloane's wedding cake as she helped tend the front with Jaye. As if on cue, Jaye entered the shop just as Moira had turned the sign and clicked the switch down into the open position.

"Morning sunshine, how'd it go?" Jaye wasted no time in getting to the meat and potatoes of what she wanted to know.

"Great, I finished most of what we'll need for today, but I want you to start on those breads for me. We'll likely run out before the day is through." Moira smiled sweetly at her, she was deliberate in her avoidance.

"Sure, sure, bread ... good. Now about your date with the coffee hottie, did I or did I not specify that I wanted details? What's he like?"

Moira chewed thoughtfully on her cheek for a moment.

"He's nice. It was a little weird at first; I was sitting there waiting for him ... "

"What? He was late?"

"Only about ten or fifteen minutes."

"Bastard."

Moira laughed. "Really, it's okay. But this restaurant, you have to go there sometime, Jaye, it's really beautiful. Candles everywhere and little tiny lights all over making you feel like you have left the city and are in some undiscovered alternate world. Jack was ... " she blushed, " ... a good date." Moira looked down for a minute, avoiding Jaye's eyes.

"Oooohh! Do we detect interest? Could it be that our fair Moira the Stoic has finally found someone to crumble her invincible wall?" Jaye was laughing with her eyes, and Moira took no offense at the barb about her personality. From Jaye, it was almost a compliment, and she knew that her friend admired her ability to be self-sufficient.

"I'm seeing him again on Friday."

"WOO HOO!" Jaye whooped and danced around the small shop just as some women came in looking shocked at this early morning insanity.

All Moira could do was laugh from her stool as Jaye exuberantly led the poor confused women through the choices, being much larger than life than she usually was, which was a feat for her, her blue hair flying out behind her. The women, the type who looked as if they might have been happy with a loaf of bread and a lemon tart for tea, wound up buying three loaves of the soda bread, two treacle tarts and a cinnamon crisp each for the way home. Jaye chirped a goodbye at them as they left the store, a great deal more animated than they had initially come in.

The women spent the morning in back and' forth conversation about Jack and the date. Jaye listened as she bounced between serving customers, running back to the kitchen to replace sold items or throw another batch of something into the large ovens. Moira sat happily on her chair, piping perfect roses onto the flower nail and then placing them to dry. By the time noon had come and gone and the coffee maker in the kitchen had been refilled three times, Moira got to the conversation with Sloane. The store was still doing a steady business, but the light mood of the morning was gone, and Jaye's' face turned stony as she listened to Moira tell her about the fight.

"Too damn right, it's about time someone told that spoiled brat just how spoiled she is. Wedding or not, you did the right thing, Moira."

"I don't know. I've never yelled at her like that before. But she had no right to ask me to pretend something for the sake of making a good impression, or wait, the *right* impression, for just one day."

"Don't dwell on it now. You probably just caught her off guard, looking all gorgeous like you did, and probably still glowing from your goodnight kiss."

Moira blushed again and momentarily dropped her gaze from Jaye. When she looked up, Jaye was beaming.

"I KNEW IT!!"

"Yeah, just one kiss, but oohh, he's a good kisser, Jaye. Really good, I felt it in my toes."

Jaye raised a mischievous eyebrow at her friend. "Tongue?"

"Jaye!" Moira threw a towel at her, and the two women collapsed into helpless fits of laughter.

***

Both Moira and Jack found that the two days between dates passed in somewhat of a blur. They worked, and they spoke on the phone twice to arrange a time and pick a movie for their date on Friday. Moira spent her time filling orders for three birthday cakes for the weekend, one anniversary reproduction of a wedding cake from the sixties that she had to duplicate from a very faded picture, and filling her regular needs for the shop.

Jack finished a rather large project that he had been working on and presented it at work to his boss and the clients. They seemed to be very happy with his work; Evan took him out to lunch on Friday to celebrate his completion and tell him that he was officially on the shortlist for the promotion. His father had been doing very well this week; he even switched from morphine to Vicodin to control the pain and discomfort of his condition, though the conversations between them had become slightly truncated since their last talk.

As Friday rolled on, Moira started to feel nervous once again. Despite the protestations of Jaye, who felt that Moira should dress up again, she adamantly refused to wear anything but jeans. After all, those movie seats could be uncomfortable sometimes, and she wanted to feel completely at ease. Jack also seemed to be feeling a little nervous about seeing Moira again. He left work at the dot of five and whipped over to see his father for dinner together quickly before going home to hose off and don some clean clothes.

Moira had dinner plans of her own first. Since she and Jack weren't meeting until 7:30 for an 8:00 show, she was on her way once again to her mother's house to join the ladies for the Friday night special, spaghetti and meatballs. She closed up her shop, grabbing a box of cinna-crisps, one of her specialties—light twisted pastries covered in cinnamon and sugar, melt in your mouth delicious—and headed out the door.

"You're just in time," Angela trilled from the kitchen. Moira had barely walked in the door and was in the process of hanging up her coat. They must have seen her through the kitchen windows. As she made her way down the hall and into the kitchen, Moira smiled at Siobhan, who winked at her and patted the place next to hers. Sloane was sitting on the other side of the table doing everything in her power to ignore the arrival of her sister.

"Hi mom, hi Nana."

She sat down and looked at the beautiful table filled with a large platter of the pasta and a big basket of garlic bread. Then she nodded across the table. "Sloane," was all she said, but there was no reply forthcoming.

Okay, two can play that game. Moira turned the charm up to full wattage as she spent her meal chatting with her grandmother, and Angela kept up banter with her other daughter. Though there was tension throughout the meal, an outsider looking in would have been hard pressed to find it, as years of bickering between the girls had made it possible for them to tolerate hours in each other's presence without uttering a single word, and had given their mother and grandmother the ability to totally ignore the strain in the atmosphere.

The evening passed with conversation on weddings, weddings and more weddings. A cousin of Martin's had married back in early summer, and Sloane was beginning to think that her own wedding was going to be held under a microscope to see if it measured up. Moira bit back the harsh comments she might have otherwise uttered, if not for the fact that she was refusing to talk to her sister. Instead, she let a small snort of indignation escape her lips as her mother smoothed Sloane's feelings over with kind words and warm food. Siobhan sat in her chair and politely listened to the conversation before leaning in to Moira and asking her about her date.

"I'll tell you about it later, Nana. I gotta get ready to go. We're going to a movie tonight."

All ears around the table perked up, and Siobhan sat up smartly, as if it had been her intention all along to draw attention to this.

"Who're you going to a movie with?" Angela asked with interest. "Not the coffee on the shirt man? How wonderful."

Moira shot her grandmother a sideways smirk, and she in turn lifted her shoulders as if to say "whoops".

"Yes, the coffee on the shirt guy. By the way, his name is Jack." Sloane looked put out that the conversation was no longer about her.

"Well, that's just great," Angela intoned. "Maybe you can ask him to be your date to the wedding. Sloane was just telling me her numbers were slightly off, weren't you honey, and that way you won't get stuck dancing with any of your unusual cousins." Angela smiled widely as if she had just solved a mystery, and Moira shot Sloane a look full of poison. Sloane twitched her lips in reply.

"We'll see, Mom. It's just a second date. I don't want to start inviting him to major family events just yet."

"Well, whatever you think, dear. Now Sloane, help me with these dishes, since Moira has to leave."

Moira kissed her mother and grandmother goodbye and avoided her sister as she quickly took the opportunity to leave the house and head back to her own. Shaking her head, she found it marvelous that Sloane could get her way in such a backward manner. The thing was, she would have liked very much to invite Jack, so that she could have someone to talk to, but she didn't want to jinx anything and *certainly* didn't want to give Sloane the satisfaction. By the time she made it back to the shop, Jack was standing outside holding a single tiger lily and smiling broadly.

"I think it got knocked out of someone's garden," he said sheepishly. "I saw it lying there on the sidewalk and thought I would rescue it for you."

Moira smiled widely at the boyish gesture. She accepted the flower with a small laugh.

"Gee whiz Jack, I had no idea you were such a girl. Did you still want to go and see a movie, or would you rather rent some Disney for the night?"

Jack put his hand over his heart as if wounded, though his playful demeanor said otherwise. He decided to play along.

"Ouch, that hurt. Okay, I was trying to show you my softer side in the hopes of seeing your softer side later. Is that better?" He chuckled.

"That's more like it. Shall we walk, or would you rather club me over the head and drag me by the hair?"

"I think we can walk. I don't want hair all over my clothes in the theatre."

Laughing, they set off together back up the slight hill and down a small side street to the theatre, where they studied the night's selections and settled on a British comedy, their original choice of movie having been sold out already. Moira made motions to get her wallet out of her purse, but Jack gently laid his hand on her arm.

"Ah-ah-ah let me, you can get the popcorn."

"Okay, deal." She smiled at the young girl who handed her a ticket and followed Jack inside to line up for popcorn. Once saddled down with their snack and a drink, the two found their theatre room and seats in the back left. For a while, they were slightly awkward again, as the darkened room and the sounds of whispers and chewing from all around them made it hard to talk. They adjusted and readjusted to the seats and cast each other small looks that wound up giving them the giggles.

"Why is it that you make me feel nervous like a little kid?" Moira asked Jack as the screen began to light up.

"I have no idea, must be my devastating good looks."

"That must be it all right. Thank goodness I'm not having that effect on you."

"Oh you do, I hide it well. See, my hands are sweating." With that he reached over and held her hand.

"They're not so bad," she said quietly. And since Jack made no move to take it back, and Moira made no move to push him away, they left their hands together as the movie began to play.

When the movie ended, Moira invited Jack to the shop for coffee and a snack. They walked in peaceful quiet, and Moira guided him through the small alley beside the store that led to the back entrance to both the shop and her home. They came into the large kitchen, and Jack seated himself on a chair in the corner while Moira made coffee and then motioned for him to follow her into the main part of the shop. She pointed to the rows of delicacies in the case and said simply, "Choose."

Jack's eyes took in the rows of the colourful and the complex of Moira's work. He finally settled on a miniature strawberry mouse cake, complete with real mint leaves for garnish and a tiny bit of gold flake picking out the intricacies of the fresh half strawberry on the top.

Moira smiled and chose for herself a hazelnut cookie with white chocolate coating the back. She grabbed her chair from the small workstation behind the counter and followed Jack back into the kitchen.

"What made you want to be a pastry chef?" he asked her as they sat companionably on either side of the steel counter, digging into their desserts.

"My Nana, she used to make soda bread and boxty quick as looking at you. Never with a recipe, mind you, she just automatically threw what she needed into a bowl, popped it in the oven and out would come the most glorious golden treats. I would sit in the kitchen after school, even as a teenager, and watch whatever was in the oven that day get higher and higher, more and more beautiful, and I asked her to teach me. She did, and the more I learned, the more I wanted to learn." Moira lifted her hands as if to say "'oh well", but Jack just looked at her quizzically.

"That's it?" he wanted to know.

"Well no, of course I went to college and studied cooking and gastronomy and even applied to a special school in France. That would have been an amazing adventure, and I was almost packed and ready to go when this opportunity came up here. I had thought that owning my own place would be a long time off in the future, so I hadn't figured it into my plans so soon. And of course the idea of leaving my family for that long wasn't the most appealing one, so I took my savings and the money I had set aside for France, and Nana and Mom gave me some money and Jaye too, of course, and we opened this place." Moira was surprised at how comfortable she felt telling all of this to Jack; normally she didn't carry so much of the conversation.

"That's amazing, and I'm actually kind of jealous. Not only can I not cook even remotely close to this, but I'm

75

not doing anything even close to as cool as you are. My job is just that, it's a job. There isn't a whole lot that a graphic artist can do if he doesn't want to get into movies or cartoons. I just don't like that side of things, or the invariable move if you're good enough to some big entertainment-based city. I like it here. But it's certainly not as amazing at working at your dream ... or owning it." He popped the last bite into his mouth and followed it with a sip of coffee. "By the way, this is really amazing."

Moira glanced up at the clock; it was starting to get late. Jack noticed and checked as well.

"Do you want me to go?" he softly inquired.

"I think so ... soon anyway. I had a good time, Jack."

Jack rose from his chair and walked over to Moira. The fronts of his legs touched her knees and he leaned in close to her. Moira tipped her head up and felt Jack's lips touch hers just as her eyes closed. This kiss was much deeper than the first, and the two became momentarily lost in the intensity of it. Jack grazed his hand over her shoulder and down her arm, but Moira pulled back.

"Goodnight Jack. Thank you for a lovely time."

Jack studied her face for a moment, he wasn't used to women pushing him away and yet didn't mind when she did. He wanted to see her again. Something still seemed to be holding her back, and he wanted to find out what. Strange that none of his usual alarm bells seemed to be ringing, quite the opposite. The more he found out about her, the more he wanted to know. Moira stood to let him out and, as she opened the back door, Jack pulled her in once more, catching her by surprise. This time, Moira kissed him back. She placed her hands on either side of his face as Jack ran his hands down to the small of her back.

Finally they disengaged from one another, and Jack asked if he could see her again.

"I'd like that."

Moira watched him round the corner and then ran through the kitchen to the front window of the shop and waved as he got into his car and drove home.

She spread her arms out in the middle of the dark, empty store and pirouetted back to the kitchen.

Chapter Eight

Jack got into his apartment and threw the mail from his mailbox onto the small table in the front hall near the door. He felt half giddy, half confused. This wasn't going at all like he thought. Usually by now, he would already have spent the night with her and be in the process of making her think that distance between them was her idea. That was his comfort zone, but she was so different from the other women he met. Something about her made him want to talk more, see her more. Shaking his head, he checked his phone for messages and headed to the living room, where he flopped onto the sofa and flicked on the television. He absently scrolled through the channels, trying to process what it was that was so captivating about Moira. There was a man on the screen doing an infomercial for work out equipment.

"What are you waiting for?" he bellowed into the camera.

"I just don't know," Jack said to the man on the screen. He clicked the television off again and headed for bed.

***

On Saturday morning, Jack bustled around his apartment, preparing for a long visit with his father. After the marvelous dessert last night, he had decided to stop in at Moira's bakery to pick up a treat for some of the staff at the hospice and maybe a little something for Kevin as well. There was a slight spring to his step as the thought of seeing her again, even if it was only for a few minutes, caused him to smile and whistle around the apartment.

Moira was up early too, as Saturday was a busy day for her. Jaye was in with her right at eight o'clock to open up the shop and man the counters while Moira lifted out tray after tray of warm breads and sweet smelling goodies from her kitchen. There was no time to talk, a steady stream of customers from the moment they unlocked the door inundated the girls. By the time Jack walked through the doors a little after nine, there were two or three people at the counter as well as several seated in the small café-like area off to the right of the door, sipping coffee and tea and nibbling on scones and biscuits. He waited his turn, admiring the spunky hair of the girl who must be Jaye bustling around with a loud laugh and a kind word for those before him.

"Hiya, cutie, what can I get for you today?" Jaye asked him with a wink.

"Lots, actually, I would like two dozen cinna-crisps, in a box please, two lemon tarts, two chocolate custards and two of those beautiful baked apples."

Jaye's swift practiced hands were already moving, gathering items and placing them into two separate boxes.

"Mmmm," she muttered from under the counter, "Having a party tonight, are we?"

"Nope, just going to visit my dad and make the day of some of the staff there with these lovely goodies. Thanks, Jaye. Hey, is Moira busy?"

Jaye froze and took a long look at his face before breaking into a huge grin and leaning over at him.

"Oh, you're Jack! Wait right here and I'll go grab her." She flounced off toward the kitchen.

"MOIRA!" she hissed once she rounded the corner. "Jack's here. He's *beautiful*, babe."

Moira stopped in her tracks and stared back at Jaye. "How do you know it's Jack?"

"Well, he knew who I was and I have never seen him

before, besides, he just bought out half the store."

"No," she flushed, brushing the flour from her front and dusting off her hands. "Not really half the store."

"No silly, but he is buying quite a bit. Get out here."

Moira came out from the back with Jaye hot on her heels, winking once more at Jack before moving on to help the person now waiting behind him.

"Hi, Jack. I'm surprised to see you here."

"Well, when you've had a bit of the best thing you've ever tasted, you somehow want more of it right away."

Jaye wolf whistled and wiggled her hips suggestively while ringing up a bewildered customer's total.

"I ... I'm flattered. Please, take them as my gift."

"God, no, I wouldn't dream of it! Actually, I was hoping I could see you tonight."

"Umm, okay. I close up at five, and then clean up for about an hour. Do you want to meet me here?"

"Sure, the front door or the back?" Jack asked her.

"The back. See you later, then?"

"You bet." Jack handed a twenty-dollar bill to Jaye, which was more than what his order came to, and left the shop, waving as he hopped into his car and took off up the road.

Moira headed back toward the kitchen while Jaye continued to bounce around behind the counter, humming "My Boyfriend's Back" under her breath and making kissing faces at Moira, who threw a towel at her, letting the laughter again take them over.

***

That night when Jack showed up at the back door of The Cakery, Moira had decided to cook for them. She led him up the stairs and brought him in to the apartment, finding him a seat where he could be comfortable, yet still carry on a conversation as she puttered around the kitchen. Seeming to have anticipated this, Jack had brought a bottle of wine with him; "conversation stimulant" he called it, in case they ran out of things to talk about.

There was a half wall from the living room to the kitchen, so as Moira began chopping and peeling and throwing things into the heated pans on her stove, Jack wandered the room, checking out her book collection and her music collection.

"This room is like a window into your brain."

"How's that?" she asked, leaning over to see what it was that he was looking at. Jack was standing in front of one of the many built-in bookcases in the room, holding a book in one hand and a picture in the other.

"Well, you have everything out on these shelves that you must love. Is this you?" He indicated the photograph in his right hand.

"Yes, that's me and my nana, before she was in the wheelchair. Wasn't she beautiful? That was taken just outside of her hometown in Mountmellic, Ireland. We went there for my fourteenth birthday, so I could get to know my roots."

"You look a lot like her." He placed the photo back on the shelf and turned the book over in his hands. It was a copy of *Anna Karenina*. "Pretty heavy book. Did you read it, or is this an ambition? Personally, I have a few heavy books on my shelves that are more of an aspiration of something I would like to say that I've read, but just haven't gotten there yet."

And so the conversation went. Jack took his time introducing himself to the place, not wanting to upset Moira by prying too much but, in all honesty, he felt like he just couldn't help himself. Moira in turn kept up a steady stream in return; ordinarily she wouldn't volunteer so much about herself, but something about Jack made her feel safe in doing so. He popped into the kitchen once or twice to open the wine, pour her a glass, or taste a proffered spoonful of her labors.

"Are you sure I can't help you?" he asked in one such moment.

"No, really, I mean you could, but I truly do enjoy doing this, and I want to show you that I am capable of more than just sugary stuff."

"I have no doubt." He traced the length of her arm with his forefinger. "One day you'll have to let me give you a break and cook dinner for you at my place, though it will be much more Green Giant and Dempsters garlic bread."

"I don't think I'll mind."

At last they sat down in the living room at the small table that Moira kept folded in the closet when there was no company.

"A toast," Jack said, raising his glass. "To spilled coffee and sugar. I'm glad I met you, Moira."

Blushing, she responded, "Me too."

For the meal, she had made a stir-fry, couscous, and asparagus spears. It was sumptuous.

The light had long faded from the sky and music was now playing softly in the background, as Jack had managed to find the CD player in his journey around her room.

"Is it strange that this feels so relaxed?"

"I don't think so ... though I will say that I have found it very hard to focus on much lately. I think you're fascinating, Moira."

"No, don't say that. I'm not even really interesting, let alone fascinating. I wish you wouldn't flatter me, Jack."

"Why not, don't you like compliments?"

"I'm not very good with them."

"So I see. We'll have to work on that, I guess. So tell me more about your family. You said your sister is getting married ... when is that happening?" Jack took a large bite of his dinner.

"In three weeks, at the beginning of next month." She sat up straight for a minute. "Gosh, it's really coming up quickly. I didn't realize it was sneaking up so fast."

"What do you think of the guy?"

"Martin? He's great. Really good for Sloane; he treats her like a princess and yet still sees through her bullshit." She shook her head, a bemused expression on her face.

"You seem surprised by that."

"I guess I can't believe that she managed to find someone like that so quickly. They've barely known each other for more than a year. I'm just surprised that everything went so fast."

"You don't believe in love at first sight?"

"No. Do you?" She held her breath slightly. Maybe not love at *first* sight, she thought, but something is definitely going on here.

"No, I don't. At least not for me, though my father might say differently. He and my mother only knew each other for three months before they got engaged. Different times, though."

"Yeah, you don't see much of that these days."

They were each silent for a few moments, soaking up the conversation, finishing the food and wine. At last Moira got up and reached for Jack's plate, which he handed her and followed her out to the kitchen.

"I absolutely refuse to let you wash dishes after making that fantastic meal. Just show me where your soap is and let me at it." And with that Jack rolled up his sleeves and started adding water to the sink. Moira smiled at him and took the dish soap from under the sink. She started the coffee maker. As Jack began to wash dishes, Moira hopped up onto the counter beside him. There were butterflies flapping around her stomach while she watched, astonished, as he did the cleaning up.

Eventually, though that had remained quiet for a spell again, they made their way back into the living room and sat together on the couch. Jack's arm rested along the back, his fingers tracing the small hairs at the nape of her neck. She turned to him as if she was going to say something, but instead was cut off as Jack leaned in and touched her lips with his own.

The kiss was warm, deep and intense. The space between them disappeared as they sank into the kiss and each other. Jack took the opportunity to touch her face, her shoulders, her hair, and Moira wrapped her arms around his neck, wanting it to go on forever, not trusting herself to give in to the sensations completely. They stayed like this for ages it seemed, kissing, touching each other's hands, hair and faces, until Moira felt the warmth of a hand on her knee start a slow journey upwards. She clapped her hand on his and pulled back.

"Jack, I can't. I ... I really like you, but I'm just not ready for this to go any further. Not yet, anyway."

"Okay, sorry. I don't want to pressure you. I promise, my hands will stay put right here." And he rested them on her shoulders. "Well, maybe here too," he said, running them through her hair. He looked into her eyes. "You're so lovely."

She dropped her gaze again. This was all a little too familiar to her, the easy flattery and the tender caresses. She didn't want to lose control of the situation.

"Maybe we should call it a night."

"Alright," Jack said, though slightly surprised. Here she was pushing him away again. "Thank you for a great meal and a memorable night." He stood to put on his shoes and coat. "Can I see you again?"

Moira followed him down the stairs to the door. "Okay, tomorrow?"

"Ummm, I have to go and see my dad tomorrow, though I'm free tomorrow night. Can I see you then?"

"Yeah, 'bye Jack." She leaned forward and kissed the tip of his nose.

"Goodnight." And he was gone.

***

Since Sunday was Moira's day off, she slept late and enjoyed a long luxurious bubble bath instead of her normally rushed shower before getting dressed and heading over to her mother's house. There were things to be done today in further preparation for this wedding of the century. Besides, Martin was expected to join the women for lunch, and even though the endless planning and re-planning was driving her crazy, Moira had to admit that she was looking forward to seeing her future brother-in-law. She laid back in the hot steamy tub in her bathroom and let the silky bubbles drift her away into a world of her own imagination. From her bedroom she could hear the faint stirrings of the low classical music she had set her radio to wake her up. She closed her eyes and replayed the kisses from the previous night again and again and again ...

***

Sunday morning in Jack's house was far different from the one happening across town. He woke, downed his customary coffee and a muffin, as well as an orange and roamed around his apartment gathering items that he thought might be useful today. No ushering him out after only an hour's visit, no sir. Today Jack had planned to spend the entire day with his father. Perhaps even take him out on the grounds for a while, if the weather held. He looked out the window, so far so good. The day had dawned with a brilliance he hadn't seen at this time in the fall for as long as he could remember back.

He grabbed a plastic bag from the holder underneath his sink and started to chuck the items he had been gathering into it; cards, some CDs, a few pictures of old friends he had come across and a few other knickknacks. He also grabbed a brush, razor, some shaving cream and a few other things from his bathroom and a jaunty looking bright red cravat that he had found in the men's department of the big mall a town over. He knew that his father would appreciate it. Finally, after about an hour of preparing, he locked up the apartment, tossed the bag into the car, and drove off through the downtown and across the river to the hospice.

There wasn't much traffic out for a Sunday morning, though he speculated that a good-sized portion of this town's population would be at one of the five churches of various denominations. Jack had given up on any aspects of a faith life when the last diagnosis had come down. He just couldn't see how any God could take his father from him, but he pushed these thoughts aside for today. This was to be a good day. His father had been in good spirits, his health was on a slight upturn, and his mood was elevated. There was no need to dwell on negativity today.

Jack let his thoughts turn to Moira and their—could he call it a relationship?—time together last night. She was still something of an enigma to him, like a puzzle that was just waiting for him to solve it. There was some kind of wall there, something that was holding her back from being really *present* with him on their dates. Guiltily he thought that this could just be him. He was holding back too. I mean, she had already filled him in on her family, her business and some fairly important aspects of her life, and what had he told her? Not much, admittedly. Oh well, there was plenty of time for that. Today was about Kevin, and Jack was determined to keep it that way.

He swung his car into the lot and discovered that his favourite spot was already occupied, so he pulled his car instead to the back of the lot overlooking the smooth green lawn, the view of the river and the other side of Fayette. Once parked, he grabbed the bag he had thrown together and let himself out of the car, across the lot and into the building.

The halls were humming with the guests that had arrived for their own leisurely visits with their loved ones on this gorgeous day, and Jack nodded a hello to everyone he passed in the hall. When he arrived at his father's room, he was surprised to see that he was not alone. There was a man in his mid-thirties sitting in the visitor's chair and looking over and making notes on some papers in a folder on his lap.

"Okay, Kev, that should just about do it. I'll see that these get filed and send a copy to your doctor for his folder." He stood up and shook Kevin's hand.

"Thanks, Brian," Kevin said. "I appreciate you giving

up your Sunday morning for this. It's the last time I'll call you in, I promise."

"Anytime, I mean that." There was a real tenderness in the man's voice. Jack thought he looked vaguely familiar, but couldn't place him.

At this, Jack cleared his throat. Kevin perked up in his bed.

"Jack! You're just in time. This is Brian. You remember him, right? He used to work for me at the station, and he's my lawyer now. I always wanted to introduce you two properly. Brian, this is my son, Jack."

If Jack had expected this strange man in the rich suit to walk over and shake his hand in a formal gesture, he couldn't have been more surprised, for Brian took two steps to cross to where he was and wrapped him in a giant bear hug.

"I've heard a lot about you. Sorry we couldn't have met sooner. It's my pleasure, Jack. Take care of this old tiger for me, will you?" He pulled back and turned once more to Kevin. "I'm just on the other side of the phone, if you need me. Take care."

"'Bye Brian, and thank you," Kevin said.

"No, Kevin, thank you," And he turned to leave.

Jack sat down on the chair that was out and looked at his father. Instead of saying anything, Kevin just smiled at his handsome son.

"Okay I give ... who was that?" Jack asked.

"Brian is an old friend of mine. He was one of the first guys I got to work for me after I bought the station. He's a lawyer now and was helping me to finalize my will and make some preparations for my wishes when this disease decides that my time has come."

"Oh."

They were quiet for a bit. The jovial mood that Jack had started out with that morning had evaporated and been replaced by concern, hurt and curiosity.

"Don't look so sad, kid. You know this is coming. Do you want to hear about my requests?"

He shrugged.

"Okay, grab that bunch of papers from the window shelf over there."

Jack handed them to him.

"Let's get this out of the way, okay, and then we'll have a great day."

"Alright," Jack choked out. He nailed a look of stony defiance onto his face, determined not to lose control of his emotions.

"Number one, DNR, that's Do No Resuscitate. I know that this is probably going to get me in my lungs. I don't want any heroic measures taken, no machines, none of that nonsense. When it's time to go, that's it, okay?" He looked to his son for confirmation, continuing when Jack nodded.

"Two, my funeral should be really simple. I don't want you buying one of these thirty thousand dollar coffins, because that's not me. I just want a simple pine one, and only a few flowers, pink roses and daisies, because they were your mother's favourite. I want poetry read and only one piece of music playing. Also, I already have a burial plot next to your mother's, so make sure there's no mistake there."

"Now, the rest of this is just inconsequential stuff, so let's get on with the fun, shall we? I thought you were going to take me for a walk today?"

Jack quickly composed himself and brushed the single tear off his face as he went out to the hallway to find a suitable wheelchair for his dad. That hadn't been easy to listen to, but he'd wager a bet that it hadn't been easy to tell either. He could understand why his dad felt the need to do it, and why he needed to tell him, but that didn't make the situation any easier. For the sake of the day, and enjoying their time together, Jack decided to push it all from the forefront of his thoughts and concentrate on having a good time. He finally located a chair and whooshed his way back towards the room, delighting the eyes of the children in the halls by making zooming noises as he weaved his way past them.

Jack had managed with the help of a nurse to get his father successfully into the wheelchair, and the two were now making their way out to the large sunroom at the back end of the hospice, hopefully to move on outside and down to the riverbanks. The bustle of the hospice was still quick paced and upbeat, an encouraging thing since most of its residents were suffering from terminal illnesses of one type or another. Jack recognized a few that he had come to vaguely know since installing his own father here. There were the two men in their mid-forties with the last stages of AIDS ravaging their faces with lesions, though they seemed to be the happiest of the bunch in the back room at the moment, engaging in a game of checkers and poking fun at each other's choice of clothing. There was an old woman with serious Alzheimer's surrounded by children and grandchildren that she didn't know, but still seemed to be enjoying the company.

It was a lovely day outside, and the large glass walls let the sun pour in, brightening the room and casting shining reflections on the faces of the visitors and patients alike. The staff bustled around, offering juice and cookies to some of the children, accepting thanks and warm looks from the families. Vicky was working, tucking a cushion under the back of a woman in the corner, who was tapping away on the computer they had for the residents. Jack knew the woman had been a great writer in her earlier years, though he did not know much else about her; she never spoke. Vicky winked at him as he headed for the door to the outside, and he nodded back at her. Kevin noticed this and looked up at Jack, though he kept his thoughts to himself.

Once they had made it outside, they followed the concrete path down to the edge of the property, where there was a small iron table and two chairs set under a tree. He parked his father facing the water and set himself down in the chair. This is where they stayed for almost an hour, neither really saying much, just saturated in the atmosphere and each other's company. Though it was mid-September,

90

the air was warm, and the wind was slight; the birds swooped in and over the river, snatching the odd bite of a fish as they prepared themselves for the long journey south that would be coming upon them soon. No one else had ventured outside, so the desire to stay quiet and still was fairly uninterrupted. Kevin would periodically turn his face upwards, soaking in the delights of the weather and the sunshine. Even the normally restless Jack didn't seem to feel much need to talk on, instead watching the trail of a bunch on ants on the tree, dragging a loose stick through the dirt on the ground, and eventually getting up and throwing a few loose rocks into the water, watching as the ripples spread outward and eventually disappeared.

After they had kept their solace for so long, Jack reached into the bag he had brought with him and pulled out the cravat he had brought, tying it around his father's neck.

"Oh, this is nice. Where on earth did you find it?" Kevin asked.

"Some shop the last time I was in Toronto. I knew it would look good on you, just your style."

"I think I'll keep it on for the new night nurse tonight, she's kinda pretty," he mused.

"Playboy," Jack said affectionately.

"Old habits die hard," Kevin stated simply. "I can't help it if I'm irresistible. At least now you know where you get it from."

"Right, my stubbornness *and* my devastating good looks, shall I go on?"

"Please, I hadn't realized you got me so well. I notice you didn't mention my staggering intelligence."

"That goes without saying."

They smiled at each other.

"C'mon Jack, get me down closer to that water. It's so gorgeous that I almost want to strip off and jump in. Remember that vacation we took when you were eight?"

"Yeah, that cottage was so cold, and we didn't get the weather until the last day before we left. You were so happy that it was finally warm that you stripped off right there on the beach and jumped into the water. Mom did too. I thought you guys were crazy."

"I'm surprised you remember that so well."

"It's one of my favourite memories, though I haven't thought of it in a while."

They headed down closer to the river's edge, Jack carefully scanning the slope for the safest spots to navigate the wheelchair. The shore was rocky and uneven, but neither of them seemed to care. Jack meandered closer to the edge, leaning down and letting the tips of his fingers trace the water's edge.

"It's warm!" he said, surprised.

"I want to feel it."

"Are you sure?"

"Never more."

Kevin leaned down in his seat and slowly removed his shoes and socks. Jack walked over to his father and knelt down, gingerly rolling up his pant legs. All of the trappings of his room had already come off for the day, the IV disconnected from the port-a-cath and the monitors disconnected. He kicked his own shoes off to the side and tucked his socks inside them. Then he leaned over and draped his father's arm over his shoulder for support.

"Ready?" he asked. Kevin nodded, so he carefully helped pull him to his feet. He was so small now, his weight barely registered. Jack moved slowly with him towards the water's edge. They looked down, the rocks of the shore digging into the bottoms of their feet, though neither of them complained. The water licked their toes and, though it was indeed warm for this time of year, the shock of it made them both gasp, and then laugh out loud at their reactions. They wiggled their toes into the mud, stirring up little pools of brown amidst the brilliant blues and whites reflected from the sky. Jack had not seen his father look this alive in weeks, months even. Kevin laughed out loud and turned his face up to the sky with his eyes closed. For a small amount of time, they forgot the treatments, forgot Jack's work and just enjoyed the moment. Words were unnecessary, instead they let the crispness of the day and the freedom of the water and sky swallow them whole. They spent a good half hour, until Jack noticed that his father was beginning to get a little shaky from the cold.

"We should go in and get you warm. I don't want you to catch pneumonia."

"Like that matters now. Don't you just love this, Jack? I could stay here all day."

"Okay, ten more minutes anyway."

"Stop worrying about me, just have fun please. Please Jack. I want to just enjoy today without you getting so worried. Watch this." And with twinkling eyes, he let go of his son and stomped his foot down hard, sending a small cascade of water spraying up Jack's leg.

"Ahh-ah!" Jack yelped. "That's cold!"

"Nonsense, you're just not used to it. Look, your feet are fine!" And with that he stomped his foot again, splashing Jack's other leg.

"Oh, it's on now old man!" Jack jumped up in the air with a whoop, bringing both feet down together in the water and showering Kevin's pants with a large splash.

They yelped and hollered like little boys, until their clothes were wet and clung to their bodies, and then Kevin's face changed, and Jack brought him quickly back to his chair. He covered his shriveled shivering legs with the blanket he had brought and gathered up the shoes and socks. Though Kevin was panting, he was smiling so largely that it fairly split his face in two.

"Thank you."

They made their way back to the building, unable to shake their smiles through their shivers, much to the chagrin of the staff who eyeballed them with displeasure and the other members of the hospice, looking on with delight and not a small amount of envy.

Jack waved off any offers of help from the staff and got his dad back into his room. He cradled an arm underneath him and helped to lift him up onto the bed. Then

93

Jack bustled around the room, getting fresh pajama bottoms, clean and dry socks and some towels to dry off their feet. Kevin was physically worn out by the activities, though he seemed jubilantly happy. He lay back on the bed, allowing Jack to fuss over him and smiling at his handsome son. Jack seemed happy too, he was humming under his breath all through his ministrations. Finally, he looked up to see that his dad had succumbed to the sleep that was inevitable after such an exhausting jaunt. He pulled a chair up to the bed, grabbed one of the many books off the shelves and stuffed a pillow behind himself. Then he put his feet up on the end of the bed and got comfortable for a while so his father could sleep.

Once Kevin was well and truly down for a long sleep, and Jack had read about a third of the book he was holding, he went back out to the hallway and started towards the room where the staff did all of their paperwork, hoping for a chance to speak with his father's doctor. When he tracked him down, they had a conversation that was not entirely to Jack's liking. This amounted to a swift repossession of the hope that he had been starting to harbor since their little afternoon adventure. Surely a man such as his father, who still had such zeal for life and managed to show glimpses of his former self, could not be so close to death's door? But he most assuredly was, the doctor had insisted. And these childish resistances to the need for simple treatment techniques such as a feeding tube, the oxygen mask and the continued use of morphine or even OxyContin would speed up the process. He was warned not to be deceived by Kevin's ability to show such a brave face and insisted that his health was well managed and under control. One of these days he would just slip into a coma while his organs and senses failed one by one.

Defeated, Jack slumped back to his fathers' room, looked in to see him still sleeping sound and walked outside to be alone with his thoughts.

Chapter Nine

At the Ryan house, the usual warm and welcoming kitchen table that held in the place of honour a pot of tea was piled high with various dish settings, a variety of flowers and vases and a plethora of food. Siobhan was seated in her chair in the small nook created by the juncture of counter and wall, and Angela, Sloane, Katie, Michelle, and Martin were crowded around the rest of the table, shouting out ideas and tasting all kinds of little dainty delicacies. Two unfamiliar people in the room seemed to be members of the hall where the wedding was being held. They kept trying to break into the loud conversation with explanations of what everything was, steering Sloane and Martin from one decision to the other and not really helping the situation at all. From what Moira could see, Siobhan seemed to be making a sport of pretending to be deaf, loudly asking for descriptions of something they had just explained over and over, and then saying WHAT as loudly as she could. Though it was giving the girls the giggles, Angela looked to be wearing thin of patience to deal with it. The whole scene was like something out of a Marx Brothers' movie, and it caused Moira to smile whilst she searched for an opening to join in the fray.

"Hi there, sis, care to grab a plate and join in?" Martin approached his soon-to-be sister-in-law and casually draped an arm over her shoulder.

"Of course, wouldn't miss it ... Hey! I didn't know you were doing this, Wayne. Good to see you." Moira recognized one of the two caterers and she shook hands with him. He was a fellow alumnus from the training college where she had gone to study cooking. He looked relieved to see a familiar face, since Sloane was in high doh, oohing over this, groaning over that and in essence picking apart all of the samples of food along with Katie and Michelle, lost in the mirth and the power of the occasion.

Moira surveyed the table, laden as it was. She had such a hard time deciding what to sample that in the end she wound up with a large plate with an equal mix of hors d'oeuvres, amuse bouches, crudités, shellfish, chicken, asparagus and a separate plate handed to her by Wayne with no less than five different dessert samples on it.

"Okay, folks," Sloane bellowed, her small frame looking deceptively tall standing on a chair in the middle of the room, "now I want you to taste everything and tell me honestly what you think. Especially the dessert, it has to be good but not overshadow Moira's cake. Raise your forks! One, two, three … EAT!"

All present scrambled to find an available place to seat themselves so that they could give some proper attention to the task at hand. Sloane planted herself on Martin's lap, who was busy feeding her little tidbits from their collective plate. Katie had hunched down in the corner of the kitchen on the floor next to the fridge, no doubt to have a little privacy should she want to enhance her dining experience with a drink or two, Moira thought. Michelle was sitting on the counter somewhat close to Siobhan, letting out a guffaw every once in a while through her full mouth as the old woman made her laugh. Angela was standing on the other side of the counter island, eating and chatting with the other caterer, while Moira wound through the people to talk with Wayne about the food.

"It's all amazing, Wayne. I especially like the chicken. Is that wine and … tarragon? It's wonderful, so light and tender. You'll have to tell me how you do this sometime."

"Well, that truly is a compliment coming from the best success story from our class. I like the chicken best as well, but try telling that to your sister. She is worried that chicken might be too bland a choice. I wish this was your wedding, Moira, you're far less concerned with appearances."

Moira chuckled, though she shot looks at Sloane to make sure those comments were not overheard. It appeared safe.

"Thanks, that means a lot, but I haven't got time to get married right now. I'm too busy keeping the business up. You know, you should really break away from that company you're working for and go into business for yourself. I know you'd be a huge success."

"You sure have a lot of faith in me. In fact, I'm starting to do just that. Would you be willing to put up a few of my business cards in your place?"

"Of course, so long as you tell your clients the best place to get dessert in town."

"Not that any folks around here need to be told that, I think you've made more of a name for yourself than you realize."

Moira gave him a sliding pat on the back and a quick peck on the cheek in response. Wayne was a good guy. They had gone out once on a date years back when they were still in school, but found that their temperaments didn't suit. They spent four hours at a dinner in a swanky restaurant tearing apart the chef's attempts at the food they ordered, talking about how they would do it all so differently. It had been a lesson in mixing relationships with business ... for them, it just didn't work. They had settled on a comfortable, non-demanding friendship instead.

Two hours passed by like lightning, the high-fevered chattering punctuated by the enjoyment of the marvelous food and the easy nature of the company. By the time one o'clock had rolled around, the family had retired to the living room with their cups of tea and coffee, and Wayne and his colleague were busy cleaning up the skeletal remains of the feast in the kitchen.

"Oohh, I'm fat," Sloane declared from her post on the

couch beside Martin, who had his head back and his eyes closed. "That was a lot of food."

"Yes it was, but totally worth it. Nice choice of caterers, Sloane. What are you going to decide on for the meal?" Angela wanted to know.

"I don't know yet. I need to know what all of you think first, especially you, Moira."

"Hmm, what?" Moira was sleepy after all that food.

"What did you think? You're the foodie here."

Moira was surprised. Here was Sloane not only being nice to her, but actually seeking out her approval.

"I thought the chicken was the best, for the entrée. That and the asparagus spears with the crab stuffed mushrooms and the starters that they brought today. Are you sure that you want another dessert to go with the cake? I'm making a really big one. It will be enough to go around to the guests and then some."

Sloane looked thoughtful for a moment. Finally she nudged Martin, who jolted his head down and gazed at her quizzically.

"Which did you like best, Martin, the chicken or the seafood?"

"I know how you feel about chicken at a wedding, hon, but it was honestly the best thing. I really think we should go with that."

Sloane shrugged. It was apparent that she wouldn't have selected this as her first choice, but she was having a hard time coming up for a valid argument against it, especially since the rest of the company seemed to be nodding and murmuring in agreement with Martin and Moira.

"Okay, I'll go talk to them." She got up to leave, and Martin joined her as they went back out to the kitchen to sit down with the caterer's again and lay out the meal plan for the reception.

In the living room, Katie and Michelle made their goodbyes and headed out to the various activities that they had planned for the day, shouting out a goodbye to the couple in the kitchen.

Only Angela and Siobhan were left in the living room with Moira, swirling around their teacups and tossing glances between each other and the animated conversation coming from the kitchen.

"I don't really know what all this fuss is about anyway. Sloane could've gotten your mother and me to cook the whole thing for far less than they're paying these guys. I still don't see why she needs this big society wedding anyway. Wouldn't a small wedding out of the house have done for her?"

"Now, Mother, this is her day. If she wants the big showy wedding, let her have it." Angela sighed.

"Yes, yes. Princess Sloane can have her day, and I won't say a word against it. You spoiled that girl, Angie, dear."

"I know."

Siobhan wheeled herself out of the room, winking at Moira as she went, and launched herself full board into the talks in the kitchen, interrupting and interjecting her ideas where she pleased.

Angela moved over and joined Moira on the small loveseat in the corner.

"What's on your mind, bug?"

"Wow, you haven't called me that in a while. Nothing really, I guess I'm just getting tired of this wedding stuff. Aren't you yet?"

"Not at all, I'm happy for Sloane. This is what she wants and I'm able to give it to her."

"I guess." She slumped back in the seat once more and laid her now empty mug on the small table to the side.

"There's something else, though. C'mon, penny for your thoughts."

"What makes you think there's something else?"

Angela leaned over so that her face was squarely facing her daughter's. "Because, my sweet girl, I can read every bit of your face like an open book. I know every expression. I do believe I can actually *see* the flickers of your brain working in your eyes. So talk to me, tell me what's

99

going on in that head of yours."

"I don't know ... confusion, really. And Sloane is just getting on my nerves lately. Frankly, I just can't wait for this whole thing to be over and she can be Martin's problem for a while."

"Martin's problem? Is that how you see your sister, as a problem? What's going on with the two of you? You used to be so close and, now that I think of it, you've hardly spoken to each other in the last week or so. Did you have a fight?"

"Sort of ... not really ... just that stupid thing about dates for the wedding and how concerned she is with how everything looks ... I'm just tired of being the one who always has to look out for her, for her feelings. She doesn't ever look out for mine. But that's part of being the big sister, I look out for her and she lets me. Only now that she's older she doesn't let me, she just resents it. Or at least that's how it feels."

Angela tipped her head to the side and studied her troubled daughter's face. She didn't speak; she just let Moira get it out.

"Oh, mom, ever since dad left I've been the one to keep her in line. I made her lunches, made sure she got her homework done and even took her shopping for her first bra and taught her about her period. I was the one keeping her head out of the clouds, or at least trying. It's not your fault," she added, seeing the look of hurt flicker across her mother's face. "I know how hard you had to work to keep this house, I just thought that the best things I could do for you at the time were to keep quiet about it and be the best help I could be for you."

A few scant tears had formed in Angela's eyes, and neither of them had noticed that the group in the kitchen had finished, and that Sloane, Siobhan and Martin were standing quietly in the doorway listening to every word.

"Maybe that's why I'm the way I am," Moira continued, sniffling. "Maybe that's why I work so hard, worried about you and Nana and Sloane, not making time for a social life let alone a relationship. Maybe that's why I let myself be so blind to Mark's true nature, because I knew he would leave eventually, and I wanted it to be sooner, rather than after a life and a marriage and children like you and daddy. I just don't want *you* to worry about *me*, or about Sloane. I thought I could do it all for you. I'm so sorry, Mom, nothing turned out how I thought it would."

Angela pulled her in fiercely for a hug and stroked her hair as Moira cried and cried into her shoulder.

"Shh, now, I never meant to put so much pressure on you. You don't have to take care of everybody, you know. It's not only your shoulders we rest upon."

Moira sat up, just noticing that her family was standing around her. "But I have to worry about you all, because if I don't, the only person I have left to worry about is me."

"Sure, you don't need to worry about yourself. Isn't your life grand already?" Siobhan piped from her chair.

Sloane was crying as well, Martin's arms wrapped around her, comforting her. Moira took in this tableau with a revelation; for all of her bravado and boldness, her baby sister was still very much a little girl who, despite what her mother said, needed someone to take care of her. She was grateful for Martin, who loved this dainty lady so entirely that her tears and dependence just made her more endearing to him. She gave him an appreciative smile, which he returned. How strange that he seemed to get this dynamic of women so well. It was not something she expected from any man, not even Jack. *God!* she thought. *I can't ever introduce him to this zoo. We're a bunch of crazy, co-dependent emotional women. How the hell would he react to that? Probably run screaming for the hills.*

"I envy you, Sloane. It's true. You have a really good man there, and you're lucky to have him. I envy you too, Martin. It's brave of you both to think about marriage, especially after what we've seen of it in this house."

Angela and Siobhan both perked up at this.

"Now wait just a minute, you're talking like you

101

don't believe in marriage, in love. That's not, I hope, the way I brought you up," Angela said with indignation.

"And not what I thought I had taught you either," said Siobhan.

"Well, it's what I feel. Look at how your marriages turned out. No offense, but they don't exactly inspire faith in the institution."

At this, Siobhan wheeled herself over so that she was in the centre of the room. "Let me tell you a little something about love and marriage, m'dear. It's not perfect. It's messy and loud and hard. Do you want to know why? Because it's human; two different people, of different backgrounds with very different ideals and opinions and you stuff them together in the same house and add small children and expect everything to be just wonderful? It can't happen like that. The trick is to see past all the hard and find what makes you happy with each other, find your glory moments and hang on to them with a vengeance. Your mother and I may not have had the ideal marriages in the end, but it was and still is the good in those men that our hearts embrace, not the bad habits that wound up being a reason to leave. I loved your grandfather, not his gambling, and your mother loved your father, not his penchant for, well, nevermind. Just because these two marriages didn't work long term isn't any reason to abandon the idea altogether. If you give up now at your young age, I don't even want to think about all the good things you'll be turning your back to before having a chance to experience them. I would rather have a thousand hurts if it meant having one more of the good days back, and anyone who's ever really been in love will tell you that. You must take the bad with the good, because the good is really, really worth it."

Everyone was rooted to her spot; it was rare that Siobhan spoke like this. Usually she was loud, brash, funny and to the point.

"Now, that was a lovely serious moment, I would like to go to the loo. I hope all you gloomy Guses have cheered up when I get back. I hate all this mooning about." With that she turned on her wheels and wound through the house to the bathroom, leaving them all staring in her wake, chewing thoughtfully on her words.

Chapter Ten

"You're still sitting here?" Siobhan declared as she once again took up the spot in the large doorway between the rooms. "What on earth for? Let's go, let's go!" Siobhan turned yet again towards the kitchen, and this time Sloane reached over and grabbed the back of the chair by the handles.

"WHEELIE!" she whooped and tipped the chair so that Siobhan's feet were now dangling down.

"Sloane, put her down this minute!" Angela barked, coming up behind them.

"WOO HOO! Once more around the park, driver," Siobhan demanded, and they howled together as they recklessly zipped around the house to the delight of Moira and Martin, watching with wide smiles from the living room door and to the chagrin of Angela, who suspected that an accident was about to happen. Martin poked Moira and pointed at his bride to be.

"That's why I love her," he said, and they both looked at Sloane, near radiant in her triumphant tour with Grandma, her hair catching the snippets of sun that were pouring in through the windows.

"I'm happy for you guys, Martin, I really am."

"Then why do you sound like you're convincing yourself?" He smiled at her though the question was fairly serious.

"Maybe I am a bit, sorry. She's still my baby sister, I don't really think of her as a grown woman about to get married. It's going to take a little getting used to."

"You thought we would have broken off the engagement long before now?" He was mocking her, though with good nature. Maybe that's why the women all loved him so much. He was forward about his feelings but never made any of them feel as if they were on trial. Maybe that's why he was such a good lawyer too.

"Sloane must have told you that. Are you offended?" Moira asked him.

"No, not really, most of my family thought the same thing. You know, there goes Martin, charmed by a young blonde and completely lost his head. But something about us really works, and I can't help just adoring the daylights out of her. I honestly can't imagine life without her."

Moira gave him a hug. *They really broke the mold when they made him,* she thought, shaking her head as they linked arms and moved off to the kitchen for a late lunch of leftovers with the rest of the family.

***

Angela beamed around the table at her family. She loved this wedding because, for weeks now, her whole family had spent far more time together than usual, and she couldn't get enough of it. Just taking a few minutes out of the moment to herself to survey the scene, she relished the thought that finally Sloane seemed to have something in her life that made her as happy as Moira. It was rare that the two girls appeared to be set on a path that made them both so happy, and both at the same time no less. She must have been standing in her position for a few moments, because she suddenly became aware that the assembled group was staring at her.

"Oh bugger off!" she good-naturedly chided them. "I'm allowed to enjoy this as much as I can, so you can all stop teasing me about it any time now."

"Who's teasing you?" Siobhan demanded. "No-one has said a single word today so far about your cow eyes and your heavy sighing, have they?"

106

Angela sniffed as everyone chuckled at the situation. She turned her attention to Moira.

"How's the shop doing these days?"

"Fine Mum, in fact, I'm thinking of shutting down on Mondays for a day to work on cake orders without the bustle of having customers in at the same time. That way Jaye can have some time off and I can work uninterrupted."

"Well, you must be doing well then. I ran into Mrs. Crawford the other day and she was simply raving about some new strawberry mouse thing that you have come up with."

Moira smiled to herself and rubbed her arms with her hands. "Yes, I have had some good feedback on that particular one." She closed her eyes for a moment and thought back to the look on Jack's face sitting in the kitchen in the evening sampling that delicacy with a smile of rapture on his face.

"Oh, have your customers been giving you compliments?" Angela was putting dishes into the dishwasher from the earlier feast of catering samples.

"You might say that."

"What might *you* say?" asked Siobhan slyly.

"*I* might say that I gave one to Jack and he really enjoyed it." Moira's face broke into a large smile.

"Well, well. I must say that it does me good to know that you are working your way to his heart the right way, with food."

"Works for me," Martin declared, setting his arms around Sloane and looking at her adoringly. "First time I ever tasted this woman's lasagna, I knew she was a keeper."

Sloane giggled and turned around to hug Martin. "You see, Mum," she said over her shoulder, "I did learn something from you. It may be all I can really make, but I'm so good at it, it's scary."

Angela smiled back at her daughters. Of all of the hardships she had worried about as a single mother as her girls grew up, she had never worried about their appreciation for food. There was always a wonderful warm meal on the go in the Ryan household, and both girls had been active participants in the kitchen from a very early age.

The banter in that warm and welcoming room continued on for what seemed like hours as the group traded ideas on the wedding, plans for the future and grazed lightly on the sumptuous food that was still sitting out on the table, having been demanded by Angela that nothing was to become a leftover for the fridge.

"So anyway, Katie is in the corner just plastered and absolutely wrapped around this guy from that fundraiser the night before when in walks Troy. He took one look at her and walked straight over, tapped her on the shoulder and calmly broke up with her. She's not even upset! She just laughed and said that she's always on the lookout for some new blood to keep her young, so why bother getting upset. The new guy's name is Mitch, and she's bringing him to the wedding as her date, so nobody say anything about Troy."

"That's nice, Sloane, wait until after she leaves so that she can't even defend her behavior," Angela quipped.

"Well, why shouldn't I? It's not like she would really feel the need to defend herself anyway, she's proud of it."

"Oh dear, should you really be spending your time with someone so … frivolous?" Angela wondered out loud.

"What a delicious word, frivolous, I just love it. It's like entanglement, tryst, decadent. Don't you just love words like that, Moira? They veritably roll off of the tongue." Siobhan was smiling as she spoke.

"Just gorgeous, Nana."

"I wish you guys wouldn't make fun of me so much," Sloane pouted.

"But you're such an easy target," Moira laughed.

"Fine, just go ahead and make fun then, I'm leaving. C'mon Martin, we've got reservations for dinner." She got up, pulled Martin after her by the edge of his sleeve and kissed her mother and grandmother goodbye.

Moira decided to leave as well. She and Jack had

plans to see each other again. She decided against mentioning that it was the fourth date they had had since meeting earlier that week. It just didn't seem so rushed to her, but her family would definitely have words to say about it, good or bad, and she didn't intend on hearing them. Walking through the streets on her way home, she congratulated herself that the constant exercise not only saved the environment from another polluting vehicle, but also saved her figure from all of the sampling at work of the rich desserts and breads that she made and tested on a regular basis. She let herself into the back door of The Cakery and spent a few minutes wandering around in the kitchen, checking things over, looking through the pantry area and the large walk-in fridge to make sure that they were well supplied for Monday. She lifted several pieces of a wedding cake from the fridge that she was in the process of doing for a small mid-week do on Wednesday night. The couple were older and having the wedding out of their small ranch-style house. Even though the guest list was small, they had insisted on a full three-tiered cake for the reception. Everything on the cake looked great. The rolled fondant was a beautiful shade of light green, and the scrollwork was in pristine white, with a strikingly rich very dark green picked out detail around the loops and sconces. She had already lifted the first two layers back into the fridge and was about to heft the third when a noise startled her.

"Moira? The door was open and I saw the kitchen light on ... "

"Aaaahhh!" she screamed and literally threw the bottom tier of the cake into the air. Both she and Jack dived to retrieve it, but it was too late. The large confection dropped onto the floor with a dramatic splattering sound.

"Shit," was all Jack could get out. They stood over the mess, staring. "Was that your sister's cake?" he finally asked.

"No, that was for a wedding this week."

Jack squatted down and lifted the bottom support piece, which was now on the top, and regarded the muddle

109

of broken dessert.

"Moira."

"Yes, Jack."

"I think it's dead." He put two fingers against the ravaged side of the remains. "Yup, no pulse, I'm so sorry."

Moira started to laugh, and once she got started, she couldn't stop, until at last she was leaning on the counter for support and, faced with such mirth, Jack began to laugh as well.

"Now what?" he sputtered.

"Now I make a new one, so much for our date."

"Can I help?"

"Sure, if you want. You don't have to, you know."

"I want to," he said simply, looking into her eyes.

"Okay, here you go," she said, and she handed him a large dustpan and pointed to the garbage pail.

While Jack scooped up the remains of the cake and wet some paper towels to clean the floor of the sugar, Moira began gathering the ingredients necessary to rebuild her creation. In no time at all, the large Hobart was whirring away, and Moira was prepping the large round cake pan for the new replacement. Jack wound up grabbing a chair from the corner to watch her as she worked.

"You know, Moira, I know about your family and about your work, tell me about your other boyfriends. Were they all as clumsy as me, or am I special?"

Moira was a little taken aback; did he seriously want to know? More important—did he just call himself her boyfriend?

She studied his face for a moment with a puzzled look.

"Do you really think we're at that point yet?"

Jack laughed.

"I don't know. It's really not my style."

"Not your style to what?"

"Ask such a personal question. I'm not usually that kind of guy."

"What kind of guy are you, Jack?"

Moira lifted the bowl of the mixer out and began scooping the contents into the large pan. She swept it into the oven and motioned to the coffee maker. Jack nodded, so she filled the base with water and spooned some fresh ground coffee into the top, switching on the button. She turned to him, waiting.

"I don't know what kind of guy I am. I'm sorry if I caught you off guard. I don't usually ask such personal questions. I just really feel like I want to know you better."

"Fair enough, I don't usually tell too much about myself, though. If you want to know so badly, it's going to cost you." She smiled at him mischievously.

"What did you have in mind? Clothing, like strip poker?"

Moira laughed out loud.

"Nothing so scandalous I'm afraid. I'll show you mine, if you show me yours. You want to know about me, tell me about you."

"I'm warning you," Jack said, warming to the idea, "I'll do it, but it won't be pretty."

"Okay," Moira agreed, pouring out the coffee and handing him a spoon and the sugar bowl. "Shoot."

"Your first boyfriend, who was he and what was he like ... and why did you like him?"

"Jason Sharpe. I met him in ninth grade in science class. We were assigned to be lab partners. He was nice looking, a tiny bit shorter than me and kind of a geek. I didn't mind, I was kind of a geek too. We used to have lunch together, and one day he asked me to be his girlfriend, so I said okay. Then he kissed me right there on the grass outside of the school and stuck his tongue right in my mouth. We broke up five minutes later, and I got a new lab partner the next week, Jaye. We've been friends ever since, now your turn."

"First girlfriend was Tracey Ann Kimble. She always went by both names, Tracey Ann, although now that I think of it, I really don't know why. She was very popular, and so was I back then. We also met in ninth, but at the time she

111

was dating a friend of mine. They didn't really get along. We dated until just after I was fifteen and then we broke up. She was also my first." Jack watched closely to get Moira's reaction to this information.

"Really! At fifteen? Don't you think that was a little young? Is that why you broke up with her? Because she had sex with you?"

"Relax, it was a mutual breakup, honestly. I went through a period where I was really intense and hard to be around. Tracey always wanted to be in the middle of the fun. She stayed quite popular for the rest of high school and I didn't. Now your turn, who was your next squeeze?"

"Colin, who was totally beautiful and out of my league. I was seventeen when I met him, and he was nineteen. He was the friend of the brother of a friend of Jaye's, and he and I showed up one night at a party we were all at. He said that I had beautiful legs and offered to buy me a beer. We wound up spending the night sitting on a roofed swing in the backyard of the house party talking and kissing each other. I never really knew what he saw in me or why he was always talking about my legs, but he was really nice and kind to me. We dated for almost a year and then broke up when he started to pressure me to sleep with him. I just wasn't ready and I was trying to focus on applying to college. When we broke up, he dated Sloane for about a month, and then they broke up too. She never mentions him. It's one of those things we just don't talk about."

"Doesn't sound like you've had the best luck in men," Jack commented softly, finishing the dregs of his coffee.

"No, not exactly," Moira said wryly. *Just wait until I mention Mark, that'll send him screaming out of here.* She poured him some more coffee and handed him a cookie.

"I guess that makes it my turn again. My second girlfriend was Amanda. We dated really briefly in college. Actually, we didn't really date, we kinda used each other for stress relief when classes got tough or we had big exams due up. I know it sounds shallow, but we trusted each other and liked each other. It sort of made it easier to cope, knowing that we could blow off steam with each other physically when we needed to." Seeing Moira's face drop a bit, he reached over and touched her hand. "This is going to sound shitty and pathetic, so if you don't want to see me anymore after this, I'll understand. Most of my relationships ... make that *all* of my relationships since then have been like this, women that understand my need for companionship, without an official relationship. They usually move on when they find the real thing, a man who wants it to go further, or I end it if it becomes too complicated. Do you hate me now?"

"Noooo," Moira said thoughtfully. "I don't hate you. It's a little shallow, though." She remained quiet for a minute, and Jack waited patiently for her to complete her thought. "Why are you so interested with me, then?"

"You really want to know? I'm not sure. You fascinate me. I feel like every time I see you, I want to see you more ... no wait, that's not coming out right. What I mean is, I like you, you're very beautiful, and you're interesting. I just can't help wanting to know all about you. Is that okay?"

It was a huge gamble. Jack hardly knew why he was doing this. *It's so unlike me, and yet I can't help myself.*

"Okay, how many women are we talking about exactly?" Moira asked. Clearly, she was intrigued. "Wait, I don't want to know. But I do want to know, are you seeing anybody like that now?"

Jack looked her straight in the eye. "Absolutely not," he said.

They spent hours in the kitchen that night. Moira eventually took the cake out of the oven and, as it sat cooling, Jack told her about his father.

"What I don't understand is why he is so calm about it all. I can't stand seeing him so helpless, and he just shrugs it off."

"Maybe that's his coping mechanism. Everyone deals with stress differently; *you* should be the first to understand that," she said to him, pointedly.

"Hmm, touché. So what do you do to relieve stress,

Miss Moira?"

"Just this," she said, sliding the cooled cake off of the rack and onto the base to prepare it for decorating. "Or I clean my apartment, or cook something fancy for myself, or take a bubble bath. It all depends on the mood I'm in."

Moira went into the walk-in fridge and brought out a funny looking round lump of pale green dough. She unwrapped the plastic from it, sprinkled some icing sugar onto the pristine marble slab that was on the counter, and slapped the mound onto it.

"What on earth is that?"

"It's rolled fondant, icing sugar that you can roll out like dough. Really useful for wedding cakes, it gives me a smooth surface to work on."

"These people want a green cake?"

"Yup, don't look so surprised; I make all kinds of colored cakes. Once I did one that was all in neon. If you want, go open that door," she pointed to the large fridge, "and take a look at the top two tiers, they're sitting on the middle self on the left."

Jack got up from his seat and opened the door, peeking in around the corner and literally sucked his breath in when he saw the beautiful creation.

"It's stunning!"

He shut the door again and came over to stand behind Moira, who was rolling out the fondant to the size of the pale sheet she would need. He gently touched her waist with his warm hands and leaned in close to her ear. She smelled like Jasmine.

"It's really beautiful," he said softly.

The little hairs on the back of her neck stood at attention, and Moira prayed that he couldn't tell that she was sweating. She could actually feel the droplets run down to the inside of her bra.

"Thank you."

Jack stayed close enough to Moira to be aware of her smell, her breathing, but not so close as to impede her as she folded the fondant gently in half and draped it over the

114

cake. She then reached over to a drawer and pulled out a queer-looking plastic contraption, something like a plastering trowel, complete with a piece rose for a handle, but with the edges tipped up and rounded. She used this to smooth the fondant over the cake until it resembled a seamless, perfectly smooth pillow. She then trimmed the excess from the bottom and wrapped it back in plastic, which she handed to Jack to store for her once again. By the time he had put it away, she had lifted the cake onto a lazy susan and grabbed a piping bag from another part of the kitchen. In a deep refrigerated drawer, there was another large bowl filled with the kind of fluffy icing that Jack recognized. She spooned it into the bag, twisted the top closed into her fist, and smiled at Jack.

"Now comes my favourite part," she said. Jack dragged his chair over to the other side of the island counter and propped his elbows onto the top, resting his head in his hands to watch her. She piped elegant curlicues and swirls over the cake, making an Elizabethan pattern with the icing as if it were no more matter than swishing her wrist. The movements had a fluidity that mesmerized Jack, and he was entranced, lost in the art of her creation. By using her other hand to slowly turn the susan, she made a series of small points along the bottom, so that there was an almost lacy edge to finish it. Then she got out a further icing bag, a new tip, and a smaller bowl of a dark hunter green icing. This she added in miniature dots that, although they seemed simplistic in conception, lent a stunning visual to the overall look of the cake. In the two and a half hours that it took for her to recreate the original, Jack found that he had become completely enthralled with the process. They didn't speak as she piped; Moira seemed to block out everything around her as she worked but, honestly, an interruption to the process would have marred the sheer joy of the experience. When it was finished she gingerly lifted it back into the fridge and emerged, swiping her hair from her forehead, a look of contentment and accomplishment on her face.

"I think I'm falling for you, Moira."

A slow, warm smile spread across her face, like the sun rising over water. Her green eyes brightened and sparkled like emeralds. In her head she was thinking, *it's too soon, it's too soon, it's too soon.* But her heart had already embraced this thoughtful, caring man, and it was all too obvious to her that she was falling for him, too. Jack got up from his seat and took her in his arms. He enveloped her in sweeping hug, burying his face in her hair and running his hands from her shoulders to the small of her back and there they stayed, swaying to the private rhythms of their heartbeats and taking in the moment completely without prejudice or fear.

It had been a long day for them, yet they were both loath to leave the warm kitchen and the comfort of each other's arms. After some light feathery kisses and some lingering gazes, Jack motioned to the time and announced that he would have to go or risk the temptation to spend the night. Moira agreed with him and walked him out to the small space between The Cakery back door and the stairs to her apartment. They parted for the night, promising to talk the next day. Moira watched him walk around the corner and out to the street. Then she locked the doors and went up to her rooms with a happy smile on her face.

Chapter Eleven

On Monday morning, Moira followed her normal routine and was engrossed in the progress of several varieties of bread when Jaye joined her in the kitchen of the shop.

"I've decided to come with you tonight," she announced.

"Okay, but why?"

"If you're going to spend a few hours with Sloane and her stupid friends in search of the perfect shoe to match those horrid dresses, you'll need backup ... after what she said to you last week."

"Oh. Okay. Hand me the olive oil, would you."

"Sure."

Jaye handed the bottle to Moira and then walked to the front of the store to unlock the door and turn on the sign to start off the business for the day. She counted the float in the till, placed some napkin holders on the four bistro style tables and checked the goods in the refrigerated display case for any signs of imperfection. Satisfied and without a customer yet, she meandered back into the kitchen and began taking fresh and scintillating smelling loaves of bread out to the front. Since it was a warm day, she opened the front door and tucked a wedge under it. The smell of fresh baked bread was always enough to bring in a few early morning wanderers, even on a Monday. Sure enough, moments later there was a pair of older ladies in matched nylon walking suits coming in with noses at work, taking in the glorious smell and the sight of the colored treats on display.

"Hello ladies, out for a morning stroll?" Jaye politely inquired.

"My goodness what unusual hair, I hope your boss isn't upset that you did that," said the first, a short, slightly plump woman in a pink suit.

Jaye patted her cobalt blue streaks proudly.

"Well, she threatened to fire me, but we're working it out."

"Oh my!" the other woman said. She was taller, with a body like a skeleton. Her suit was purple.

"I'm just kidding." Jaye winked at them. "Now, what can I do for you on this beautiful day?"

"Oh, we don't eat sweets anymore," the skeleton said, though her partner was staring longingly at the choices. "But I couldn't help smelling that wonderful bread. I assume that it's fresh."

"Right out of the oven."

"I'll take a loaf of marble rye," she said.

As Jaye was sliding the still warm loaf into a white paper bag, the second woman piped up from her position, now leaning way down over the much sweeter of the selections.

"Excuse me dear, but why are these cupcakes so small?" She pointed to a huge arrangement of cupcakes half the size of normal ones and twice as colourful.

"Those are our baby cakes, very popular with small kids and moms that don't want to give them more than they can handle."

"I'll take six, assorted colours," she announced, ignoring the scowls of her friend. "I'm having my grandkids over later," she said as explanation.

"Of course, I'll just throw in an extra for you both to split now, that way you'll know what you're giving them." Jaye was smooth, handing the treat over the counter before they had a chance to protest and depositing it directly into the hands of the skeleton, who broke it in half and handed her plump friend the smaller piece. They popped the bits into their mouths whole and chewed thoughtfully as Jaye

118

finished putting the aforementioned six into a box.

By the time the ladies walked out ten minutes later, they had not only the rye and the baby cakes, but a box of cinna-crisps, a pecan pie and an order for a tray of assorted goodies to be picked up on Thursday night for their bridge game.

Moira came out when she heard them leave.

"You missed your calling, Jaye," she said to her friend. "You would have made a deadly litigator or lobbyist. Something that would pay you some real money."

Jaye laughed.

"This stuff sells itself. They just didn't know that they wanted it so much until they did. Now look how happy they are. Besides, if I were a lawyer or a political stooge, I wouldn't be able to spend so much time with my best friend, now would I?"

"I guess not," Moira said wryly.

Jaye bounced around the shop as Moira went back to replace the sold items with backups from her stores in the kitchen and rearrange the contents of the display.

"So, how are things going with Jack?"

"Fine." She blushed slightly. "Really good, actually. He was here last night."

"Reeallly?" Jaye drawled out. "That was quick."

"Not like that. We just talked in the kitchen while I redid the Bakker cake."

"Sounds romant— wait, what happened to the Bakker cake? I thought you finished that already."

"I did, but I dropped it."

"That's not like you at all." Jaye was playful in her sarcasm. "What is it about this guy that makes you so clumsy?"

"I don't know. But it wasn't clumsiness; he startled me when he came in. I just dropped it. I actually think the new one looks better."

"So what did you talk about?"

"Past relationships."

"Hmm, heavy topic. Did you tell him about Mark?"

119

"Actually, no. We didn't get that far. I did find out that he hasn't had a relationship in a long time, he's more of a short term guy."

"Oh oh. How do you fit into that?"

"I'm not sure yet. We aren't sleeping together, which by the sounds of it isn't how he usually operates at all, and he says he feels differently about me than the girls he usually dates." Moira frowned. This all sounded so much more convincing when Jack said it.

"Be careful, okay. You sound like you might really like this guy, but I don't want to see you get so hurt again."

"I know, Jaye, thanks."

The arrival of more customers put a stop to their conversation then, but it gave Moira a lot to think about.

***

In Jack's office the mood was light, as it usually was when a project was completed. There was a team meeting first thing to announce projects for the week, give out assignments and give feedback from clients. So far, Jack's clients were the ones that seemed to be the most satisfied, having nothing but positive things to say, which is probably the reason why he was chosen to handle the creation of a new company corporate logo to represent a mid-sized bank chain hoping to revamp their image. He was flattered and took the folder of specs from Evan with a smile. At the end of the meeting, Evan called him over to the back of the room, where there was bottled water and a coffee urn. He filled his mug and turned to Jack.

"Busy day today?"

"Not too busy, I'll start reading through this material and see what I can come up with. Maybe do a little internet recon on what the top five banks in the province have going on so that I can compare. Why?"

"I'd like you to join me for lunch today. Say around 12:30?"

"Sounds good. I'll look forward to it."

Evan patted Jack on the shoulder and left the room. The two or three other employees still in the room gave Jack a thumbs up. Word was out on his possible promotion, and they were all rooting for him. Jack grabbed a water bottle and headed down the hall back to his own office, where he sat pouring over the information on the bank.

It was a smaller yet growing chain, with fifteen branches now in several midsized towns. They were doing well with growth and profits on the rise. They were gearing to a younger demographic after noticing a large portion of their clientele were retired. Not that there was anything wrong with retirees, but the real money was not to be found with frugal spenders with bulging portfolios, it was with the earn-and-spend generation of which Jack was a member. Looking at their website and the boring logo of intertwined letters, Jack could see why they wanted the help. It was not a place that he would give a second look to. He clicked on the internet portion of his computer and began researching what the big banks were doing in terms of looking fresh and inviting. By lunchtime he had a pretty good idea of what kind of look would be appropriate and had already drafted a few ideas on paper. He saved his work and headed out the door behind Evan. They got into his car and drove to a quaint restaurant that had taken over a smaller building in this industrial part of town; a genius move, as it did a tremendous lunch trade for all of the workers on this side of the river without congesting the charming streets of the town that were already busy enough with the tourists. They secured a seat in the rapidly filling room and placed orders for sandwiches and cool iced tea. Evan adjusted his position in his seat and threw a bemused look at his companion.

"Well, aren't you wondering why I asked you here?" he asked Jack.

"Of course. I was waiting for you to tell me."

"The promotion, Jack. We'll be making our official announcement sometime this week. Wednesday or Thursday, I think. It's come down to you and Jerry Vale, and since both of you are about to turn in some fairly important work, a lot of it will hinge on that and the response of our clients. I encourage you to keep your mind on your job and make sure that copy comes to me with absolutely no mistakes." He took a bite of his food, which had arrived silently and swiftly during his short speech.

"That's very good to know. I have a question for you, though."

"Fire away."

"Why are you telling me all this and not telling Jerry too? Isn't that a little bit of favouritism?" He smiled at his boss.

"What makes you think I haven't talked to him?" Evan retorted calmly. "It's no secret that you would be my choice of preference, but I'm not the only one making the decision, Jack. It just so happens that I met with Jerry for breakfast this morning. Something told me you would be more of a lunch person." He chuckled and took a deep sip of his beverage.

"Oh, of course, I appreciate it."

"Don't look so surprised, Jack. You do a good job. That's why we hired you, but it's no secret that you're not on your A game with your father ill. Don't worry, the executives are aware of your situation and are more than sympathetic to your personal needs right now. We just want to see you keep your performance level at the height we know that you're capable of. The game is in your hands."

"Thank you for the advice, Evan. I have to tell you, it's been a real help to me to have such a good mentor. Not just since I came on, but the last few months especially."

Aww, flattery gets you nowhere in business. But I'll take the compliment as your friend. Now, what do you think of the bank specs we gave you this morning?"

"I'm glad you asked. Actually, I spent most of the morning doing some research on the trends with some of the leading banks in the country and where their advertising and commercializing is aimed. Our guys have their focus on the wrong demographic, but we're going to fix all that for them."

"That sounds more like the Jack I know," Evan said, brushing the crumbs from his hands. "Now, what do you say we head back to the office and give 'em hell?"

"You got it."

They stood up and carried their plates back to the counter, where Evan waved away Jacks motions towards his wallet. Jack went back to the table and left a generous tip instead. They drove back to the office and marched straight to their respective offices to get on with the work of the day. For Jack, there was more market research as well as a few phone calls to some old college buddies who now worked in the financial sector in Toronto. He was determined to knock the socks off of this client and turn around their revenues to heights they had only dreamed of. The excitement and the thrill of possibilities and outcomes kept Jack working at the kind of pace that he had possessed when he started out at the firm. Moira may have the luxury of a job that she loved and was passionate about, but Jack knew that he was very good at what he did and, when the fire got into his belly, maybe even the best. Feeling like a giant of industry, he began pounding out the outlines of his ideas early into the afternoon, and his fingers didn't stop moving until shortly after five, when it was time to leave for the day. Even so, he was one of the last ones to leave his office, in a bright mood and on his way to visit Kevin.

Chapter Twelve

When Moira and Jaye closed up shop for the day, they had decided against the idea of staying closed on a Monday, at least for now. Business had been nonstop today. At this rate, they would be able to hire a girl or boy from the high school to come and help out on weekends. It was encouraging to know that, in the short few years that she had her business, she had already managed to pay off the loans of her mother and grandmother and was now functioning completely in the black, with profits that were looking better and better every month. She was now the premiere supplier of the birthday and wedding cake trade in town, with some orders starting to come in from neighboring communities. That business alone was making it possible for her to consider buying a company van, something large that could transport some of their more spectacular creations safely to their destination and allow for some advertising on the side, a point which Jaye had been making for some months now. They safely stored the items away that needed away, made a list for tomorrow morning's baking and locked the doors. They had planned to grab a bite upstairs in Moira's apartment before meeting Sloane and the girls at the mall to shop for shoes. As they set about the apartment's kitchen preparing some light fare for themselves they chatted about the amount of turn around that day and the diversity of their clientele. Jaye told Moira about her boyfriend and his requests for her to change her hair. Moira told Jaye about the feelings she was having for Jack and how she was becoming a little less guarded, yet unwilling to fall into another relationship that would end up with heartbreak.

"You need to be a little easier on yourself," Jaye told her friend between bites of chicken salad. "Seriously, I've been thinking about this all day. If anyone deserves to be happy, it's you. I know that I said you need to take your time, blah blah blah, but honestly, if you start out every relationship thinking that it's going to end up like the one with Mark, you're just going to end up sad and alone and pushing every man away. Jack seems like a pretty good guy so far. Give yourself a break."

"I know. In my head I say the same thing to myself. Is it crazy that this is all going so quickly?"

"Yes, but that's what's so great about it. You've had a crazy big smile for the last week, so anyone that can do that to you can't be all bad."

They finished their meal and tidied up, still talking.

"So, Sloane and Martin, they going to make it?" Jaye asked her friend.

"I think so. You know, when she's around him, she's so different. He doesn't put up with any of her pouty bullshit, but it's like she just accepts that about him; they don't fight about it. Besides, anyone can see that they utterly adore one another. I wouldn't be surprised if they stayed married for a very long time. Sloane never would have agreed to something so serious if she didn't really and truly love him."

"If he's such a good influence on her, maybe you should bring up some of your beefs with her when he's around. That way she would have to not only deal with them, but do it with some modicum of maturity."

"It's a good theory, but I think I'll just let it be. I don't really want to get into it with her."

"Why are you always avoiding confrontation with Sloane?"

The two ladies headed out to Jaye's car and turned towards the mall at the south end of town.

"I'm not avoiding confrontation, I just don't see the point in fighting with her anymore. She doesn't see things from the same perspective as I do, and unless we can go back in time to when we were kids and switch places, she never will. It doesn't make sense to try to make her see how things were, and sometimes still are. In a way she has a point too, and I'll never understand her perspective either."

"Okay. That makes sense. I just get so frustrated for you when I see how hurt she makes you sometimes."

"Thanks. You're a good friend, Jaye."

Jaye harrumphed in her seat. "Well, if you want to get all mushy about it."

"Mushy, with you? Never. What I meant to say is thanks for having my back, bitch!"

"That's more like it. Now, tell me again who are the two musketeers that we are meeting with today."

"Michelle and Katie."

"Which one is the one with more money than God and a drinking problem?"

"That's Katie. Try not to pay her too much attention."

"Sure, I would never do anything to embarrass you in front of your sister's friends."

"Sure you wouldn't."

"Oh, do I detect sarcasm?"

Moira laughed at her. "You really are a bitch."

"Thank you."

By the time Moira and Jaye arrived at the first shoe store in the mall they were slated to prowl, Michelle, Katie and Sloane were already established on chairs surrounded by what seemed to be at least half of the boxes from the stockroom. Even though the dresses were turquoise, they had shoes of every colour and style imaginable out, and Katie was twisting a rather horrible patent leather pump in neon pink onto her slender foot, much to the hilarity of her friends and the chagrin of the shop keeper, who seemed torn between making a sale and suffering through an embarrassing defense of his choice of stock.

"Moira! You made it. And you brought Jaye." Sloane leaped off her chair and over the pile of shoes and boxes in

127

one graceful movement. She hugged her sister hard, her bony shoulders pressing into Moira's chest.

"Of course I made it. You command, I show up." She turned to Jaye. "It's our process."

Jaye laughed as Sloane put on a pouty face. "I don't command, Moira, stop joking around."

Moira and Jaye picked their way over the heap and took a seat in the chairs facing the other girls. "Tell me you're not considering making us wear those monstrosities," she said to Sloane, pointing to the shoe that was now wedged on Katie's foot.

"Why not? Pink and turquoise go together. I'm also still thinking of the yellow." She indicated a mustard-coloured wedge that Michelle was turning over in her hand.

"What did I tell you?" Moira muttered to Jaye, who was eyeing a pair of black snakeskin sling backs.

"Hmm, oh. Hey, these aren't bad. I might get these for myself. Excuse me, do you have these in an eight and a half?" she asked the owner, who nodded and scurried off into the back to bring forth yet another box.

Moira took a few moments to watch the girls chatter and squeal over the various types of shoes laid out before them. Once again she wondered why she had agreed to be in the wedding. It wasn't as if she and Sloane had the kind of relationship where they rushed to one another's side in moments of need or triumph. It had become something more akin to tolerance and obligation. Still, her only sister had wanted her here, and she was determined to make the best of it.

"What exactly are you looking for, Sloane? Do you really want to have us wear something that will clash so spectacularly with the dresses?"

"I don't expect you to understand. It's a statement. No one ever wears wedding clothes again anyway; why not wear something that will stand out in your memory?"

"Not to mention all the photographs. *And* keep everyone looking down at our feet at the service instead of at you."

128

"Good point. I don't want to detract attention. Maybe we should just get those plain satin pumps and have them dyed to match the dresses."

"Can you do that?" Michelle asked.

"Sure you can. I've seen it done lots of times. Mom must have gone to about four weddings when we were teenagers." She turned to Katie and Michelle. "All of her friends married late. Anyway, it's not a bad idea." She pulled down the generic white satin shoe from one of the top shelves in the store. "We'll need these in a seven, a nine and a ten, please."

The poor man who ran the store began gathering up some of the other now discarded designs and stuffing them back into their boxes. Then he ducked into the back once more, arms loaded, and emerged a moment later with three new boxes.

"Do you dye them on the premises?" Katie asked him, slipping one of the shoes on her foot. She quickly removed it and tossed it at Moira. "Here, I'm swimming in these; they must be your size. Hand me that box down there."

Moira rolled her eyes at Jaye, who was standing in front of a mirror admiring the snakeskin shoes on her feet.

"Why do you keep doing that?" Sloane asked.

"Doing what?"

"Rolling your eyes and muttering to Jaye. I'm right here, you know. I can see you and I can hear you."

"Sorry. It's just some of your ideas for these bridesmaid outfits are a little ... "

"A little what, Moira?"

"Juvenile," said Jaye.

"Exactly."

Now it was Michelle, Katie and Sloane's turn to exchange a look.

"You see, I told you she wouldn't get it," Katie smugly informed her friends. "Moira, you're just too old and frumpy to get it. It's too bad. I would have thought that you'd have more of a sense of adventure. But I guess those days are over for you, huh."

"Moira has plenty of adventure," Jaye defended her friend. "It's takes a huge leap of faith to go into business for yourself. Remind me Katie, what do you do for a living ... nothing, isn't it?"

"I do whatever I want. Unlike you, I don't have to schlep around all day in my best friend's store to earn my living."

"Right, right, you had it handed to you on your silver platter. And just for the record, I own a quarter of that 'shop', so maybe you should back off a bit."

"Ooooh. A quarter of a shop. My, but we are ambitious," Katie barbed, causing Sloane and Michelle to twitter.

"It's fine, Jaye. You don't have to defend me to Sloane's friends. I don't expect them to understand."

"You can just get off your high horse now, Moira." Sloane turned to the owner once more. "We'll take these. Do you dye them here?"

"Yes." He was obviously uncomfortable with the exchange going on between the five women. He busied himself making out the order slip and setting up the bill for the shoes. Sloane stood by him at the counter, chattering about the urgency in timing and the date for pick up. Jaye was beside her, the box of black shoes in one hand, wallet in the other. Michelle had begun to pick up some of the mess that they had made, jamming shoes into boxes without looking to check for size and style coordination, probably creating more work in the process. Katie took advantage of this distraction to most of the party to belt back a quick shot from her trusty flask in her pocket.

"Couldn't wait until we left the store? I hope you're not driving tonight."

Moira's voice suddenly appearing at the back of her neck startled Katie. She spilled a little of the amber liquid down the side of her mouth, wiping at it with the back of her hand and slipping the flask away again.

"You're not fooling me," Moira continued, "it's not

the first time I've seen you do this. Just promise me you'll stay sober on the wedding day until at least after the ceremony and the speeches."

Katie rounded on her, two pink circles now visible on her cheeks.

"You have no idea what you're talking about. And it's you who should check your behaviour for the wedding, not me."

"What's that supposed to mean?"

"It means, in about two weeks you won't have Sloane to push around anymore, so maybe you should find yourself a new hobby, miss high and mighty, and stop making *her* the excuse for your pathetic life."

The room had frozen, the other ladies having all finished what they were doing in time to hear this last statement from Katie. They left the store together in a huddle, Jaye gripping her hand on Moira's elbow, Katie whispering furiously to Sloane. Michelle was left pulling up the rear of the group, once again on the sidelines of the conversation, but showing her support for Sloane by standing on her right flank while Katie held the left. They kept this formation in quiet solidarity out through the throngs of people and into the parking garage, where the two groups finally split off as Sloane and her friends headed towards Michelle's car and Moira and Jaye headed to theirs. Before they got too far, Moira called Sloane to her.

"What do you want?"

"I'm sorry. I really didn't mean to get into a fight with your friends tonight."

"Sure." Sloane looked at her feet.

"I'm serious. I don't want to fight with you before your wedding. It's just Katie ... "

"What about her?"

"You really should keep an eye on her, Sloane. She's drinking all the time. This must be the third time I've seen her do it in the past week and a half."

"So?"

"What do you mean, so? Aren't you worried about

it?"

Sloane stole a look back to her girlfriends, who were now sitting in the car chatting.

"You have no idea what she deals with or how she copes with it. Stop trying to fix everyone's life for them."

"I'm not trying to fix people's lives, I'm trying to help! You never want my advice anymore. What happened? You always used to listen to me."

"I didn't really have a choice, did I? You're always just there, sticking your nose into my life and giving me advice even when I don't ask for it. Why can't you just let me live my life my way?"

The sisters' voices started getting higher. Jaye came closer to lend Moira her support if she needed it, but it was too late. The gloves had come off, and nothing but fireworks seemed to be following the girls these days. Even Michelle and Katie got back out of the car and came over to see what the commotion was all about.

"You think you didn't have a choice?" Moira shot back. "*I* didn't have a choice. Mom was so busy working just to keep the house and Nana was always sick or trying to bring in some money to help out, I had no option but to be the one to keep you in line. But you didn't see that, did you? You never see that people always have to bail you out or clean up your messes. All you ever see is you, and getting what you want and what you need. Did you ever once say thank you to mom for keeping you in your fancy clothes and your frivolous lifestyle? No, because you always just assumed that she'd do what you needed. If it wasn't for me watching out for you, well, I don't even want to think about where you might have ended up."

Sloane looked as though she'd been slapped. Finally, she responded slowly and coldly: "I'm sorry I've been such an inconvenience to you up till now. You can take that job description off of your résumé, 'cause I'm a big girl. I can take care of myself."

"Fine, or rather Martin can take care of you, you don't know how not to depend on someone."

"Martin and I take care of each other, but you wouldn't understand that, would you? I may have depended on you, all of you, but you've never depended on anyone but yourself. That's why you haven't had a decent relationship yet, you never stop being in charge. Mark was suffocated by it, and eventually your little friend Jack will find that out too and he'll leave you. Even though he may love you, he'll leave you because you'll never need him."

With that stinging remark, she stalked off, pulling a stunned Michelle by the sleeve and propelling her to the car, where Katie stood with a smug look on her face. Moira was rooted to the spot, shocked disbelief on her face, and it took Jaye several minutes to finally propel her down the stairs and into the lower lot where she had parked barely more than an hour before. After getting Moira seated and buckled, Jaye slid into the driver's seat and guided the car down the street and back to the apartment over the store. Once inside, they went up the stairs, and a still stunned Moira collapsed on the couch while Jaye reached into the small cupboard above the stove and fished out a bottle of brandy. She poured two large measures into some glasses and went back into the living area, seated herself beside her friend on the couch, and wordlessly handed her the drink. Moira took a grateful deep sip, looked up at Jaye and, with a deep shaky breath, burst into violent tears. With the patience and anticipation that comes with years of practice, Jaye waited while her friend cried. Then she rooted around in the bottom of her large purse and came up with a pack of cigarettes and a lighter. She slid two out of the pack and lit one, handed it to Moira, and then lit the other. Moira gratefully took it and got up to get a tissue and a small dish to use for an ashtray.

She inhaled the biting brown taste of the nicotine and blew out a large cloud of smoke.

"Thanks, I didn't know you still had any, thought you quit a month ago."

"I did. These are for emergencies only."

"Oh."

They sat longer still, enjoying the vice in silence and making the most of it with long drags followed by gulps of the brandy. The combination of the alcohol and the smoke made Moira feel heady, foggy. Sloane's words washed over her like a cloud, fuzzing her head and keeping tears close to the surface.

"Am I really such a control freak?"

"Don't do this. You let her get to you way too much."

"But she's right! I push people away, try to manage them and fix them and correct them and I never let anyone get close. How can I have missed that all this time?"

Jaye took a deep breath.

"Okay, we've been friends for a long time, right?"

"Yeah."

"So I'm going to say this with love, not with the poisonous intent your sweet little sister has, okay? You are a little authoritative, in the best possible way though. If you weren't, there's no way you'd be a success at running the business. You never would have gotten through some of the things in your life if you weren't so strong. But it does not, I repeat *not* have any bearing on your personal relationships. Not that I have ever seen. Mark didn't leave because you didn't need him; he left because he was a cheating asshole who only had eyes for what he could get out of you. If anything, you're sometimes too trusting. Don't let Sloane's personal insecurities make you feel bad about yourself. You're the best person I know, and that's a fact."

"You're wrong. I'm insecure and I cover it up by acting so tough and strong. It's not just Mark, or Sloane, or even how I am with you. Think about the relationships in my life, Jaye. Every one of them has ended in some kind of disappointment. How can you love someone who never lets you in? Tell me that. I don't let people in."

"You let me in."

"You're different."

"Why? Because we've known each other since high school? I'm no different than anyone else you care for in you life. And I know that you deserve the best, you deserve to be happy, and you deserve to let Sloane stew in her own juices for a while. She's just stressed about the wedding. She'll come around sooner than later and apologize. And because I know you and the kind of girl you really are, you'll forgive her when the time comes. I've never known anyone as loyal and bighearted as you, Moira. Just remember that."

Moira leaned over and hugged her friend gratefully.

"Now, I know what we should do," Jaye announced.

"What?" Moira sat up again, wiping off her face.

"Let's have a sleepover. Like we did when we were teenagers."

"Okay, I'll go get some pajamas." Moira went into the bedroom.

"I'll get some more drinks and put on a movie." Jaye shuffled on her knees across the floor to the low sideboard where Moira kept her movies. She thumbed through them.

"Dirty Dancing or Beaches?"

"Dirty Dancing, definitely," Moira said with a smile, coming out of the bedroom in some baggy pants and a t-shirt and carrying some similar clothes for Jaye. "I'm a sucker for Patrick Swayze."

"Really?? I always like that Neil guy."

"Liar, he's a creep." She tossed a couch cushion at her.

Jaye tossed the pillow back. "I like creeps. Oh, I better call Rick, he'll be wondering where I am."

As Jaye called her boyfriend, Moira grabbed her keys from the side table and went down to the shop, where she took a chocolate cheesecake from the fridge. Smiling to herself and feeling much better, she locked back up and went up the stairs to slough off the events of the night and just relax. The movie was already on opening credits when she came back in.

"Mmmmm. Shall I get plates?"

"Nah, just grab two forks from the kitchen."

The girls settled on the floor amidst pillows and poured themselves more brandy as they feasted on dessert and laughed at the movie. By the time Patrick was getting

Baby out of the corner, they had eaten more than half the cake and finished at least a third of the brandy.

"Jesus, I'm drunk."

"It's good for you, puts hair on your chest."

"Gross!"

They turned off the movie, put the cheesecake in the fridge and stumbled into the bedroom, where they crashed together on the bed, the alcohol aiding in a swift departure into dreamland.

***

Earlier that same night Jack had packed it in after a rewarding day at the office and headed over to the hospice for a visit with his father. He was carrying a book of dirty jokes and limericks that Evan had given him a while ago, something to keep him laughing in hard times. His step was light, the fruits of the day and the warm memories of the weekend to keep him jaunty. The main hallway of the hospice seemed brighter, despite their lurid colour choice, with beams of the indian summer sunshine breaking in through every nook and cranny available and casting soft light on each surface it touched. As Jack rounded the corner towards his father's room, the smile seemed to drop from his face as the familiar voice could be heard in a tone that was barely recognizable. He paused, just for a moment, wondering if he was imagining the whole thing. But no, it was definitely Kevin, and he was angry. At first the other voice was hard to make out, but eventually Jack recognized Vicky, the nurse who managed his father's case during the day.

"Please, Kevin. You can't just pull these out, there's a procedure. You're going to wind up hurting yourself."

"I don't care, just get them out! I'm tired of being hooked up to machines." He wheezed for a moment, and then a deep rumbling cough emanated from the room.

"Kevin, come on. You're going to wear yourself out." Vicky was trying to be soothing, but the frustration and

136

concern was crystal clear in her voice.

"That's the point, isn't it? This isn't living. I don't want any of this, I didn't ask for it. Did you read my file? Well, did you? It says DNR! DNR, Vicky! I don't want heroic measures. I don't want tubes and lines or any of this shit."

"If you don't have this, the end is going to be very painful. You said that you wanted to stay lucid as long as possible, right? You have things that you want to talk to your son about, right? Well, if I take out the feeding tube and the IV, the pain will get too intense to bear and you'll starve to death."

Jack held his breath as the sounds of his father's broken sobbing filled the hallway. He was in shock. For as long as the terminal sentence had been handed down, he had never seen or heard Kevin be anything but accepting of this fate. It was almost too much to bear to hear him so upset. He was about to leave when Vicky appeared in the hallway before him. She took one look at Jack, closed the door behind her and gently but firmly propelled him down the hallway.

"How much of that did you hear, Jack?"

"That depends, how long were you in there?"

"For a few minutes. He was throwing some of his equipment around the room and took off the heart monitor we put on him."

"Why was he wearing a heart monitor?"

"He's been wearing one since your little excursion on the weekend. That cold water was a bit much for him; we think he has a touch of pneumonia."

Jack shook his head.

"I've never, not since the first diagnosis, heard him get this upset before. Something must have triggered him off. What happened here today?"

Vicky looked at Jack with a sad smile on her face.

"Nothing happened here today out of the ordinary. You have to understand something about your father, about all people who are facing their own mortality. He is angry. It's normal, and it happens to everyone at one point."

"He's never said anything to me, and I ask him all the time. He never complains."

"He never complains to *you*, Jack," she said gently.

"What's that supposed to mean?"

"It means that people in your father's position rarely want to put added stress on their loved ones. He doesn't want you to hurt anymore than you do already. Sometimes it's just easier to be angry, frustrated, or in pain with someone who has no emotional connection."

Jack digested this for a moment. He hated seeing and hearing his father like this, hated everything about this disease. He was upset, but in a way relieved that there was someone his father could lash out at. He felt guilty and yet thankful that it was not he who had to deal with it. Vicky must have sensed this, because she gave his arm a squeeze and walked away down the hall, letting Jack be the one to decide whether or not to go in and see his father in this weakened state. Inside the room, he could hear Kevin shuffling about on the bed, barking out wet coughs and sniffling.

For what seemed like an eternity, he stood steadfast, listening for the sounds of his father, the one that he knew, to return to the room, instead of the broken down and frustrated noises of a sick and dying man that were currently emanating from within. It was a practice in patience, a skill Jack had presumed he had in abundance, until now. It was almost more than his heart could take, standing in the dank and pale green washed hallway, which only a few minutes ago had seemed to him to be so bright and cheerful, waiting for the right time, the right moment to enter the room. In the end, he decided to give his father the night. It was quite apparent to Jack that he would be in no mood for false pretenses today and, with the renewed efforts of the staff to maintain his health for the lingering days he had left, Jack thought it would be best to leave him a night to recuperate and rest before giving him cause to put on a brave front yet again. He turned on his heel and walked back down the hallway and out the door.

As Jack drove his car home, he made sure that he

passed by Moira's. The lights were all off, of course; she was out shopping for shoes for her sisters' wedding today. The windows of the shop looked as inviting as ever to him, and the pristine beauty of the white wedding cake in the window shone in the twilight sun like a beacon. Of course, now that he had seen her at work, Jack knew that this was just a fraction of the talent she possessed and found himself grinning broadly at the memory of sitting in her kitchen watching her create a cake from scratch, with colours and techniques that, if asked, he never would have thought would work, but when completed made the most visually stunning edible tapestry he had ever seen. He turned on the radio and sang off key to the songs until he pulled into his own driveway and turned off the car.

Once Jack had let himself into the apartment, he tried to survey it through her eyes. A dirty dish here, an empty cup there. It was full of things that would have to be dealt with before he ever brought Moira here. As he started cleaning, a new revelation struck him: although he had brought many women here over the years, he could not recall the last time he had gone to the effort of cleaning before letting them in. Notwithstanding the fact that many of those incidents had occurred with very little planning and forethought, there had been a few who had lasted long enough for him to have certainly tried to make the effort, yet none had merited it. In spite of himself, Jack was quickly falling for the fair Moira, and he knew it. Stranger still was the fact that this didn't seem to bother him as he might once have thought it would. Despite all of the conversations with his father, his boss, his few acquaintances from work, despite all of his ingrained reservations against it, sooner or later he was going to have to admit that he was falling in love with her. With renewed vigor, he examined every nook and cranny for errant items that might have previously escaped his eye. There was a spoon stuck down between the cushions of the couch, no doubt a relic from a hastily prepared and drank coffee in the early hours, or late as the case may be. Dust had accumulated over nearly every surface worth looking at, and he searched the house for any cleaning supplies that he might still have stowed away. Surprisingly, he found an arsenal of cleansers and dusters and the like in the bathroom under the sink. Relics from before his father had become sick, from when he actually spent time keeping his home looking neat and tidy. Hauling out the bucket that contained the items, he hastily threw out an old sponge that had become hardened as a sea star and an old spray bottle of window cleaner that only had bright blue dregs swirling around the bottom. He smiled in spite of himself and shook his head as a sort of reprimand for how slovenly he had let himself become over the last months.

It took Jack almost two whole hours to achieve the level of cleanliness that he had been going for. His apartment was still by no means perfectly clean, but at least it was freshly dusted and swept, surfaces wiped and glass shining. There were no longer dirty dishes piled in the sink, no empty coffee cups in the bathroom or the bedroom. He had even run to the laundry room in the basement and threw in a load of clothes, something that his bachelor habits usually reserved for a once a week occasion. There were four shirts hanging in the closet near the front door ready to be dropped off at the cleaners the following morning, and he had recycled any newspaper or magazine that had been sitting stagnant for more than a few weeks. Now, all that he needed to do was to go shopping. It becomes a shock to the system, when one does this kind of overhaul, exactly how poorly one eats, or how sparsely one chooses to use space that should, in essence, describe oneself, Jack reflected. He realized that he really didn't eat very well at all. His kitchen had a lot of pre-made muffins in their plastic snap-shut containers and some rather humiliated looking fruit, but other than that he mainly ate pre-made meals when he was at home. Almost everything in his fridge and freezer was in a box, ready to have its wrapping removed and to be microwaved or baked accordingly. His cupboards contained soups and several half used packages of chips and crackers. The only thing about which he could feel truly proud in terms of kitchen stock at the moment was his wine collection, stored in the neat wine cooler beside the end of his short counter. A purchase that had been his first big splurge after getting his own place, good wine was something Jack had fallen into in college along with a lady friend of his after taking an evening elective appreciation course to add something creative to his rather dry-looking portfolio. It was about two thirds full, each wine in it having been bought for a special reason, and being kept for a special occasion. Not so long ago, in fact only about a month and a half after Kevin's diagnosis, Jack and Evan had traveled to wine country California. A local vineyard was preparing to launch its new vintages after some serious overhauls to both staff and production procedures. They had hired the firm to do their entire online PR, everything from website to advertising to creating a new logo and slogan. It had been a boisterous trip, as the new proprietors were both congenial and generous, sending both Jack and Evan home with two cases of their most popular selection, a combination of a pinot and a chardonnay, as well as two bottles each of a very rare gamay merlot, bottles that were worth over a hundred dollars each on their own. It was not viewed as a kickback, since Evan had since not only booked the vineyard as the location for the Annual General Meeting, but had thrown tons of business their way through friends and family.

Jack had yet to open either of his bottles. Evan, he knew, had already consumed one and had declared it to be the best wine he had ever tasted and well worth its price, if not undersold.

Wanting to call Moira, yet knowing that she would be tied up for the rest of the night, Jack resigned himself to a warmed up meal from one of his several boxes, and made a grocery list to replenish his sad supplies. Then he grabbed a book from one of his shelves, settled down in his large and comfortable bed with the pillows propped up behind him, and read well into the night.

Chapter Thirteen

In the morning, after a shower, locating clean clothes and putting together a small breakfast (all of which seemed to be remarkably easier after last night's efforts), Jack made a quick phone call to the hospice to inquire about Kevin and his situation and, even more importantly today, his state of mind. It was Vicky who took the call, which was a relief since he did not relish informing any other member of the staff that he had been there yesterday but had run away like a scared little boy at the sign of his father's pain. Vicky told him that it had been both a quiet and yet a disheartening night as Kevin had dealt with the ravages of the infection in his chest and had responded by having a fitful, largely drug-induced sleep. Even now he was out soundly on his narrow bed, the rattle in his chest mimicking the beeping intervals of the heart monitor. She told Jack that they had explained to Kevin that the monitors were not actually treatment, they were just keeping a better watch on his system than the doctors were able to do, barring actually standing over him for hours at a time with a stethoscope pressed into his chest, a finger over dry lips to indicate quiet to all as they listened and tried to distinguish the myriad of sounds that a dying body makes. He had accepted this information as well as some antibiotics for the infection, some morphine for the pain in his joints and bones and something to help him sleep for dessert. It was a chemical meal, but one that had granted him at least a few hours at a stretch uninterrupted. He had also left word for Jack that he wanted some time to himself for today, and that Jack was to give him a night off, with a promise not to die just yet.

Jack thanked Vicky for the information and for her words to him the day before. He was glad to hear that there had been some weak attempt at a joke about dying; it could only mean that Kevin's spirits were once again on the rise. Buoyed by the news that he would be okay, or at least that he was managing for the time being, and with the reprieve of a night off, Jack set off for the office, smiling as he now did whenever he passed by Moira's shop just before he turned off to cross the bridge to the business sector. He tried to ignore the heavy feeling that engulfed his chest as he passed the long driveway for the hospice. Part of him wanted to ignore his father's wishes, disregard the pending promotion and just fly into the parking lot and then park himself at his father's bedside for the remainder of the day. There really couldn't be anything more pressing, could there? But he knew better. He knew that once his weakened father opened his purpling eyelid to see that Jack was sitting holding vigil at his bedside, he would immediately kick him out. If there was one subject that Kevin had been adamant on since becoming ill, it was that Jack not disrupt his life to stand watch over him as if he were a child. There was to be no role-reversal here, Kevin wanted his life to end with dignity, and on his own terms. If he needed a day to himself, then that is what Jack would have to give him, and he knew deep down that honouruing this simple request would mean far more to Kevin than his helpless presence in that lonely room.

Sighing, he drove on and pulled into the parking lot at work. There was much to be done today, and he was actually not only on time, but a little early this morning. A quick glance around the lot told him that not even Evan was in yet. This was a good sign. It could only help his chances in the long run of securing the promotion. He moved through the still fairly quiet office, noticing that Rebecca was already in and had already filled his inbox with the day's mail and projects. She said good morning and gave him a wink, never pausing in her movements around the room. Jack said hello back and slid himself into his own office, grabbing the stack of papers from his desk and leafing through them while he waited for his computer to warm up. There were several clients requesting updates, a few inner-office memos to address and a list of pro-bono work that Evan had attached to a sheet requesting that all of the employees try to take on at least one of the projects. Jack scanned the list and decided on helping a school to design a website for their fundraising programs. It was a fairly new phenomenon, a school using the internet to raise money, but it had many benefits. For one, it allowed the public to have access to what exactly they were raising funds for, a breakdown of costs and progress and an opportunity to gear donation dollars to specific projects. It seemed this particular school (a high school) needed a new gym, since the old one had flooded and the school board could only cover about half the costs of replacement. They had drawings from the architect, floor plans and wish lists for equipment. Judging by the sheer size of the school, it would have to be very large indeed to accommodate the students. This project was quite obviously beyond the fundraising capabilities of a chocolate bar campaign or bake sale. It needed heavy promotion, the sooner the better. The more he read, the more Jack knew that he would help this school out. He buzzed Rebecca and asked her if anyone else had requested the project yet.

"Nope, you're the first one. Do you want all the contact info?"

"Absolutely. I plan to set up a meeting as soon as I can."

"Okay, I'll notify Evan that this one is now taken."

"Thanks."

She went back out to her desk and a moment later popped back in again, dropping a further packet of stapled sheets onto his desk. Jack thanked her and removed the staples, re-arranging the sheets to suit his own organizational proclivities. He started a new file on the school and

145

picked up his phone to call the principal and set up a meeting. The more he became engrossed in the plight of this school, whose Phys. Ed. department was struggling to keep a curriculum, the more passionate he felt about the cause. It wasn't long before Jack's fingers were flying, both over his computer keys and with a felt tip pen across his notepad, the ideas for this promotional site literally leaping from his mind, his fingers struggling to keep up. Every so often, he would stop mid action and jot something down on another sheet of notepaper, the creativity of this project sparking ideas for another and another of his existing clients; such was his method.

By late in the day, he had come up with some pretty good preliminary ideas for the school fundraising site, as well as made it through a fair chunk of his research on the bank. He was in the process of saving his work and separating the two very different files back into their own folders when he realized how late it was getting. His first thought was of Moira. Knowing that his father wanted a night to himself, no doubt to sleep and try to regain a bit of strength, all he could think about were her green eyes and her smile and her lovely, lovely lips.

A quick glance at the clock on the wall told him that if he left now, he might get to her store before it closed. Technically, he should really stay until five, but with all that he had accomplished today, he didn't feel bad about taking the early leave. As Jack slipped out through the main heavy glass doors and into the parking lot, he couldn't suppress the smile that was slowly setting over his handsome features. With a light heart, he drove into town.

***

For Moira, the day had been less than perfect. She awoke with a serious hangover to the sounds of Jaye singing in the shower, loudly. The right side of her body was aching, since it turned out she had fallen asleep with her bra still on, the cheap one where the wire kept poking out and, upon further

146

investigation, found that the rogue wire had indeed been sticking out and had implanted itself in the soft flesh just under her arm for who knows how much of the night. There was a loud angry purple and red mark where it had assaulted her flesh. She got up and fished through her drawers for the one bra she owned without wire. It was terribly ugly, so old that the once white material had become faded and grey, little tiny balls of cotton were stuck to it everywhere, and the straps were fraying. No matter, it was a moot point. The objective was comfort, not allure. It's not like Jack's first glimpse of her in her scanties would include this bra in the scenario!

The water in the bathroom had shut off, and Jaye walked in, soaking wet and toweling herself off. She was oblivious to still being naked and mostly exposed, but that didn't faze Moira anymore. She had seen Jaye naked too many times before.

"Earth to Moira. What's with the look? Good lord, what an ugly bra."

Moira cast a quick glance down at herself. She shrugged, and then showed Jaye the mark from the wire of her bra from yesterday.

"Ouch. That's no good at all. Listen, you should hop into the shower. Even if you stayed in the kitchen all day today, the karma of you looking like that at work won't help us with business."

"Fine, as long as you didn't use up all the hot water."

Jaye swatted at her with the towel as Moira went past her to the bathroom. She looked into the mirror as she closed the door. *Big mistake,* she thought. Her hair was so thoroughly knotted on the one side that it actually looked as though some kind of weird animal had died on the side of her head yet refused to fall off. Her eyes were black and sunken from too much alcohol and lack of sleep. Speaking of alcohol, the previous evening's imbibing had led to a faint yet pungent smell of it seeping from her pores. Yes, a shower was indeed called for.

She dropped what little clothing she had left onto

147

the floor and let the comforting water cascade over her. The shampoo felt like balm on her skin as it ran in large foamy rivers down her back. She took her time, though ordinarily it would have been a rushed effort so that she could run down to her beloved business and open up, but knowing that Jaye was in the other room, and in much better shape, she decided that it wouldn't hurt to take a little more effort than usual. Besides, the longer she stayed under the spray, the better she began to feel. Moira turned her face up slightly to let the spray bathe her face and shoulders. She grabbed a razor from the little corner shelf and carefully shaved her armpits and legs, cautiously, taking her time to make sure that not a knick or a hair would be left to besmirch her skin. In fact, the longer she stayed, the more time and effort she took. She used conditioner, a beautiful smelling body wash that filled the small shower with the scent of jasmine and lathered every inch of her body. By the time she turned the water off and stepped out to grab a towel, she was feeling significantly better. She dressed carefully in a crisp white shirt and some jeans and pulled her damp hair back into a ponytail to keep it away from her face as she worked. She even applied a little mascara and lip gloss, something which she had been doing with less and less frequency lately and finally headed downstairs.

As she suspected, Jaye was already established in the shop. The coffee machine was purring away, the tables were clean and set with fresh napkins, and the cool display cases were stocked. She was just switching on the sign and unlocking the door when Moira joined her, catching her off guard with a hug before heading back to her kitchen sanctuary to start on the day's work. Jaye said nothing, but smiled and swatted her friend on the bum before opening the till and making ready for the first wave of customers to come in. The two laughed the day away, trading off with preparing yet more tantalizing treats and taking care of the store front and till. Not even the darkening sky in the late hours of the afternoon could dampen their spirits.

"That's it! We're out of the mousse cakes again,"

Jaye announced, coming back into the kitchen around three thirty that afternoon. "They're selling like mad. I can't even keep them on the shelves. You'll have to make more, and we should talk about doing more than just strawberry. I'd be willing to bet that any other flavor you could come up with would be just as popular. What do you think?"

"At this rate, we are going to *have* to take Monday or some other day off, just to keep up with the demands. I can't cover all the baking needed anymore just in the morning or while you're running the shop."

"That's a good thing, right? Business has been getting better and better. In fact, we might be able to hire some help again soon, and afford it this time!" Jaye flounced back to the front as the jangle of the bell announced another customer.

Moira smiled and hugged herself. She knew business was good, booming in fact. It had been a hard lesson learned, as when she and Jaye had first opened The Cakery they had hired two youngsters to work the store front for them while they prepared items all day long in the kitchen. But when a brand new business is getting off the ground, and a customer base has yet to be cemented, it does not make sense to be paying out salaries to untrained employees who really don't understand the difference between a rye bread and a pumpernickel, or how they should arrange the goods in the display to their best advantage, or that they should keep the free samples to their friends to a minimum. It had only taken a month to realize that the operating costs were far outweighing the sales and, with a heavy heart, the two women had let go of the extra help. All good intentions aside, it made no practical sense to have them in when they could manage between themselves. Now, of course, was a different story. The business had been up and running for quite some time and showed no signs of slowing down. In fact, Moira was even giving the grocery store a run for its money in the bread department. She was constantly filling orders from customers and was beginning to consider setting up a website so that she could expand her cake services to a broader base of patrons. Maybe it was something she could talk to Jack about. Yes, business was very good, and Moira couldn't be happier about it. The smile became plastered to her face as she went into the walk-in to grab a large bowl of sourdough starter that had been sitting and fermenting for a week. She set the bowl on the counter and dipped her large measured scoop into the gigantic bag of flour she kept in a deep pull out drawer in the work island. The large steel bowl would take four additions of flour before she needed to turn the soft lump out onto the marble surface to knead the remaining flour in. This was her favourite part, using her hands and arms to roll and re-roll the dough from a gooey mess into the firm perfectly smooth ball of dough that would eventually rise into golden fragrant bread. She relished this, rolling the large lump under her hands and deftly using her fingers to keep the edges from wandering too far out onto the counter. The acute smell of the fermented yeast filled her nostrils and she drank it in. Sourdough was amazing, it was sharp smelling and soft and made the best toast in the whole world. When the dough had absorbed the last of the flour and was smoothed into a gorgeous pale mound on her work surface, Moira grabbed a long sharp knife and a bunch of bread pans. She used the knife to score deep cuts into the dough and then took the smaller sections and shaped them with her hands to fit the pans. In no time at all, there were twelve perfect loaves to be, resting in the bread pans and waiting to rise to their full height before being baked. Moira set them on a tall multi-shelved rack in the back of the kitchen near the ovens, where the residual warmth would assist in the rising process. She had been so absorbed in her ministrations that she hadn't noticed two things: one, that it was nearly five now, and two, that Jack was standing in the doorway watching her with a large smile on his face.

"Oh! You startled me." She smiled shyly. "How long have you been there?"

"Long enough. You look so beautiful when you're concentrating like that. I didn't want to spoil it by telling you I was here. Are you getting ready to close up?"

Moira's hand flew to her forehead to wipe away a streak of flour. "Yeah, I was just setting some bread for later."

"Good, I was hoping I could take you out. Actually, let me re-phrase that. I wanted to take you to my place, make you a terrible and not nearly enough to impress you meal, and maybe have some wine and talk for a while. What do you think?" His sheepish grin made her blush a little.

"I'd love to, but I need to be here in about one and a half hours to put the bread in the oven. Sourdough is finicky. If I let it raise too long, the bread will be too soft and will be hanging down over the side of the pans. Is that okay?"

"Sounds great. We'll come back here after an early dinner then, deal?"

"Deal."

"Let's go then. C'mon, grab your coat."

Moira started to laugh, "Oh Jack, I can't go right now, it will take me at least a half an hour to close everything down, put things away, you know. I can't just take off."

"Of course you can."

"Especially when he has already recruited your very smart and savvy business partner to finish all the boring stuff so that you can go and play," Jaye stated, having appeared in the doorway beside Jack and giving him a surreptitious wink. "Now bugger off! I have work to do."

Moira gave her friend a grateful smile and grabbed her jacket from the landing out the door at the back of the kitchen, then grabbed her purse from its place on the small shelf near the door. Jack had already headed back out to the main door to open it for her, so Jaye took advantage of his turned back to wiggle her hips suggestively at Moira, who stifled a giggle.

Before Moira could rattle off a list of closing things to remember, Jaye shot her a look that said "I can handle this", warning her from going into superwoman mode instead of just letting herself be kidnapped by this tall handsome man.

"Be good, kids!" Jaye shouted from the doorway as they got into Jack's car. Jack saluted her.

As they drove off, Jack turned to Moira.

"I was a little worried you might turn me down," he said. "I know how much you love that shop, kind of like it's your baby. But then I thought, what's the point of having a business partner if you can't let her close up once in a while, and it's obvious how much you trust her, so I took a chance."

"I'm glad you did. I think I went into automatic pilot for a while today. It'll be a nice diversion for me to get out."

"I hope I'm more than just a diversion for you," Jack said quietly, reaching over and touching her hand.

"I hope so too," she said.

Chapter Fourteen

Jack's apartment, newly cleaned, was really everything Moira had come not to expect from a man's apartment. It was, actually ... quaint. Though it was not too large, it was comfortable. She was touched that he appeared to have cleaned up for her. He ushered her to a seat in the living room while he put together a lovely light meal in the kitchen. Moira gazed about the room as Jack darted in to pour her a glass of wine, or set out two place settings on the coffee table before her. She was enjoying watching him nervously flutter about the room. It was like he had suddenly become a different person, a more timid one, more anxious to please or to prove something—she didn't know which yet. Finally, as he set down some food, which had obviously started out frozen, but which he had equally obviously gone to such lengths to dress up and look more presentable, Moira burst out laughing.

"Oh Jack, this is marvelous."

He stood, crestfallen, which only made her laugh harder.

"If you could only see your face right now! You look like a petulant child. I'm not poking fun at you, Jack, honestly. I don't think any man has ever gone to so much trouble for me before. I think it's wonderful."

Finally Jack's face broke into a smile.

"Well, I told you I couldn't cook. But this is the best I can do. I'd do it again if I knew it would make you smile like that, though. C'mon, let's eat some freshly unfrozen dinner."

They dug into their meals, lasagna portions with a side of salad that he had made to dress up the rather rubbery layer of cheese and the too dry layer of beef and vegetables. Although the food was admittedly terrible, the two enjoyed each other's company, talking and laughing throughout the meal, terrible as it was, and the wine, magnificent as it was. When Jack offered to drive Moira home, she accepted, since the sky was growing very dark and murky and she didn't want to walk home and risk being caught in the downpour. They stowed the dishes in the sink and rinsed out their wine glasses, then Jack locked the door behind them and they drove off to the shop, where Jack left his car in the space in front of the store. By the time they had walked the small distance through the narrow path that led to the back door and ultimately, the stairs to the apartment, the rain had already started to fall. Moira fumbled briefly with the key, having trouble getting it into the lock in the rain. Moira tore the note from the door of The Cakery kitchen, which stated that Jaye had taken care of the bread and not to worry about it anymore tonight, which was good, since Moira had long forgotten it in the comfort of Jack's company. They climbed the stairs and let themselves in through the door just as the rain went from gentle mist to full downpour.

"Can I make you some tea before you head back out into that?"

"Absolutely. Is the car going to be okay there, or should I move it?"

"It's fine. I have one designated spot that I can occupy, since I'm a business owner. Most of us on the street do, and the city doesn't tow from those. Take a look." She indicated the window as she turned to the kitchen to put on the kettle. Jack glanced out the window that overlooked the street and noticed that there were indeed one or two cars that were parked in front of businesses.

"Why don't you come and sit down," he said, taking a seat himself on the smallish sofa in the living room.

Moira came in and snuggled down into the corner of

154

the couch, and Jack reached out and lifted her legs off the floor and rested them on his lap. They sat comfortably for a few minutes, waiting for the water to boil and listening to the sounds of the rain on the window.

"Your feet are a little wet," Jack told her and proceeded to take her socks off, giving her toes a gentle rub as he did. She closed her eyes and tilted her head back for a minute. When she opened them again, Jack was watching her, his hands still resting on her feet. He leaned over and kissed her softly. Moira kissed him back, sinking against the warmth of his body. When Jack finally pulled away, he remained close to her on the couch, his hand tracing the lines of her face, her shoulders. The sudden loud wail from the kettle startled them from their embrace, and Moira got up to go and fill the teapot. Jack opted to get up himself and put on some music. He selected a soft jazz CD from her collection and was sitting again on the couch when Moira returned bearing a tray with a little antique teapot, two teacups, two smallish bowls and a small plate of cookies. Jack laughed out loud when he saw that they were Oreos.

"What's funny?" Moira asked as she once again sat down with him, pulling a throw blanket from the back of the couch and draping it over her legs.

"You, the baker, have store bought cookies in your house. I find that really funny."

"I know, I know, but sometimes you just need an Oreo, you know. That and ... I didn't want to upstage your lovely dinner." She had a twinkle in her eyes.

"Touché. It's okay though, I like Oreos." He lifted one off the plate, twisted it open and took a couple of licks of the white filling, winking at her. She giggled back and leaned over to pour out the tea.

"What do you like in your tea, Jack?"

"Just a little bit of sugar, like the tip of the sugar spoon."

He watched as she dipped the end of a small teaspoon into the sugar bowl, shook off any extra and stirred it into his teacup. Then she took the smaller bowl (which, at

155

closer inspection, resembled a little pot with a queer lid) from the back of the tray, lifted it and dipped her own spoon in. It was honey, and she deftly swooped her spoon around so that the golden substance wouldn't run off onto the tray. She stirred this into her tea, taking time to make sure that it was all dissolved, and then set the spoon down on the saucer. She caught Jack watching her with interest.

"What is it?"

"You're so deliberate about everything. It's like watching a performance just to see you make a cup of tea."

"Stop, you're going to embarrass me."

"I hope not. Don't be self-conscious with me, I love this. I like who you are at home."

"I'll try. I just ... well, I worry a lot."

"Believe me, I understand."

And with that they fell once more into the comforting silence of sipping tea and gazing at one another. The awkwardness in Moira began to slip away as she realized that Jack was actually comfortable and enjoying himself.

She cleared away the tea tray and settled herself once more on the couch with Jack, draping the blanket so that it covered them both and setting her legs once again in his lap, where he immediately took the opportunity to massage her feet, touch her legs and encircle her ankles.

"What are you thinking about?" Jack asked as he rubbed Moira's bare foot.

"I'm trying to figure something out."

"What?"

"Whether or not you really like me."

He smiled and ran his hand up her leg, stroking her calf.

"I think you already know that. What is making you wonder?"

"Well, you don't do the relationship thing. At least, you haven't, from what you've told me."

"That shouldn't make a difference. What's the other option?"

"What option?"

156

"Well, you're trying to figure this out, so either I like you, or ... "

"Or you don't, I suppose. You could be just killing time with me, and are morbidly interested in what I have to say."

"What else?"

"Or else ... " She dropped her gaze for a moment. "Or you're the first one who's really understood me, and this is something really real."

"Oh, I definitely like that option. You need to stop worrying so much. I like you, I can't say that I understand you, but I like you enough to find out."

"Okay. I like you too, Jack."

They went back to sitting quietly on her couch, Jack rubbing her leg under her jeans and Moira tracing the tiny hairs on his arm with her finger. Outside, the gentle rain from earlier was starting to come down much harder.

"Moira?"

"Yes, Jack?"

"Why won't you tell me what happened with Mark?"

"I don't know. I don't want to cry in front of you."

"He really hurt you, didn't he?"

"Yeah, he really did. It's my own fault. I saw a relationship, and he saw a meal ticket and free rooming. I projected onto him things that weren't there."

"I don't think you should fault yourself for that. He obviously knew what he was doing. Otherwise he wouldn't have acted like a boyfriend."

"I know. If I think about it now, the signs were all there, I just didn't want to see them. And Sloane had always had such an easy time with men, I was happy that for once I had someone too. Maybe that was part of the problem; I used him too. But I did care, and that's why it hurt so much."

"Have you told your family about me yet?"

"Sort of. They know we're seeing a lot of each other, but I'm not giving any details. I don't want to rush things, Jack. I don't want to push anything. Besides, my family is so wrapped up in this wedding right now, there's not a lot of interest in what I'm doing, which is refreshing."

"Why, are they so bad?"

"No, not bad, they're just really involved in my life. All we have is the four of us, and now Martin, so everybody is always in everybody else's business. Most of the time it's nice, comforting. But sometimes it makes me feel a little claustrophobic and I need a break from it. This has been nice. Sloane loves the attention, and I love the privacy."

Moira shifted slightly, allowing Jack's hand to travel further up to her knee, still massaging and caressing her skin. She tilted her head back on the cushion, relaxing into the mood. Outside, the rain came harder and thunder started to rumble.

"My family isn't really involved in my life like that, but then again, there are only two of us," Jack said reflectively. "I'm not sure if I'm missing out on anything, because I've never had that big family dynamic."

"Hmmm, but you and your dad talk a lot."

"Sure we do, but ever since he got sick, the conversations have all been the same. I worry about him, he worries about me. We try to have a nice visit, but it's hard when the reminders of his disease are all around us."

"How sick is he?"

"The doctor thinks a few more weeks. It's really just a waiting game now. It's hard to know for sure, though. He's eating again, so if you talk to the nurses, it's a good sign, but if you talk to the doctors, it's a sign of the final calm before the storm."

He stopped, and a flicker of emotion played briefly across his face. Moira decided not to press him.

Just then, a large flash of lightning darted across the window, and the resulting boom took out all of the lights.

She sat up, and Jack yanked his hand from its resting place on her leg.

"I'll get candles."

"Is your kitchen okay, you know, downstairs?"

"Yeah, I have an independent generator for it, just in case of such an emergency."

They got up, and Moira went into the drawer on her bureau for candles. She slipped Jack a box of matches, and they began lighting the various candles around the room. Jack looked out the window.

"Wow, that's quite the storm," he said. "Come and see."

Moira came over and put her hands on the sill to lean over and take a look at the scene out the window. The lights of Main St. were all off, with a few of the windows above the shops like hers showing some flickering flames dance against the glass. The rain was falling in giant sheets, covering the streets and shop walls with a slick shine. Trees were bending in the wind, and debris was being tossed through the air like toys.

"Looks like it's getting serious," she said.

Jack put his arms around her from behind. He buried his face in her hair. "Maybe I should go now, before it gets worse."

Moira twisted in his arms and turned to face him. Her heart was pounding in her chest at the thought of what she was going to suggest.

"I think you should stay."

"Are you sure?" Jack whispered.

"Yes."

"What about that stuff you just said," he murmured, brushing her cheek with his lips. "I don't want to rush you either."

Moira turned her large green eyes so that they were staring right into Jack's. She took a deep, shuddering breath. "It's okay."

They went around the room and blew out most of the candles, taking one each and going into the bedroom. Moira placed hers on the small table next to the bed, and Jack put his on the dresser. He came over and kissed her deeply, gently removing her shirt from her shoulders and kissing the exposed flesh as it emerged. Moira rolled her head back

159

and shivered slightly as the touch of Jack's lips made her skin tingle and goose bumps formed on her arms. She pushed him gently down until he was sitting on the edge of the bed and stood before him in her bra and jeans. Jack looked at her, eyebrow raised as if to ask whether he was permitted to touch, and she nodded ever so slightly, lifting his hand up to her breast, then letting go to let him explore at his leisure. Jack touched her hesitantly at first, the tips of his fingers barely brushing the flesh. Her skin was so smooth, so soft. The little jabs in her breath making him take just as much pleasure in her reaction as in the actions themselves. Moira sank down onto his lap, lifting his shirt over his head and pressed herself against him.

"We don't have to, you know," he whispered in her ear.

"I know," she said. "I want to."

With those words, Jack knew that he was being given a gift of sorts. Moira was not the kind of woman who gave herself freely to men, and from the conversations they had had about previous relationships, didn't have the best track record with them once she did. Likewise, Jack didn't normally operate like this either. A more complex and compelling woman than those with whom he normally associated, and he was addicted to her, wanting to take things slowly, more slowly than he ever had before and really *be* with her in every sense.

She kissed his chest, marveling in the soft patch of hair in the center and how her fingers threaded through them so easily. Then she kissed his mouth, deeply, first his upper lip, then his lower one, opening her mouth and letting his tongue lick and taste her. They moved cautiously, carefully, and with utter fascination of one another, relishing every new exploration. The clothes tumbled carelessly to the floor, and they moved together on her bed, naked and warm, with the soft flicker of the flames casting brief shadows and illuminations on their bodies.

Against his usual urges, and with an intensity that surprised him, Jack bathed in his discovery of her, wanting

160

to get to know every inch of her. He kissed her from her toes to her shoulders, long sliding kisses. When he turned to take her nipple into his mouth, she gasped out loud, and he looked up at her face and smiled. Everything about Moira was beautiful. Jack found himself wishing that they could stay like this forever, kissing and caressing each other in the dark of a storm, in the warmth of this room with the light dancing over them.

He gently lifted her leg slightly and dipped a finger inside her, covering the moan from her lips with his mouth, then moaning himself in response as her hand found his erection and her fingers wrapped around it, feeling the slow pulse of his blood boiling beneath the surface. Their motions began to take on an animal urgency, as they moved in sync on the bed. Finally, Jack moved and shifted his body, and Moira raised her hips to allow him ultimate access to her. He entered her slowly, savouring every sensation, the heat of her body, and the look in her eyes as she locked them onto his. Her hair was strewn on the pillow, and her lips were slightly parted as she kept his gaze.

"Jack ... " she whispered, then closed her eyes again and arched her back as he filled her completely. Their bodies were a perfect fit, and they held for a instant, suspended in the moment and in the beating of their hearts.

"You're so beautiful," Jack told her. "You have to know that, I can't believe you're really here."

They moved together like poetry, their bodies becoming aglow with a faint layer of sweat and lust. First Jack guided their movements, traveling his hands from her hair to her breasts to her thighs as he possessed her, then Moira took over, trading positions so that now she sat astride him, touching his chest, teasing his nipples and letting her hair drape over him. They danced thus, until the urgency of orgasm became unbearable, then exploded in succession, first Moira, then Jack, and lay in each other's arms as their breathing came back to normal and the heat faded away into a warm glow that emanated from them in the aftermath of their lovemaking.

Finally Moira got up and went into the bathroom. When she came out, she had draped a short robe over her shoulders, leaving the middle unfastened to allow a strip of flesh to peek through.

Jack leaned up on his shoulder and looked at her. He could scarcely believe that this phenomenal yet guarded woman had allowed him to share her body so intimately. She crossed to the dresser and blew out the candle, then rejoined him on the bed.

"Still waters ... " Jack said to her, kissing her briefly as she snuggled down next to him and lifted the blankets to cover them.

"Hmmm?" she asked. "What do you mean?"

"It's just an expression. You seem a little shy and withdrawn a bit in the daylight, but I've never felt so ... how should I put it ... enveloped in a woman before."

"I'll take that as a compliment."

"You should. Do you still want me to stay?"

"Why, do you want to leave?" Moira looked momentarily stricken.

"No, I don't want to leave. I feel as though I could stay right here for a long time."

She sighed in relief. They drifted back into the softness of the pillows and fell asleep, while outside the storm settled down into a gentle rainfall once again.

Chapter Fifteen

In the morning, Moira awoke to the sound of the radio in her living room and the artificial brightness of all the lights that weren't properly turned off the night before when the storm took the power. She glanced at her clock, *12:00, 12:00, 12:00* ... well, that was going to be no help. Beside her, Jack was still asleep, one arm thrown carelessly over his forehead. *Man,* she thought, *I can't believe I slept with him already.* Thank goodness no one knew about it, she'd never hear the end of "history repeating itself" lectures.

She had promised herself that she would not be thrown so recklessly into another of these physical relationships before they really knew each other, and now here she was. She carefully got out of bed and slipped into the bathroom. There she splashed water on her face and studied her reflection briefly. She scowled at herself. Slipping back into the bedroom, she hastily started to dress. Just as she was pulling a t-shirt over her head, Jack stirred, lifted his tousled head up and smiled openly at her.

"Good morning, sunshine. You look lovely."

She blushed and, adjusting her shirt, smiled back at him.

"Umm, good morning. I'll go make some coffee, so you can have some privacy to get dressed."

And she hastened out of the room to the safety of her kitchen. Before she could even pour the water into the top of her coffee maker, Jack came out in his boxers and shirt.

"Why are you running away?" he asked gently. "Are you sorry about last night?"

Moira nearly spilled in her flustered response.

"Maybe we shouldn't have done that so soon. I'm not usually so forward." She avoided his eyes, instead busying herself with the filter and the packet of ground beans on the counter. But Jack was having none of that. He walked straight over to her.

"Look at me."

"No."

"Moira," he said softly, "look at me."

She looked up; her eyes were huge and wet.

"You are beautiful, and I don't want you to feel bad. Last night was wonderful, and I am grateful for you."

"Okay," she whispered.

He leaned in and kissed her gently on the lips, lifting his hand to touch her waist. When they broke away from their kiss, Jack smiled at her, tracing her cheekbone.

"Is it okay if I use the shower?"

"Sure," she said, and then added playfully, "and you can use my toothbrush too."

"Cheeky." He smiled and turned back to the bedroom to get ready for the day.

By the time Jack emerged once again from the bedroom and bathroom, he was clean and fresh, with his damp hair still tousled on his head and an impish look on his face. He joined Moira, who was setting out cups of coffee, fresh fruit and some muffins on the small table in the living room in front of the couch.

"Breakfast?" she asked.

"Sure, thanks." Jack sat gratefully down and helped himself, watching Moira's movements closely. He loved how she shook her wrist to straighten out her sleeve. If she noticed that he was watching her, she gave nothing away. Still slightly avoiding his eyes, she poured milk into her mug and stirred in a spoonful of sugar, then sat down opposite him on the couch. They ate in harmonious quiet, the silence only a little frayed around the edges, as Jack suspected that Moira still had slight reservations about the night before. When they finished, Moira brushed the crumbs from her lap and stood up to gather the items and return them to her kitchen. Jack got up and began to help. Almost as if by learned habit, they moved in sync, each cleaning and putting away the efforts of their meal. When at last they bumped into each other as they both turned to leave the room, the humour of the situation caused them to at last laugh out loud.

"Okay, so you still feel bad. Why don't we see each other tonight?"

"Are you sure?"

"Yes, I want to prove to you that I still want to see you. Why don't you come to my place? I'd really like to see you tonight." *And every night,* Jack thought. He felt like he was bewitched, he just couldn't get enough of her.

"Okay," Moira agreed. "Just come and get me here later."

"Right after work, I promise."

They gathered their things and left the apartment. At the bottom of the stairs, Jack kissed her once more, not wanting the magic that had captured them that night to dissipate. Reluctantly, he left, shutting the door behind him. Moira sighed again and went to turn the key in the lock to the shop, but found to her surprise that it was already open. She walked in and found Jaye sitting on the counter, piping icing onto some sugar cookies and wearing a very coy smile.

"Nice night, Moira?" she asked, raising her eyebrow.

"What do you know?" Moira demanded.

"Oh, nothing. Just when I was out last night and drove by, there was a car parked out front, and when I came in this morning, the same car was still here. And I'm not sure ... but I think there was more than one set of footsteps wandering around up there this morning."

Moira smiled, and then frowned.

"Oh my GOD, Jaye, what the hell did I do??"

"Had a little somethin' with Jack, by the sounds of it."

"I can't believe I did that so soon! I mean really, after all the bullshit with Mark, I promised myself not to do anything like that again. What's the matter with me?"

Jaye hopped down from the counter and picked up the now full tray of cookies, looking at her friend.

"There's nothing wrong with you, Moira. Stop comparing Jack to Mark. There is no comparison. This guy genuinely likes you, anyone can see that. Was it bad? Is that why you're so freaked out?"

"No, it was very, very good. It felt ... right."

"Then quit your bitching. I don't want to hear another word."

Now it was Moira's turn to look amused. "Not another word?"

"Weeeell, if you insist on giving me details ... "

***

As Jack drove into work that morning, he couldn't help but smile. He could still practically smell Moira on his clothes, his hands. The events of the night kept playing over and over in his mind. He was sure that it would be a difficult day at work; he just couldn't stop his mind from racing. He pulled his car into the lot at work and fairly bounced into the office. Whistling, he walked through the hall, nodding hello to the various staff he passed by, and into his office. He had a lot of finishing work to do on the project that he was wrapping up. The initial presentation had gone well, and now it was up to him to polish the work, get it ready for being post-ready on the internet. He settled into a comfortable position, turned on his computer and checked the messages in his inbox. There were only two, one from Evan to remind him of a lunch meeting they had, and one from the hospice. The doctor in charge of his father wanted to go over some things with him. Jack decided to return this call right away. He picked up the phone and punched in the numbers.

"Good Morning, St. Jude's Hospice, how may I direct your call?"

"Hello, this is Jack Wallace, returning Dr. Morgan's

call. Is he in?"

"One moment, please."

Tacky musak filled Jack's ear as he waited to be transferred. *Who gets the commissions to make instrumental versions of pop music?* Jack wondered as he listened to the guitar and fiddle pick out a crude version of a Dixie Chicks song. Terrible was the only way to describe it.

"Jack Wallace?"

"Yes, good morning, Doctor. How's my dad holding up today?"

"Not so good, Jack. We've had to reinsert the feeding tube."

"What? But he was doing so well last time I was there! I don't understand how; did he take such a downfall in a matter of under twenty four hours?"

"It's the nature of this stage of the illness, Jack. We've also hooked him up to a heart monitor; it seems that during the storm last night, he suffered a small attack, probably due to the lightning we had touch down at the back of the lot. It was very loud, and quite a few of our residents reacted poorly to the intensity of the storm."

"What does this mean?"

The doctor paused, gathering his thoughts and searching for the best way to put it to this distraught young man on the phone.

"It means, I think you'll find that if his heart is starting to struggle with overcoming small disturbances, the illness will run its course sooner than you might have been preparing for. We'll keep him comfortable, but you should be ready to see some rapid changes in the next week or so."

"Okay, tell him I'll be in tonight to see him, please."

"We will, Jack. Right now he's still sleeping due to the medication we gave him to regulate his heart. He'll be very tired from the drugs, but so far hasn't refused treatment for his heart or for his nutrition. Don't upset him tonight, Jack. He knows his time is getting short and needs you to be supportive and realistic, okay?"

"Okay. Thanks for calling so quickly with the update."

"Of course, Jack. I'll leave word with the staff to call you if there are anymore changes."

"Thank you."

He hung up the phone feeling terrible. Why was it that he couldn't seem to have something positive in his life without something horrible happening to balance it out?

He tried to recapture the euphoric feeling of the morning but found that it was impossible now. Like the air being let out of a balloon through a pin-sized hole in the side, he slumped in his chair for a minute. Then he straightened up and buckled down to work, the only factor that he could control right now. Jack opened the files that contained the collection of work needed for this client. He bent in to his computer and fiddled around with the graphics, sharpening a line here, cleaning up a layout there. There was really so much to do that he barely noticed as the time ticked on, the memories of his night with Moira mingling with the thoughts of his father and the update from the doctor that morning. All the distractions in his head made him work even harder this morning, contrary to his normal mode of operation. Usually thoughts of his father made him feel restless, distracted, but today they just seemed to make him even more determined to do a good job, fix every possible fodder for critique and correction from Evan. Jack looked up at the clock, an hour to go before he and his boss left for their lunch meeting. They were headed to a small deli on the far end of the street from Moira's shop. There was a lot to go over, campaigns to plan, the promotion to discuss, and he was sure that there was some final feedback on the last piece of work he submitted. It should be a fairly positive meeting, he thought.

He tucked his nose once again down to his computer and scanned the images on the screen and read and re-read the copy, making sure that everything was crystal clear and lucid. There was no room for mistakes when there was a promotion at stake. Everything was looking crisp. Time to save and backup all of the files. He reached into his desk for a blank CD and inserted it into his computer. It was the policy of their work that everything was saved twice, attractively first, with nice looking icons to mark the files for the company that it would go to, and secondly for the archives. To Jack it was now second nature. Although most of the employees used standard company icons to mark out the files on the disc, Jack preferred to personalize his for the account. He knew that it was small touches like that that had led to his being listed for advancement, personal attention to detail. And it didn't hurt that it made his work stand out in the industry either. When the last of the two discs popped out to indicate being complete, Jack printed out a customized sticker cover from his printer and attached it to the first disc. This was the one that would go to the client. He then put it into an envelope and got up to drop it off with Evan. He walked down the hall from his small office to Evan's larger one in the corner, where the door was closed. Jack knocked somewhat quietly on the door and heard his boss call out for him to enter. Opening the door slowly, in case there was someone else in the room, Jack stepped inside. Evan was sitting alone at his desk, staring at his computer with a frown fixed on his face.

"Just a minute," he said without looking up.

Jack took a seat and waited patiently for Evan to finish what he was doing. Years here had taught him that with Evan, it was better to wait for his full attention when handing in work. After a few minutes, Evan looked up, still wearing the frown, and regarded Jack smoothly.

"How's the work coming?"

"Done," Jack announced, placing the disc in its jacket on Evan's desk.

Evan's face broke into a smile.

"Thank goodness. Apparently they have moved up their launch date and were wondering about speeding up the work. You know how much I hate to rush things, we get sloppy when we do, and something invariably gets missed or overlooked."

He slid the CD off the desk, slid it out of its cover and popped it into his computer. The frown returned as his practiced eyes danced across the screen, taking in every detail down to the tiniest copyright marker in the bottom corner of the screen. Finally, something akin to relief spread across his face.

"Nicely done, Jack. I think we can send this out as is."

"That's great!"

"You've come a long way from the days when I used to hand your work back to you two or three times before we sent it out. I'm happy with this effort, it's air tight."

Evan paused, as if he were waiting for something. Jack waited patiently for his boss to remember whatever it was he was struggling with. Finally Evan looked at Jack expectantly.

"Was there something else?"

"Umm, lunch, I thought."

"Oh, was that today?!" Evan quickly swiveled in his chair and flipped open his palm pilot, tapping at the screen with the little pointer.

"Gosh, I'm sorry Jack, there's been a lot going on for me this morning. I completely forgot."

"Did you want to reschedule?"

"No, no." He checked his watch. "It's a quarter to twelve now, why don't we head out?"

"No problem." Jack scurried back to his office and grabbed his jacket from the hook behind his door. He was just making his way down the hall, jamming his arms into the sleeves as Evan emerged from his door, already with his jacket on and looking completely put together. They headed out together to the parking lot, where Evan indicated to his car. Jack nodded, and they got in and drove off.

Traffic was light as they made their way across the bridge and turned onto the lower end of Main St. As they passed by The Cakery, Evan turned to Jack and smiled.

"That place has the greatest rye bread I've ever tasted. My wife is crazy about it. You should try it sometime."

Jack began to chuckle and blush, the mere sight of the place making him picture Moira's green eyes in the candlelight, looking up at him trustingly.

"What, did I say something funny?" Evan asked, clearly confused by his companion's reaction to the harmless statement.

"No, not at all. That's Moira's store."

"Moira, Moira ... the coffee/icing sugar girl?" Evan asked incredulously.

"Yeah, we're seeing each other."

Evan smiled broadly.

"It's about time. Tell me, do you still throw food on one another?"

"No, no. That was total happenstance. She's wonderful, really. And you're right about her food, though next time you should take your wife one of her strawberry mousse cakes. They're like heaven."

"Hmm, okay. I'll have to remember that."

They parked the car outside of the deli and went in. Ten minutes later, they had a comfortable booth near the front windows and two Reuben sandwiches with coleslaw to attack in front of them. They ate comfortably, the formalities of the office behind them. Evan leafed through a newspaper as he munched on his sandwich. Finally, when nothing remained of their lunch but some errant crumbs on the plate and a cup of coffee each, he began to get down to business.

"First things first, Jack. I would like to formally offer you the position of Creative Director. You've worked really hard, even in the face of some extremely trying circumstances, and that does not go unnoticed. It will be effective two weeks from this Friday, and will come with a handsome raise and some more holiday time. What do you think?" It was obvious that Evan had caught Jack off guard with this information, which must have been his intention; he did love the element of surprise.

"I'm thrilled. Thank you, Evan. Of course I accept."

171

"Good, now that's out of the way, how's your father doing?"

Jack's handsome eyes clouded. "Not so well. For a little while there, he was doing great. He was eating again and just seemed to be so energetic. I even took him outside for a few hours on the weekend, but this morning he slipped back into some problems."

"I'm sorry. The ups and downs must be hard on you."

"Yeah, there's no way to know how to be if he's improving one minute and on a downslide the next. I wish I could know what to say to him, but I'm finding it harder going the longer this drags out."

"It's not easy to lose family," Evan said quietly. Jack remembered that the year he had come to work for him, Evan had lost a sister to ovarian cancer. No one was immune from the far-reaching hand of this disease.

"It will be a relief to you, when it's over," Evan said quietly. "To see him be released from the pain."

"I know. I mean, in my head I know, but it will still be hard-going."

"Of course. Nothing about this illness is easy."

They were quiet for a spell, each reflecting on the experiences of their past and present. Finally, Evan spoke up again.

"So, Maria?"

"Moira."

"Yes, what's going on there?"

"She's so different from the women that I usually go out with. I really like spending time with her. In fact, I'm seeing her again tonight."

Evan smiled at his colleague.

"Jack, you need some good friends. I can't be the only one you have to talk about these things with, can I?"

"Sort of," he said with a wry smile. "I guess I'm not much of a socialiser."

"Understatement of the year. Why don't you bring Moira out to the house next month for the wife's birthday party? I could use some people to talk with besides her

172

friends and their husbands and boyfriends. They're all too interested in status for me. I don't relish a night of conversation on whose car is newer, or who just bought a new boat. Besides, it'll be good for you to get out."

"I'd love to ... only ..."

"No pressure, I understand about your father. If you are able, come out. If not, I'll understand. Bring your lady out with you, show her off. You know how much my wife likes to fawn over new love."

They laughed together, then paid their bill and headed back to the office for the afternoon. Jack found that he was feeling light, accomplished. What great news he would have to tell when he spoke to his father tonight! The promotion was his officially.

As he and Evan approached the office main doors, Jack was immediately aware that something was up, something that he couldn't put his finger on. Evan opened the door and said, "After you."

Jack walked in and was inundated with a rousing cheer from the employees, who were gathered in the main hallway/reception area.

"Congratulations, Jack!" yelled Rebecca.

He thanked her and turned to Evan.

"How long has everyone known?"

"Oh, since this morning. I thought a nice reception would be a good way to welcome you into your new role," he said. "Everyone, meet your new Creative Director, Jack Wallace!" he bellowed to the renewed cheers of the assemblage. Jack took a mock bow as the ladies from the office wolf whistled at him.

Chapter Sixteen

By the time work ended for the day, Jack was already feeling emotionally spent. There had been far too much for him to process. Like it or not though, his first order of business for the day was to go to the hospice and see his father. The phone call this morning had been playing around in the back of his head all day. It seemed impossible to him that the same man who had eaten soup and sweets on the weekend could now be once again a slave to the frailties of a body that was refusing to go on living. To the continued cheers and congratulations scattered throughout the hallway on his way out the door, Jack left feeling the weight of the world crushing his shoulders. He felt tense, uncomfortable and not a little bit nervous. It only took him minutes to arrive at the hospice and park his car, but the brief walk from the parking lot to the door felt like a marathon. He nodded hello to the few members of the staff that he now recognized on his way in, then steeled himself at the door to his father's room and, finally, entered.

There on the bed lay Kevin, grey, shriveled and hollow looking. His purpling eyelids were closed, wires rose up from various parts of him, and the monitors on the bar mounted beside him blipped in time with the reluctant rise and fall of his chest. Jack carefully pulled the visitors' chair closer up to the bed, lifting it gently so as not to wake him with the noise of wood scraping on the linoleum. He sat, touched his father's hand and steadied his nerves. At the contact, Kevin drew in a shaky, raspy breath. His eyelids fluttered, as though a breeze had grazed them, and he opened his watery eyes to regard his only son.

"Jack," he barely whispered. "How do you like my new look?" The thin face cracked a weak smile.

"Its nice, Dad, nurses into bondage these days?"

"They all want to keep me tied down, it seems." He tried to chuckle, but only managed a small cough.

"How are you feeling? I mean, if I go by how you look, I'd have to say pretty shitty."

"No, shitty would be an upgrade, I feel like I've been run over by a truck. Like there's a two-ton elephant sitting on my chest. Heart attacks, not so much fun. Who knew?"

Just like him, Jack thought, *cracking jokes at a time like this.*

"What happened exactly?" Jack asked. "The doctor said you had a heart attack."

"What can you expect when a bolt of lightning drops down outside of your window? That storm last night was responsible for more than one resolution, I can tell you. I heard from Nurse Vicky today that four people died last night. Guys like me just aren't meant to weather big shock like that anymore. The system can't handle it." He pointed weakly to his chest to illustrate his point, but at mention of the storm, Jack's eyes flickered with the realization of *his* resolution as a result of the storm, his night with Moira.

"Mmmmm, seems you would agree with me." Kevin's eyes twinkled momentarily. "Did you not see the lightning?"

"No, must've missed it," he mumbled.

"I see."

Jack dropped his gaze. He did not want to tell his dad that while he was lying in this horrible place, his heart arresting and feeling scared and in pain, he had been lying in Moira's bed making love to her. It felt like betrayal. It didn't matter, though. Kevin knew him so well, he had already guessed as much.

"I hope this is not the last you see of her."

"Of course not. She's not like the other girls I've dated."

"If you can call that dating," Kevin kidded with him,

softly. "Don't feel so bad about it, son. If I still had my vitality, it's how I would have spent my night too. You know what this means though, don't you?"

"What?"

"Now you have to let me meet her. Otherwise, I'll hold a grudge."

It was Jack's turn to chuckle. Leave it to his father to turn *this* situation of all into an advantage.

"Okay Dad, you win. I'll bring Moira in to meet you."

"When?"

"By the end of the week, I promise. Just let me give her a few days warning and you a few days to get your heart back to normal."

Kevin looked thoughtful. "Good plan. I don't want to spark another attack. If she's as good looking as you say, my heart might not be able to take it."

"End of the week, Dad, I promise."

At that point, one of the nurses (one that Jack did not recognize) came in to change the bag on the IV.

"Hi there, you must be Jack," she said, smiling a warm and winning grin. "I'm Gloria. I've just got to change this young man's saline bag and give him his shot of meds for the night. You might want to get out whatever else you have to say before I administer this. It knocks him out pretty good."

"Don't listen to this vixen, she just likes to keep me in bed," Kevin chided her. Gloria laughed out loud, showing a row of beautiful pearly teeth.

"Oh, you rogue." she said. "He's my favourite, this one." She lined up her syringe with the attachment on the side of the tubing and inserted it. Then she patted Kevin on his shoulder.

"Anything you need, doll, just buzz me."

"Thank you, my dear," Kevin said slowly. His eyelids quavered briefly as Gloria left the room, gently swinging the door shut behind her.

Jack stayed and watched as the medication took its toll and his father gave up to the deep sleep that it induced.

177

When he was sure that Kevin was truly asleep, he stood, picked up his jacket and left the room.

***

Moira sat on the chair in her kitchen and looked at the clock for the umpteenth time. It was getting close to seven thirty. She was a little surprised and a little disappointed that Jack had yet to show up, and worse, yet to call. All she could think of was his revelation to her about his past relationships and wondering if she had become another notch in his bedpost. She really had thought that last night had been special, and although she had spent a good deal of the day berating herself for her actions so soon in this relationship—if she could call it that—something in her heart had been telling her that it would be okay. She grabbed a soda from the fridge and popped it open, then paced a little more as she became more and more nervous. Finally, she gave up sitting down in the dark and locked the bakery, dragging her tired feet upstairs to her apartment. Everything looked as it had that morning when she left. The soft blanket that was thrown over them last night loosely as they sat together on the couch was now lying in a heap on the floor. She smiled a wry smile as she remembered the reason why it had been dropped there. Abruptly, she felt the hot flush of tears coming to her face. *Well, this is just great! Not only have I broken every promise that I've made to myself about getting involved again, but I've gone and slept with him, and now he's avoiding me. The first man I've felt truly interested in for ages.* She turned and kicked the side of the sofa.

"Shit," she said out loud. "Double shit."

The phone jangled loudly, making her jump. She ran over and grabbed it, hoping it was Jack.

"Hello?"

"Moira, I'm glad I caught you. I need you to do something for me."

It was Sloane. Probably some favour for the wedding.

"What do you need, Sloane?"

"Martin has some relatives coming in for the wedding and they can't find a room. I think it's his great Aunt and Uncle, actually. Can they stay at your place? Pleeease."

Moira closed her eyes. If Sloane had her way, she'd have about five or six people staying here in her apartment, and she would end up being some kind of personal chef/chauffeur service for them. It was getting harder and harder to say no to her baby sister.

"I guess so, Sloane, but that's it. I only have one bedroom, so I can only accommodate the two people. Don't ask me to take anyone else."

"Oh, no. Of course not! Thank you thank you thank you. You're such a life saver. They're coming on the bus because neither of them can drive anymore, so just pick them up at the station the day before the wedding around 4pm, okay? Thanks."

Sloane hung up the phone, leaving Moira feeling a little run over. But that was just Sloane: get a yes to the main favour, throw in a few smaller ones and hang up before she could protest. It was her formula, and one that Moira had grown accustomed to. The phone rang again.

"Yes?"

"Moira, thank goodness. I don't think we've had a chance to go over the plans for the stagette this weekend. God, I can't believe the wedding is in less than two weeks! Can you?"

"Oh, um, hi Katie. Actually, can we go over those plans later? I'm kind of tired, it's been a busy day."

Katie laughed. "Sure, Moira, like selling cookies is hard. Honestly, girl guides do it all the time." In the background there was a tinkle of laughter to this remark. Katie warmed to her subject. "I mean, I don't know how you manage to stay in business, what with all the kids who sell the same thing on their front lawns." This stupid remark even got a laugh from the rowdy entourage that was with Katie. Moira realized that she must be in a bar somewhere.

"Oh ha ha, Katie, good one. Yeah, well, my stupid job
179

was actually kind of busy today, so I'll talk to you about the stag night later. Okay?"

"Whatever. You know, you could get just a little more excited about this. It is your sister that's getting hitched. I don't know how Sloane puts up with your bad attitude. Just call me when you decide you actually want to be the maid of honour, okay?" Katie hung up her phone and Moira hung up hers. She found herself shaking her head. She stood staring at her phone.

"Ring again, I dare you," she said to it.

It rang.

Expecting Michelle to be the next caller, now that she had spoken to the rest of the wedding party, she answered rather saucily.

"What?"

"Hi Moira, it's Jack." *Triple shit,* she thought.

"Hi, I was wondering where you had gotten to." *Please don't let him break up with me.*

"It's been a ... busy day. I'm really sorry I wasn't there earlier, but I swear I had a good reason. I was hoping to take you out tonight, if you still want to. A few of my colleagues are meeting at the Dunwoody Inn tonight, at the club in the basement. If you want, we could go and meet them there. There's a jazz trio in tonight."

"Okay. Should I meet you there?"

"Of course not, I'll pick you up. Be there in about half an hour."

"Okay, bye."

Moira hung up the phone and stared at it for a moment. Then she went into her bedroom and changed out of her work clothes and into something more comfortable for sitting in a bar.

Chapter Seventeen

The bar was noisy already, and the few colleagues of Jack's that had arrived already let out a cheer as they arrived, congratulating Jack on his promotion and pointing the pair to the only seats still available, a couple of bar stools at the back corner of the counter. They grabbed them quickly and ordered a couple of drinks. Although she wasn't positive, Moira thought the barmaid seemed to give Jack a brief wink as she set the glasses down before them, though it wasn't acknowledged by him. She didn't have time to dwell on it, though; Jack proudly filled her in on his news from work, and a quick explanation of his father's worsened condition, which attributed to his lateness and the reason for not calling. Finally the members of the small band walked out to the performance area and took up their stools to begin playing. They were pretty good too, as was evident by the several young ladies up near the front that catcalled and whistled at them as they played and hollered loaded comments at them in between songs. The elevated mood in the joint made the drinks go down easily and the familiarity of conversation rise to include several highly charged conversations around them. Every so often, Jack would lean in to whisper in Moira's ear. A song he liked, a funny looking drunk on the brink of falling down, it didn't seem to matter what it was he was saying, the warmth from his body and the faint smell of shampoo and cologne were enough to plant a firm smile on her face for most of the night. He frequently found reasons to touch her, a hand on her knee, brushing a lock of fallen hair from her face, and the two were finding themselves connecting more in the clatter of the noisy bar than they had on almost all of their previous dates, save for the last one. Jack was making no mistake about staking his territory with Moira. One or two men seemed to send appreciative glances in her direction, though she either didn't notice or didn't want to, and Jack was enjoying letting the world know that she was here with him and no other. Maybe that's why they were both so shocked when the pretty girl with the red shirt on walked up to him with such purpose and planted a kiss on his cheek, cutting Moira right out of the way. "Hey there, lover. I thought you were going on a trip out to the west coast for work. You never called to tell me you were back," she practically purred at him.

Jack gently but firmly pushed her back to an arm's length distance.

"Hi, Christie. Ummm, yeah, I did go to California, just for a week to present some stuff for work. When did you get back from Montreal?"

"Moncton. And I got in about two weeks ago." She looked straight at Moira at this point, as if to say "who's the girl?".

"Hi," Moira said loudly. "I didn't catch your name. Mine's Moira." Jack seemed embarrassed and didn't volunteer any information of his own.

"It's Christie." She swooned and then, turning to Jack once again, the voltage turned up to high volume, "Is this your girlfriend, Jack? My, but you do move fast. I'll leave you guys alone, then. Bye, babe."

"Yeah ... " Jack started to say but with a swoosh of her hair she was already gone back into the crowd, leaving a sputtering Jack to deal with the quizzical and slightly hurtful look on Moira's face.

***

After they returned to her apartment, Moira and Jack sat on the couch in her living room and settled in for a nightcap. Once they had their glasses in hand, they sat quietly, companionably for a few moments, letting the events of the evening wash over them as they each waited for the other to be the first to talk. Moira shuffled uncomfortably for a time, not wanting to voice the reservations she was beginning to feel.

"That was interesting," Jack said, finally breaking the silence between them.

"Maybe not the word I would have chosen. Uncomfortable, yes, slightly embarrassing, yes, illuminating, absolutely."

Jack cocked his head to the side to study her face with more clarity.

"Illuminating, huh? I told you, there's nothing to worry about. That part of my life is so over."

"Are you sure?"

A deep sigh sent Jack's body sinking into the back of the sofa. He knew what was coming. She was starting to distrust him. Not that he could really blame her after that run in, but honestly, it just seemed too soon to reveal the depths of his feelings. This was truly uncharted territory. How to explain?

"I don't know what else to say to you, Moira. I can see why you're bothered, but I can't be the one to set your mind at ease. I've been more up front with you than any other woman in my life. So I have a past, a not too attractive one, and every now and then it's going to see us out, whether it's in a movie theater, a restaurant, or just walking into your own shop. I'm not proud of it, but there it is. I can't do any more than just tell you that I don't sleep around anymore. Up until last night, I wasn't even sleeping with you."

"Maybe that's part of what bothers me. You say that you used to have these one or two night stands, and that almost all of your relationships with women for the past eight years have been like that. So what am I? What are we doing? If you were just waiting to have sex with me so that you can move on, I wish you'd let me know. My last rela-

183

tionship went like this too. Everything was great, the dates were great, the connection was there, and we moved it forward. The only problem was his little nagging need to sleep around. I don't want to go through that again. How do I know what you're really doing when you don't call and say that you're busy, or you have to postpone or cancel a date? I mean, really, Jack. It's only been a week and half. You don't owe me anything, just be honest about what you're doing. I don't want to get into this if it means questions all the time. I don't even know if you really have a sick father. Maybe that was just your way of getting me into the sack the other night."

Jack's face froze. He was totally stunned. *I'm falling for a crazy woman!* he thought. A tear welled up in his eye as he struggled to answer her onslaught without letting his emotions get the better of him.

"I think I should leave. But before I go, I want you to know something." Jack rose from his seat and took a steadying breath. "My father is all I have. For a long time now he's been all I've had. And yeah, I don't do relationships so well and have had a really shitty past when it comes to women. But I feel bad for you, Moira. Someone has screwed you over pretty good if you think that a guy can't show a genuine interest in you without an eye out for the next thing, the next woman. I really felt like we had something building here, but I can't do *this* and deal with my father at the same time. If you really think that I'd make up his dying just to fuck around with other women, then we should end this before it gets harder to walk away. Good night, Moira."

Jack placed his glass firmly on the table and strode to the door. Without looking back at Moira, he threw on his jacket, stuffed his feet into his shoes and stalked out, leaving Moira reeling. She had done the unthinkable. Really, she hadn't meant to question the existence of Jack's father, but neither did she want to put herself into a predicament of being the last to know ... again. What she said to Jack was both cruel and unfair, but the words were out of her mouth before she had a chance to stop them. When she looked back on it, he had actually let her into his world a little tonight. He had brought her out, introduced her to a small group of his co-workers and let her share in his triumph over the promotion. And how had she repaid him? By throwing accusations and insinuations in his face. Maybe he was right to storm out like that; she sure would have. Moira picked up her phone and dialed his number. Of course he wouldn't be home yet, but she felt the need to apologize before her harsh words had too much time to sink in. She waited for the machine to pick up.

"You've reached Jack Wallace. I'm not in right now, so leave your message. If this is a wrong number, leave a message anyway. I hate hang ups."

Moira smiled, it was cute.

"Jack, it's Moira. I hate hang ups too, so don't. I'm so sorry about what I said about your father. I had no right. It's just ... I'm scared. I don't do relationships well either, and I keep thinking that everything with you is so right that something about it has to be wrong. I don't want to push you away. Can you come and see me tomorrow and we can talk about it, or maybe I can apologize in person. Again, I'm so sorry."

She hung up, hoping that when he got home he would check his messages right away. In the meantime, she decided to make one more phone call.

"Hello?"

"Hi, Jaye. It's Moira. Are you busy?"

"Nope, just sitting here with a glass of wine and Hugh Grant on the TV. Is everything okay? There's nothing wrong down at the shop, is there?"

"No, no. Nothing is wrong at the shop. I just wanted to ask you a question."

"Shoot."

"Do you think I'm distrusting?"

"What happened?" she demanded. "Did you and Jack have a fight or something?"

"Kind of," she said in a small voice. "I sort of said

185

some things."

"You better tell me what's going on. Do you want me to come over there?"

"It's no problem. You don't have to drive all the way over."

"Okay, I'm on my way. Be there in ten minutes."

Moira tried to tell her that it wasn't absolutely necessary, but Jaye had already hung up the phone.

She took a look around her room, wondering if she should tidy it up, but there was nothing to tidy. Instead, she dug around in the cupboard over the stove and unearthed a new bottle of brandy. Ordinarily, she didn't drink all that often, but from time to time she really enjoyed a little something spirited, usually when she was upset or bothered by something. When Mark had left, she had drunk and entire bottle of scotch in one night. Jaye had stayed by her for every minute of it, heading off the phone calls from her family and holding her hair when she vomited beautifully in the bathroom, the kitchen and even in her bedroom. Of course it was also Jaye who saw her through the skirmishes with Sloane and the early tough months when the business didn't do as well as she would have liked. She was really lucky to have her as a friend.

Jaye arrived in just under ten minutes, carrying a small bag in one hand, a DVD case in the other, and with a bag of ice tucked under her arm.

"Now," she said, marching into the room and depositing the bag on the floor, the movie on the table and heading into the kitchen to put away the ice. "The last time you went through something big with a man, you didn't have any ice for your scotch, which might have diluted it a little bit, so I— Oh, you're drinking brandy. Well, that certainly doesn't call for ice. It'll be just like the last time then, after that fight with your sister. Thank goodness you replaced the bottle." She chucked the bag into Moira's freezer and pulled out two crystal snifters from the cupboard, into which she poured a neat measure of the golden liquid. Then she sat down in the living room next to Moira on the couch.

She stared at her.

"What's with the bag?" Moira finally asked.

"If I'm going to stay at your house tonight while you wallow, I'll need fresh clothes for work tomorrow."

"You're staying the night?"

"Of course. So tell me all about what happened." Jaye sat back comfortably on the couch and took a sip from her glass.

Between drinks, Moira told her of the planned get together for after work, the delay, the lack of phone call from Jack with an explanation, or even a "hey, it'll be a little late", the eventual date at the jazz bar with his colleagues, the woman who came up to him so intimately and how Moira was left out of the transaction, and how it was glossed over by Jack. She told her about how uncomfortable it was to think that there were still women out there who might feel like Jack was someone they could just call on whenever they needed a little physical connection. She told her about the fight in her apartment, only a little more than an hour ago now, and the hurtful words she had spouted about his father. She even went into her guilty feelings about sleeping with him the previous night and the amazing physical connection they had, which only increased her worries. When she was finished, she was crying and her glass was empty. Jaye wordlessly filled it up once more and took a deep breath and looked at her friend.

"Sounds like you really fucked up this one."

"I know." Moira sniffed.

"So why are you so paranoid? Do you honestly think that he made up a sick father just to get you into bed?"

"No, of course not. Jack wouldn't do that. In fact, I was the one who asked him to stay that night."

"Really?? That's not like you at all. What made you do that?"

"It was something about the mood. It was storming out, and we were having this really quiet lovely night, talking and stuff. I just felt this really strong connection between us. I suppose I just missed that so much, I didn't want it to end." She looked slightly petulant, as if she were defending her position, as a child would defend an act of defiance to a parent.

"I don't know what to say to you, babe. Obviously you're still really messed up about a lot of things. Why have you never gone to a therapist to talk?"

"I don't need a therapist."

"Maybe you do. I've known you a long time, Moira, and I've never known you to be reasonable when it comes to relationships. You and your mother hardly talk beyond polite conversation, you and Sloane are always fighting, you push away good men with excuses, and you fall hook line and sinker for the bozos who are plainly feeding you a load of bullshit. I could have told you Mark was an asshole. In fact, I think that I tried to, but you wouldn't listen to me. What do you want me to tell you? Did you at least say sorry to him?"

"I called and left him a message."

"Well, that's something at least."

"One thing's for sure, though."

"What's that?"

"I gotta stop doing this when I get upset." Moira looked down at her drink. "I don't even really want this."

Jaye wordlessly got up and took her drink and Moira's to the sink, where she dumped the contents without a word. She replaced the bottle in the cupboard.

"What do you want?"

"I want Jack. I want to stop being such a bitch. I want to make up with Sloane before this wedding. I want to stop feeling like I'm always pretending with people."

"Well, that's not a tall order at all, is it? Let's start with the first one. You want Jack. Fine. Give him his space to cool off and talk to him, tell him how sorry you are. What was the second one?" She came back into the living room and sat on the floor facing her friend. "Stop being a bitch?! Well, I hate to tell you this, babe, but you're not a bitch. You can't be. If you're a bitch, what the hell does that make me?"

"Über-bitch?" Moira started to smile.

Jaye shook her head slightly, "Naw, I don't like the word 'über'."

"Wonder bitch?"

"Much better. Like Wonder Woman, but with claws."

"Jaye."

"Yeah?"

"What am I going to do about Sloane?"

"I don't know. She's under a lot of pressure right now too, right?" Moira nodded at her. "So maybe part of the reason you guys are fighting so much is because she's just as wired up as you are right now. Everything feels amplified around a wedding."

"No kidding. She's so difficult, though. Or is it me, am I being difficult?"

Jaye sighed another of her heavy sighs.

"You are right now." She threw a pillow at Moira. "Would you just de-stress? This is getting ridiculous! You know what you should do tomorrow? You should go and talk to your mom and nana. Don't worry about the store; I can manage for a few hours. That's why you have me, right? Go, go and see them. Get some older woman of the world advice."

Moira wrinkled up her nose. The thought of seeking advice on men and sisters from her mother and grandmother was a little alien. She hadn't directly gone to them for personal advice since, oh, early high school. It surprised her when she thought about it. She had just assumed that they all had this great, close relationship with one another, but when scrutinized, it appeared to be mostly superficial.

"Maybe I will. Thanks, Jaye."

"Don't mention it." She got up from the floor. "I'm going to change for bed."

She grabbed her bag and went into the bedroom to change her clothes. When she came out, Moira was looking at her phone.

"Don't," Jaye said to her, softly.

"Okay."

They cleaned up the glasses and shuffled off to bed, Jaye climbing in beside Moira and wrapping her arms around her for a brief minute.

"What was that for?" Moira asked her when she let go.

"You needed a hug. Now shut up, please, I'm trying to sleep."

As Jaye rolled over Moira laughed softly to herself. A "Thank God for" friend was what she thought as she drifted off into the black pool of a dreamless sleep.

Chapter Eighteen

Jack awoke suddenly the next morning. He had come home angry, listened to Moira's message and decided that he needed to give her some distance, at least for the night. He was well aware of his track record and how that little interruption in their night at the bar must have come off to her. But it still didn't excuse what she said about his father. For the first time, he began to wonder if he had it right all along to stay out of relationships. *Women are crazy*, he thought to himself as he showered. He resolved to go and see his father straight after work and talk to him about it. There must have been something else bothering her. Maybe it had something to do with her sister and the wedding that was coming up. Whatever it was, Jack wasn't going to let it dwell on him all day, this first full day in his new position at work. He began running through his mind all the things he had to do, not the least of which was to get some more work done for that school gym. He had a few ideas that he wanted to bounce off of Evan, and a meeting with a few of the teachers later in afternoon. Jack grabbed his keys and locked the apartment as he headed out the door. He drove away with his mind awash in his work, too busy to stop for coffee and too upset still to give up more than a fleeting glance at the little bakery across the street and a few doors down from the bridge. He attacked his day for two reasons: one, so that he would not stop and think of Moira, with her soft skin and green piercing eyes; and two, so that he could show his boss that he was up to the challenge, ready to prove himself in this new role right from the get-go. He was a machine, pounding at the keyboard of his computer for several hours before taking a break and grabbing a coffee from the lounge to stretch his legs. It did not go unnoticed. Evan gave him thumbs up sign as he headed back to his desk, but Jack made no time for pleasantries today. He wanted the work; the work would save him from dwelling, from thinking too much. It was a channel, a means of escape and a creative outlet. There seemed to be so few things that he had control over these days, it was a welcome diversion to immerse himself in a world where the control was almost exclusively his own. As such, the frenzied pace made the day go all the faster. He barely noticed four o'clock speed by, missed four-thirty altogether, and nearly jumped out of his skin when Evan knocked on the doorframe at twenty past five.

"Time to knock it off, Jack. You've already gotten the promotion. You don't need to prove anything to anyone here, and we all know you're up to the task."

"Right-o, boss. Just wrapped up in what I'm working on. I honestly wasn't trying to prove anything to anyone." He started the process of shutting down the computer.

"See you in the morning, then." And Evan left.

It took about ten minutes to save and back up all of the work that he had out on the computer that day, and a further five minutes to correctly file all of the papers and discs that he had strewn over his desk. Finally, after making sure that his private filing drawers were securely locked, that absolutely nothing was left out, and that he left a few important notes on Rebecca's desk for morning, did Jack finally throw his jacket on and head out. The near-six sun was causing amber and rose coloured jets of light to crack through the thick billowing clouds in the sky. Like a violent jet of two-toned light had ripped through the paleness of the sky and the huge white columns of clouds. It held his attention for a spell, thinking about how such a beautiful scene could also resemble something angry. As though God had decided not to share the magnificence of the sunset but had eventually torn a few pieces away in or-

192

der to not completely deprive his people a glimpse of this glorious sunset, but just a small glimpse, as if they didn't deserve the full grandeur. It in fact reminded him of his father. The grey exterior of his wasted form just a covering for the full and colourful glory of his true self, the self that occasionally peeked out through the shroud and made him laugh and cry. It was humbling, this sky, and this illness.

The feeling of his stomach rumbling was what finally tore his gaze and attention back down to the ground again. If he was going to spend any decent amount of time with his father today, he was going to have to get something to eat first. And, he knew, he was going to have to talk to Moira. Finally he jumped into his car and took off across the bridge, stopping in front of The Cakery. The lights were off now in the store, as he suspected they would be this time of day, but there were a few shining down from the upstairs windows, and he knew she would be home. Jack decided that, as angry as he had been at her the day before, and as hurt as he was by the words she had thrown at him in her confusion and her frustration, that is just what it had been: a confusing and frustrating situation that had spiraled out of control more quickly than it was possible to diffuse. The talks they had had, the night they spent together, all of them seemed too significant to toss aside, at least not yet, not without fulfilling a promise to Kevin first. Jack walked to the back door, found it open, and went up the narrow stairway to knock on the apartment door. After a minute, Moira answered, her hair wrapped in a towel and a spoon sticking out of the corner of her mouth. She was clearly not expecting anyone to call.

"Hi," she stammered. "Uh, come in."

Jack didn't speak, but he came in the door and turned to shut it behind him. Moira ducked back into her small apartment kitchen and dropped the spoon onto the counter. He could hear her hastily putting away some dishes of some sort, though he wasn't about to peek in at her.

"I got your message last night," he stated from his

station near the door. "Thanks."

In the kitchen he could literally hear her freeze in her motions and hold her breath. Then she appeared around the doorway. Her eyes were huge and wet, her expression timid.

"I'm so sorry for what I said about your dad."

"I know. But the rest of it ... I think I understand why you were so hurt. Is that why you wanted to hurt me back?"

"Sort of, I mean ... I think so ... I didn't actually want to hurt you. It's all so blurry. I'm feeling a lot more than I'm ready for, more than what I should be at this stage, and it scares me."

He took a step closer into the room. "I understand."

She looked at him quizzically. "Do you? I get the impression that you don't feel the same way I do."

"Moira, if I didn't feel something strong for you, something real, I would have walked out that door last night and not come back at all, no matter how many messages you left on my answering machine."

Moira just looked at him for a minute, unsure of what to say, how to react. This was completely uncharted territory. Finally, she mustered out a feeble response.

"Is that why you're here, to clear the air?"

"Yes, and more than that. Are you busy tonight?"

"Not really," she said slowly. "I had planned to go to my mother's house and visit with her and my grandmother, but they didn't know that I was planning that. Why?"

"I want you to meet my father." He didn't blink, didn't give away a single thing with the request. It was as if at the mention of his dad he had shut something down or built something up to protect himself. *If only I had noticed it before,* Moira thought, *the emotional barrier he puts up about his dad, maybe I would have known better than to attack at that.*

"Jack, you don't have to do this. I believe you."

"I know I don't. Any more than you had to let me spend the night the other night. You don't have to let me into your bed, and I don't have to let you into my family, but there it is, the two most significant things we could do for one another. And besides, he's not doing well, and he wants to meet you. So go dry your hair off, I'm taking you there in ten minutes."

Moira had no argument for this. A part of her really wanted to meet him, but she had hoped it would be under better circumstances. She told Jack to grab a bite from her kitchen if he had just come from work while she dried her hair and changed. Jack gratefully strode off into the kitchen, while still maintaining his air of control and coolness. He spotted a muffin in a bowl and grabbed that and a peach from her fruit dish. He was almost done the muffin when Moira reappeared from the bedroom.

"Did you have any dinner?" she asked him.

"No, but this will tide me over, thanks."

She shrugged, "I'd tell you to grab some of the pasta I made myself tonight, but if we're in some kind of hurry ... "

Jack looked back on the stove, where there was indeed a pot half full of ziti and some kind of cream or white cheese sauce. It was tempting, but he wanted to do this before it got late and his father got tired. Besides, the uncomfortable rumble in his stomach only reminded him that he was still a little miffed at her, which was hard to do when she stood before him looking sumptuous in a white t-shirt and dark blue jeans, her still slightly damp hair framing her face.

"Yeah," he finally stammered out, "I want to get there before he gets his night meds."

"Let's go, then."

Moira grabbed her purse from the small side table and her keys from the hook. She locked the door behind them and followed Jack in silence down the stairs and out to his car. If Moira was getting uncomfortable with the tone of the evening, she was giving nothing of it away. Perhaps just as determined as Jack to maintain her air of disappointment over the argument, perhaps just to be contrite.

Whatever the reason, they drove in full poker face, like a couple of wax figures staring straight out at the road before them. In fact, neither of them spoke until they arrived at the hospice, when Jack turned off the car and turned to Moira, his expression still very much unreadable.

"I want to tell you something."

"Okay."

"I meant what I said the other night. My past is going to run into us around town every now and then. Sometimes, it's going to be embarrassing and inappropriate as it was. Sometimes it's going to be harmless. But I want you to know that I didn't sleep with you for a conquest. And I also want you to know that I'm bringing you here not to prove a point, but because he asked me to, and at this stage of the game I am doing my best to live up to any wishes he has. Okay?"

Moira's face looked slightly stunned.

"Okay," she practically whispered back.

He walked around and let her out of the car, then took her hand purposefully and led her into the building. *He's nervous!* Moira realized, which made her nervous. They walked slowly down the hall, Jack's steps almost soundless beneath his sneakers, Moira's making loud clicking noises with her chunky heeled shoes. It was not the most inviting looking place, she noticed. The walls were not a warm or inviting colour, and it smelled ever so slightly of disinfectant and medicine. Jack finally stopped next to a door that was only very slightly ajar. He carefully lifted his hand and used the flat of his palm to push the door open. His hand left a sweaty imprint. She followed him into the room cautiously, shyly. Moira had never seen a dying person before. She stood in place by the corner of the L-shaped room, just close enough to see Kevin, but with enough distance to allow Jack to alert him to their presence, and leave quickly if needed.

She watched as Jack placed the chair from the corner next to the bed and sat in it, resting his hand on the chest of the pale and beaten looking man lying in the bed.

196

"Dad," he whispered lovingly. "Dad, do you feel like a visit?"

"Hmmm?" Kevin mumbled, his eyes still closed.

"I brought you a present." He looked toward Moira, motioning for her to come forward.

"What present?" Kevin laboriously muttered. "Is it your lady?"

"Yeah, Dad, this is Moira."

Kevin opened the corner of his right eye, making the wrinkle of skin that would have been his left eyebrow, had he still any hair, contact and pucker.

"So, he finally brought you to meet me, eh?"

"It looks like it," she said.

"Come over here and sit on the bed, dear. It takes my old eyes a little longer to adjust to the light these days."

Moira came over and sat down near Kevin's knees. He opened the other eye and gave her a real good look up and down.

"Oh dear," he said slowly, turning to Jack. "Green eyes?" Jack nodded at his father with a faint smile playing on his lips. "You're in big trouble, son."

"I know, Dad. It was the first thing I noticed about her."

"I'll bet." Kevin intoned. His weak snicker became a loud and wracking cough that shook him from shoulders to shins. Jack looked alarmed and almost jumped to his feet, but Kevin stilled him with a gnarled finger held aloft.

"It'll pass," he hacked out.

Jack eased back fully into his seat again, letting Kevin be the one to guide this conversation.

Kevin did not speak for several minutes. He lay calmly in his bed, the head raised into the semi-sitting position that gave him the most comfort. His gaze never wavered from Moira's face and, although she felt his eyes on her, the minutes felt like hours as she mustered the courage to look this dying man back in the face. It was daunting to literally look death in the face, and she just had to work up to it. The gentle blip of the monitor connected to Kevin's

197

chest ticked away as she eventually managed to raise her head and look into the eyes of Jack's father. He held her in those deep watery pools for a time, letting the silence morph from a barrier to an encompassing calm, where all feelings that Moira had had of trepidation and tension melted into something so sweet and mellow that the change in the air between them grew soft and deep.

"You're uncomfortable, aren't you?" Every syllable was a bit of an argument between what his tongue wanted to form and what his chest allowed him to get out. "I don't mind. Most people don't like to be so close to a dying man. Even my nurses seem to have trouble talking to me the way they used to. I think they're trying to disengage themselves."

"It's okay. I mean ... I'm okay." Moira tried hard to be. She wanted to talk to him. "You must be really proud of Jack."

"More so in the last two weeks than ever before. I don't have to sing his praises to you, though, do I?" Moira shook her head.

Everything about this man went against what she had built up about him in her mind. He was patient, measured and deliberate. His words were slow in coming, but she got the sense that every one of them was spoken with complete intention. She began to relax, and she looked around the room, drinking in the items that Kevin had chosen to surround himself with in his last weeks of life. There was a photograph on the bedside of what must have been a much younger Kevin and a beautiful woman. Moira leaned in and lifted it to have a closer look. In his youth, Kevin looked a lot like Jack, sandy hair, the same slightly sideways smile, the same ease in his posture. Kevin let out a long slow hiss with a smile as he watched her ponder the photo. The woman in the picture was truly breathtaking. Her eyes twinkled, and she gazed at the younger Kevin with complete adoration. He, in turn, was looking at her as if there were no one else on the planet. The picture was almost naked in its emotion. *This is what love looks like.* She placed the picture back in its place.

"That's Jack's mother. Lovely, wasn't she? That's my favourite picture of her. Jack took it when he was just fifteen. She died in a car accident soon afterwards. It just proves to me that you have to snatch moments like that one and hang on to them. Life is not absolute, love is."

Moira gazed at this peaceful man in astonishment. She had never heard such a declaration from a man before. It went against all her preconceived notions. She shook her head.

"You sound just like my Nana, but I hate to tell you that I don't believe her either. Love is not absolute, Kevin. It is something that can disappear. It's fragile. How can you not know this? Love can't feed you, it can't keep you healthy or cure cancer. How can you say something like that when you had love and it was ended by a car crash? That's not absolute." Her eyes begin to shine and Jack, she noticed, was looking resolutely out the window so that they couldn't see his reaction to this conversation.

Kevin smiled sadly at Moira and took the remote control for his bed into one of his ravaged hands. He raised his back support to a nearly fully seated position.

"That is why I wanted to talk to you, Moira. Jack is just as jaded as you are. He lost his mother at fifteen. I spent a great deal of my time in those days getting my business going and shutting off from him, because he reminded me of her, of what I lost." His gaze bore into her, but she did not break. "When I realized that Jack was doing the same thing, I felt so sad. Here was a young man with everything to offer, and he was already cutting himself off from the world around him. Jack's whole life has been about work, tangible accomplishments. I assume he has told you of his previous history with women?"

Moira raised her eyebrow and nodded.

"You see!" He exclaimed triumphantly. "No connection. It's like he has been afraid to let someone in because in the end, he'll just lose them. When I got my diagnosis, I could see the door closing even more. I am all he has left, and now he's losing me too."

Warm tears began to form in Moira's eyes. She tried to blink them away, but the motion just ensured the slow journey down her cheek. Kevin drew a few more difficult breaths. Then he continued.

"Jack told me that you have been hurt. Men in your life have not been good to you, and women in Jack's life have not been connecting with him, not since his mother."

Moira was now weeping openly.

"You don't understand," she sobbed. "Love doesn't happen for everyone like it did for you. It's wonderful that you had that, but every relationship that I know of has had some flaw, some problem, and eventually the problem becomes bigger than the feelings. Love isn't everything, anyway. It's enough that we like each other, and that we get along and share interests. It's enough for us, it works."

"Love *is* everything, Moira. It is enough for a life. When you love someone totally, completely, absolutely, there are few things in this world that can take that wholeness away from you. That is what I am talking about. My wife may have been taken from me, but my love for her is eternal. Death, negligence, accidents and anger are going to happen; the *love* stays. That is why you must love. Love is life."

Moira blinked through her tears. Kevin smiled through his. The effort of such a long speech drained him. She reached over and touched Kevin's hand.

"You're good for him," Kevin coughs out. "If I wasn't dying, I'd take you to dinner sometime myself."

"Thank you, Kevin. I will think about what you said."

She turned to look at Jack once more and was surprised to see that he looked angry again. He was gaping at his father with shocked surprise on his face, naked hurt.

"Why are you so angry?" Kevin's voice remained calm.

"I don't know," Jack replied without looking up.

"Yes you do, what is it?"

"Why aren't *you* angry?" Jack didn't feel that this was exactly the time to let his father know that he had overheard his tantrum, but he did feel that, under the circumstances, now would be a good time to ask the question that had bothered him for weeks now, months even.

Kevin let out an involuntary coughing laugh. "What?"

"I said," Jack looked up, "Why aren't you angry? I just don't understand. *I'm angry!* I'm angry and I'm not dying. *You're* dying. You're dying, Dad, and you aren't angry. I don't get it. You lie here all day wondering whether or not today is going to be the last day, and you want to meet Moira and talk with her about all this personal stuff, as if you're going to be some kind of friends, and yet you can't because *YOU'RE DYING*. Why aren't you screaming with anger? When mom died, you were so mad. I remember it, you shut down, and you stopped talking, and nothing made you smile. It took years for you to find your smile again and now ... " He trailed off, looking at his father as if waiting for him to complete his thoughts, lend credence to the fury, show some sign that he knew where he was coming from, but Kevin just stared up at him, his glassy eyes penetratingly still, and waited for his son to purge.

"Now. I've never seen you so placid. I don't understand it, and I don't like it. At least when we first heard the cancer diagnosis, you reacted. You fought. I just don't see how you can take all this so lightly. Because I sure as hell can't, and you're throwing me off what little sense of reality I have when you want to do things like talk with Moira, like there's some kind of future in it. I can't wrap my head around it."

His chest heaved with the exertion of letting so much off his chest, and his eyes shone with tears. There was a large lump in his throat that he could not force back down.

"Jack." Kevin looked at his son. "My Jack, how I have ruined you. What is it you want? You think I don't get angry? Of course I do. But you don't need to see any more anger from me. I've let you have enough of that to last a lifetime. Do you want me to yell and scream and tear out my tubes? I can't do that for you to feel better about my fate. I was so wrong to show you all of that after we lost your mother. Diving into work, shutting out life ... what a legacy I gave to you in your formative years." Kevin's shook his head slowly and laboured to breath, to finish what he must say. Jack opened his mouth to talk some more, but was stayed by Kevin's frail blue veined and punctured hand rising up to silence him.

"I've watched you, Jack. As every parent watches their child, I've watched you move purposely through the motions of your life with all of the frustrations that I felt when we lost her, and none of the joy that she was. I thought at the time that the best way to help you was to encourage this push you gave yourself through life. Higher grades, later nights, early graduations, work and work and work. No time for fun or for girlfriends or for being still. Even when I was happy again, we didn't share happiness together. By the time I re-found life, you had turned your back on it, and I didn't know how to bring you back into it. That is my shame, Jack. There lies my anger. But it's my own. I am not angry to die." Again he paused to wheeze and cough, but with his hand up once more to stop Jack from interjecting. This *would* be said.

"Every day we wake up and we choose. We can be happy, and be *alive* in the moment, or we can put our heads down to the world and begin another day of dying. I choose to live. I may be dying, Jack, but I'm not dead yet. I choose to let what's left of life in. And I want to do that for you. The only legacy I can give now is one of peace and real happiness. Let me, Jack. Let me give you this gift."

He sank into the mattress of his bed and seemed to pale further before Jack's eyes. His body appeared to shrink by the second as the air left his lungs and his skin grew more translucent, as if someone was sucking the air out of a bag of meat to seal it for freezing. Both men allowed tears to travel down their cheeks in silence and held hands in the small room as the sun dwindled in the sky behind the window. Moira stayed and kept vigil over this scene, allowing the men to cry and to have their moment, in complete and total awe of being let in to the heart of this small family. When Kevin reached for her hand and placed it simply on top of Jack's, she smiled at the old man. Words had passed their usefulness in this small room, and the world shrank around them and filled them up with everything that never needs to be said when love is present.

Chapter Nineteen

It didn't take much more than twenty or so minutes for Kevin to slip back into the deep sleep that consumed most of his time these days, yet the stillness of the moment held Jack and Moira captivated for the best part of an hour, hands on each other's and resting lightly on Kevin's lower chest, rising and falling with the broken breaths he took. Finally, they got up, an unspoken agreement that the time had come for them to leave. As they walked away from the room, back down the pale green hallways and out into the parking lot, they kept their hands entwined, the anger and frustration that had followed them there that night having been evaporated by the strong words and convictions of the gentle man in the bed. They drove back toward the main part of town, not speaking, but saying volumes with their silence. When Jack pulled up in front of The Cakery, he turned off the car and walked around to open Moira's door. Then he locked it and followed her quietly to the door at the rear. She gave him a searching look, studying his face as she unlocked the door and stepped aside for Jack to enter first, confirming that she wanted him there with her, needed him there.

They opened the door to the apartment and kicked off their shoes. It was getting late, close to ten o'clock, which for any normal couple in their late twenties might seem like the most opportune time to start a night, head out to the clubs or the bars and begin the prowling for a companion, but for two workaholics who had just spent the night in the presence of a remarkable man whose life was being snuffed out far too soon, the energy they might have felt had been sapped, and they wanted nothing more than to lie down.

Again, as they had on one or two occasions now, they moved as one, anticipating the other's moves, putting together a simple snack of some cheese and crackers, a glass of white wine and some cut fruit. Sitting side by side on the couch, they ate, they drank, and they occasionally touched hands, or let their knees rest against one another. Once or twice, it seemed as though Moira wanted to speak. She opened her mouth, a quizzical look on her face as if a question was resting on her lips, but then she looked at Jack, his face drawn and tired but with a look of completion, and she let it go. Thus they sat for an hour, until the gentle beep of Moira's clock announced that eleven had come and gone. And when the heavy blanket of night was firmly in place over the city, they rose, placed their dishes in the sink and walked simply into Moira's bedroom. They removed their clothes, Moira donning a large t-shirt and Jack keeping his boxers, and climbed together into the big bed that they had shared only a few evenings ago. They snuggled tightly together, Jack wrapping his body around Moira's and holding her closely as she planted light feathery kisses on his forearm and he nuzzled the back of her neck and her hair. It didn't take long for sleep to claim them, and they were sound and relaxed until the morning sun peeked in the windows to rouse them.

***

Not even the brightness of a fresh morning seemed to snap Moira and Jack from their quiet reflective moods. Although they both knew that some kind of corner had been turned between them, it was yet to be spoken out loud. As it was, they both went about their morning routines alongside one another; at least Jack did as much as he was able, considering that this was not his place, and he had none of his own things here with him. Suddenly, mid pre-work ministrations, Jack stopped in the middle of the small kitchen and kissed Moira deeply. She responded by sinking against his warm body, kissing him back with fervor and passion.

"I don't ever want to fight again," Jack stated as they broke apart several minutes later. He reached up and stroked the back of her head through her glorious hair.

"Okay. I'm so sorry I hurt you."

"Don't be. It's done now, let's just let that go."

Moira looked him in the eyes. He had such beautiful, sad eyes. She momentarily flashed back to that moment almost two weeks ago when they collided on the street and the coffee went flying. She remembered noticing his eyes then, too. How was it possible to be here in so short a time? And yet, there were none of the same alarm bells going off that there had been when she first became involved with Mark. *It all just fits,* she thought, *even the argument we had feels more real to me than anything else.*

"What is it?" Jack asked her, noticing her eyes moving, the wheels of her mind churning behind them.

"You'll think it's silly, but I just can't believe what I'm feeling. Do you think it's all too soon?"

Jack chewed thoughtfully on his lower lip. "I did, sort of. I mean, I just didn't think that this would ever happen for me, and I had sort of accepted that. But everything feels so ... I don't want to say perfect, because we both know there's no such thing. But it feels right. Like we fit."

Moira smiled.

"You have a better way with words than I do, but I know just what you mean."

"You know what?" Jack pulled back from her for a moment. "We should take a day off. Together. I don't think I have taken more then three days off voluntarily in the four years I have worked for Evan. Can you take a day from the shop?"

"Of course I can, it's my business. Jaye can manage it for a day. Did you have anything in mind?"

"Do I have to? I would like to spend a whole day with you, and I'd like to go back and see my dad again later today, with you, if you don't mind."

"Sounds perfect, why don't we go visit my mom? I'd like you to meet my family."

Jack grinned. "Sounds perfect."

***

Like the opening of floodgates, the quiet, reflective mood of the last several hours since they had left the hospice melted away. Jack called in to Evan and announced that he would miss the day to the surprise but not the chagrin of his boss, who seemed to understand his need to spend some quality time with his father in these last few opportunities he would have before the disease claimed him. A great track record with attendance didn't hurt him. Besides, he had finished his last bit of work ahead of schedule and could afford to miss some time. Jack thanked him and hung up the phone, accepting the cup of coffee that Moira proffered him. He handed the receiver to Moira, who shook her head at him.

"Nah," she said, "It's almost time for Jaye to be in, we'll just go down and tell her ourselves."

"Okay. Do you want to go to your mother's house first?"

"Yeah. I'd really like for you to meet her, and my grandmother."

"Sounds good to me. Shall we, then?"

Moira laughed. "Let's finish our coffee first. Do you want anything else?"

Jack gave her a long lingering look up and down, a slow smile playing on his face and laughter dancing in his eyes. "Not yet."

She smiled back at him, thinking of the many, many things that they could spend the day doing, but there would be plenty of time for that later. Instead, they finished drinking their beverages and bustled around tidying up the place. Then they locked up and went downstairs, Moira letting them into the back door of the shop. Jaye was not there, but a quick peek at the clock told Moira that she wouldn't be long. Instead, Jack helped her set up for the day, wiping down tables and setting out napkins, sweeping the floor and turning on the lights for the display coolers along the counter. Moira counted out the float for the till and made notes of items that would need to be baked and replaced for tomorrow. Then they went into the kitchen, grabbing fresh loaves of golden bread from the warming rack against the back wall and beside the walk-in. Jack made a show of deeply smelling and then swooning over each, which made Moira laugh. This is where Jaye found them when she came in, a pair of clowns in the kitchen smelling bread and unable to take their eyes off of one another.

"Well, good morning. This is a welcome sight. Hi, Jack."

"Jaye, did you know that this woman here makes the best smelling bread in the world?"

"Umm, yes, I do believe that I've heard that once or twice. Are you working here today?"

"Not at all, I'm kidnapping this fair lady and we're taking a day off."

Moira shrugged sheepishly at Jaye, who winked at her friend and put a mock stern look on her pretty face.

"Then what the hell are you both doing? Get outta here! I have work to do."

Jack saluted her and turned to Moira. "You heard her, boss, we have to vacate the premises. Are you ready to go?"

Moira smiled a grateful smile at Jaye and then held her hand to her forehead in mock-faint. "Take me away from all this," she said sweepingly, letting her hand drape across her face and then pretending to loose her balance. "I have been banished." Then she gave Jaye a quick hug, and whispered to her a thank you, and to call if she needed anything. Jaye gave her a swat on the bottom and shooed them both out the back door. By the time they got through the alleyway and to Jack's car, Jaye had turned on the open sign and could be seen hustling about the inside, glad to have her friend so happy, and thrilled for a chance to give her a day free from the store. The car roared to life, and Moira pointed Jack the way to her mothers' house. They sang along with the radio, Elton John and John Denver on the easy listening station that Jack had on, which of course Moira had to tease him about. He had terrible taste in music, even though he just insisted that it was so that he could have something on that wouldn't be a distraction to him as he drove. She turned it up even louder for Jeff Healey, singing loudly along with him, making dramatic gestures to Jack, who laughed loudly and rubbed her leg.

"Okay, I get the point," he said, reaching up to change the station.

"No, leave it," Moira said. "I know the words. Besides, we're almost there."

They drove down Marksam until the beautiful house rose up before them a street away. "That's it," Moira said, pointing. "Just turn here and pull up on the side of the road."

Jack did so, and commented on the house. "This is your mother's place?" he mused. "I love this house. I used to drive past here sometimes when my dad still had the gas station. I've always thought it was one of the most beautiful houses in Fayette."

They stopped the car and got out. Moira walked Jack up to the garage and in to the door. It was unlocked, so she walked in and kicked off her shoes, motioning for Jack to do the same. There were two other doors in here, one directly in front of them and one off to the left. Moira pointed to the door on the left.

"That goes out to the backyard, Mom's pride and joy," she said.

"Show me?"

"Of course, but you have to come meet them first." Then she pushed open the door in front of them and walked into the bright spacious kitchen. Siobhan was sitting with her chair pulled up to the table, nursing a cup of tea and nibbling on a biscuit with jam on it. She looked up as they walked in.

"Well, this is a pleasant surprise," she said, wiping the crumbs from her mouth and shirt. "I was wondering whose car it was that had pulled up. Angela, get out here!"

Angela came bustling out from a small hallway on the left. She had her blonde and silvery hair swept up into a messy bun and was holding a sheet.

"What, mother? Oh, Moira. Good morning, dear. I'm just doing the laundry. I'll be out in a sec, grab a mug and a cuppa, won't be a jiff." And she disappeared once again.

"Well, how do you like that?" Siobhan mused, "Not even a glance at your young man." She looked at him. "You must be Jack. It's nice to meet you."

Moira propelled Jack into the room and pulled out a chair for him. She reached into a cupboard and pulled down a mug, and then with a questioning glance at Jack and a nod from him, a second one.

"Jack, this is my nana, Siobhan."

"Siobhan," Jack said, extending his hand and rolling the taste of the Irish name around his mouth. "Shi-vohn. I love your name. It's lovely to meet you."

Siobhan reached out to meet his hand and shook it vigorously. "Likewise, my dear boy. You must be the one Moira dumped coffee on. How nice that you didn't hold that against her."

"I would never. It was purely accidental. Besides, didn't I go and do the same to her a day or two later, with icing sugar?"

"Really? I didn't hear about that one." She raised her eyebrow at Moira. "Would this handsome young lad be the reason we haven't seen much of you lately?"

"I was just here last week."

Angela came back into the room again, this time her eyes actively seeking out the male voice in the room.

"I thought I heard a man in here. I'm so sorry, I'm a little in my own world today. You must be Jack."

"It's nice to meet you."

"My mother, Angela," Moira said.

Jack shook her hand as well.

"Moira, what on earth are you doing here in the middle of the morning? Who's watching the store?"

"Relax, Mom. Jaye has it under control today."

"Oh, well, is anything the matter? It's not like you at all to come here in the middle of the day."

"Not that we mind," added Siobhan.

"It's my fault," Jack explained. "" wanted to kidnap her and demanded that she introduce me to her family. Of course, now that I know where you live, I'm going to need a tour as well. This house is outstanding."

Angela blushed a little. "It is rather lovely. I can't imagine not living here. This house is like a member of the family. I'd love to give you a tour, unless you'd prefer Moira ..."

"I wouldn't hear of it, I'd love for you to do me the honour." Jack stood and waited for Angela to lead him around. When Moira made to join them, he turned her down.

"Let your mother show me around. I promise I'll be back." He kissed her cheek.

Moira sank back into her chair as her mother led Jack out of the room, already chattering about the restorations that she had made with her husband, and the further work that she had done with the girls in the later years. She grinned as she heard their footsteps ascend the stairs, Jack's exclaiming voice carrying down, then leaned back in her chair with a long grateful sip of her tea.

"Well, he certainly seems nice," Siobhan quipped. "Come on, take me out back. No doubt that's where she'll end the tour." Moira scooted in behind her grandmother and wheeled her out from the chairs and table and into the backyard. There was a lovely cedar deck with a small ramp from the door that led out and a rounded corner that Siobhan liked to park her chair in, with the best view of the expansive garden. Even in the fall, the greenery was something to behold.

If Moira thought she was going to get away with a few minutes of quiet to herself, she was sorely mistaken. Siobhan barely waited for her to get settled in a chair when she fixed her with an unwavering look.

"Well?"

"What?"

"What is going on with you and this Jack?"

"A lot. We really like each other. We've been spending a lot of time together lately. I think he's the best person I've met in a long time."

"Really? Because the last time you got so wrapped up in a man so quickly, it didn't turn out so well, did it?"

"Nana! Really, I understand you thinking that, and believe me, I've thought about it more than once, but Jack simply isn't like that. You'll see. He's so different from Mark, from most men I've ever known, really. He's just wonderful."

"Uh huh. I think I'll reserve judgment on that for myself, thank you very much."

"Okay. I know you'll like him. I don't need to sit here and sing his praises to you. You'll find out on your own."

This line of logic took Siobhan slightly aback. No one had really fallen too hard for Mark's lines of bullshit in the beginning, and then less as time went by, but no one had questioned it because Moira was so quick to defend him. This abandonment of argumentativeness struck a chord with her. If Moira was satisfied to let them draw their own conclusions, maybe there was something there after all. She'd decide when she got the chance to talk to him more.

Changing the topic, Siobhan asked, "How's the shop doing?"

"Oh, just great! I have three more weddings booked for October, and it's still early. Plus the Christmas orders are starting to roll in. Remember that suggestion you made last year about having ready-made desserts and platters made?" Siobhan nodded. "Well, if we thought it was a good idea last year, it's bloody brilliant this year. I've already got enough orders to keep me busy for several weeks leading up

213

to the holidays. Jaye and I were talking the other day about taking on some more help as we get closer to December. God knows we can finally afford it, and I'll need to be in the kitchen full time to cope with all of the outgoing orders. Jaye is even going to have to help me with some of it, so we'll definitely need someone else who can cover the front of the store."

Siobhan was delighted to see her granddaughter's face light up like this. The business was indeed going from strength to strength these days. Moira had paid back the start up loan from her ages ago now, and was operating in a surplus balance.

"That's wonderful! Really dear, I couldn't be prouder of you."

"Thank you, Nana. You know, I never would have been able to do all this if you hadn't helped me out in the beginning. I really appreciated it."

"Nonsense. I would have given you that money, you didn't have to pay it back. And that's not how family should be." Her voice had a slight edge to it that Moira failed to pick up on.

"I know, I remember, but I wouldn't have felt right. I want this business to be a success in every possible way, not because my relatives gave me pieces of it."

"Believe me, I can understand that. It's hard to be beholden to anyone, but harder still when it's family." Now the hardness was reflected in her face as well.

"What is it?"

"Oh nothing, just old memories."

"I wish you'd talk about it more."

"I would, but it makes your mother unhappy."

"What makes me unhappy?" Angela asked as she and Jack emerged from the house and into the backyard.

"Wow! This is amazing. You did all this?" Jack exclaimed over the breathtaking garden.

"Yes, it's a bit of a hobby of mine." She turned back to the women. "Mother, what makes me unhappy?"

"Talking about the past. Moira and I were just talking about her business and loans. She's doing much better, stronger every day down there."

"Don't change the subject, what was it that made you stop like that? Why is Mom unhappy with talking about it?" Moira wanted to know, now that the topic had been broached.

Jack looked slightly confused. "Should I go inside?" he asked.

"No, don't be silly," Siobhan told him. "I was referring, my dear, to the strangeness of being beholden financially to family. Moira was just thanking me for helping her with start up costs, and I was telling her that my money needn't have been a loan, I would gladly have given it to her."

Angela shrugged. "I don't see why that would bother me." Then she fell silent for a moment.

"Okay, what's going on here? You two are acting weird," Moira stated.

Angela looked at her mother, who turned and pointedly stared in the opposite direction.

"Is this about your move here?" Moira piped again. "Why don't you ever talk about it? Something is obviously still bothering you about it."

"There's no need to talk about it; different time, different place. It used to upset your mother, so I don't bring it up anymore," Siobhan stated simply.

"May I say something?" Jack inquired.

"Sure," Angela said.

"I don't know if Moira told you, but my dad is really sick. He has advanced pancreatic cancer. I took her to see him last night. One of the things that he has been most adamant about since this illness took place is how sorry he is that he didn't get to work through some painful memories with me while he still had the time. I don't want to interfere in your family, obviously, but if there's something that's still haunting you from long ago, you should get it out and over with. Just say the words out loud so that you can move on and finally leave it behind you."

215

The three women stared at the handsome Jack as he spoke. Here was this man telling these three women how to deal with their demons, and the craziest part of all was that he was making sense!

"We need Sloane. It wouldn't be right to go through this without her," Siobhan said.

"Well, where is she? She isn't working right now, would she be at home?" Moira asked.

"Probably. Oh, wait. She's coming here for lunch to get some boxes of things that we put aside for her. Can you wait until then?"

"I guess." Moira was slightly giddy that she was going to uncover some huge family secret. Of course she didn't want to wait for her sister, but it made no sense to call her over if she was going to be there in an hour or so anyway. Instead she brought Jack down through the winding paths in the garden and pointed out all of the plants and flowers that her mother had lovingly nurtured through the years. Then she took him down a short hill into the lower garden, which was framed by a high hedge, where all of the vegetables grew. Grateful for the late season they had due to a particularly long winter and delayed summer, a good portion of the garden was still very much in bloom and alive. They snapped some late blooming snow peas from the vines and split them open, eating them on the spot. They were sweet, with a satisfying crack when they bit down on them. Angela walked down into to join them, obviously pleased to have someone else enjoying her beloved garden; she was smiling warmly at the two.

"These are delicious, Mom." Moira told her, about to open another fat pod.

"You're lucky. With the late start we had this year and all the sun we've been getting lately, it's been a fantastic time for gathering the last of the late vegetables. Some of them just keep sprouting more and more. I can't remember when we've eaten so much fresh food this late in the season." She turned back in the direction of the deck. "Isn't that right, Mother?"

"What?" Siobhan yelled back, "I can't hear you down there. Never mind me, dears, I'll just sit up here alone and count the seconds till you come back, shall I?"

"Hmm, she's getting difficult," Angela said to her daughter.

"Oh Mom, she's just pulling your leg." Moira laughed. "Aren't you, Nana?"

"What?! I really can't hear you. I think my hearing is going. It'll be my eyes next. Can't even see the hand in front of my face any more." There was a hint of mirth to her voice as she complained. "And I'm not difficult."

Chapter Twenty

Jack left the two women to wander the aisles of plants and walked back up to the deck, where he pulled up a chair next to Siobhan. He began to talk to her quietly, and Angela and Moira could see her warming, occasionally raising her hand to point something out to him.

"He's very nice, Moira. It's good of you to bring him home to meet us."

"Actually, it was Jack's idea. We went to see his father last night. He's very sick."

Angela raised an eyebrow at her handsome daughter. "You two are getting pretty close, then?"

"Yeah, you could say that. It's funny, but I feel so relaxed around him."

"Going a little fast, isn't it? Not that I'm criticizing." Angela had dropped her voice even lower so that Jack and Siobhan would not hear her.

"I thought you might think so, but in all honesty, it feels right."

Angela studied her face for a moment. She seemed to be struggling with something, chewing back a statement that was crawling on the tip of her tongue. Moira watched her with interest and not a little bit of trepidation.

"He's not Mark, Mother."

"I didn't say anything!"

"You don't have to, I can see it on your face. We've talked about it ... well, sort of talked about it. But we've got this connection. I don't really know what it is, but somehow I just know Jack wouldn't hurt me like that."

"You're putting an awful lot of stock in your hunch. Are you sure that's wise?"

"You're too worried. Honestly Mom, you need to let go a little. I don't remember hearing you complain about rushes when Sloane got engaged in under a year."

Angela looked slightly affronted. She reached for an explanation that would placate her daughter. "That was different. Sloane's always been fairly direct about what she wants and what works for her. What I mean is, she and Martin are so alike in that respect. It's hard to imagine either of them rationalizing drawing things out. They knew what they wanted, and it just works for them."

Now it was Moira's turn to look irascible.

"In case you failed to notice, I go for the things I want too. I would never have gotten the shop if I hadn't been prepared to just jump on in with both feet and go for what I wanted."

"Sure, you've always been able to do that when it comes to your business or making important decisions, except when it pertains to your personal life. I meant your track record with men."

"You meant Mark, and Jack is not Mark."

Angela sighed heavily. "I don't want to fight with you, that was not what I intended. Lately it just seems like when I want to talk to you, it all comes out wrong, and I wind up hurting your feelings. What can I tell you, Moira? I just don't want to see you get hurt again."

Moira softened a little at this. "I know. I always know that you mean well, it's just that sometimes it comes out wrong."

"I admit it's a problem. I had this problem with your father too. This is probably why things ultimately didn't work out between us. I wish they could have, for the sake of you girls."

Moira put a hand on her mother's arm. This was a side of her that she rarely saw. She was about to open her mouth to say something back when wicked laughter erupted from the deck. They looked up together to see Jack

220

and Siobhan both roaring. Deciding to walk back up and rejoin them, they tucked their arms in to one another's and ambled back through the winding paths of plants to the upper part of the garden and the deck.

"What's so funny?" Moira asked as Jack wiped a tear from his eye and caught his breath.

"Your nana was just telling me about how you got potty trained. I've never heard anything so funny in my life." He crumpled into debilitating laughter again.

"Nana! Why on earth would you tell him that?"

She shrugged, trying to appear nonchalant, but quite obviously fighting off another attack herself. "He asked me what you were like as a child. It's one of my favourite memories."

"I think there's a picture of it in the house," said Angela, now clearly remembering the time herself, her face loosening into smiles and the corners of her mouth twitching as she fought off the laughter as well.

Moira, as a small child, had been afraid of her training potty. There was no rational reason why, she just didn't like it. So Siobhan, ever the creative genius, had one day, when Angela was at work, dug out a very old pot from the pantry, one that had not been used in a long time, and had decorated it with as many stickers and glued on pictures as she could. When it was completely covered, she presented it to Moira, who happily plunked herself on it and had no trouble using it.

"It was like a little chamber pot for a child. The best part was I had found a large, plate-sized picture of a smiling face, and I stuck on the bottom of the inside and glued it so that it was sealed in. I told Moira that face was how happy I would be if she could learn to use the pot instead of her diapers. She ate it up. Your mother was so mad at me, at first, but I reminded her that it was nothing much more than the flowery chamber pots we used to use back in Ireland in our youth. And Moira was happy with it, so why not. Funnier still was Moira running round the house, so proud that she had peed on the 'pot'. When all other kids were using a potty, she used a pot, literally."

"And you wonder why I have issues," Moira said dryly.

This made them laugh all the harder, and by the time Sloane had come in through the backyard to find her family, she was surprised by the scene of the entire assemblage rolling out of their chairs unable to control their merriment.

"This is a nice cozy picture. I didn't expect to see you here, Moira. Who is running the store?"

"Jaye is. Sloane, I'd like you to meet Jack."

Moira moved over slightly, and Jack stood up to shake hands with Sloane. He was surprised; the two sisters couldn't have looked more different. If it weren't for the bright green eyes that seemed to run in the family, he might have assumed they weren't related at all.

"Nice to meet you," he said, as she enthusiastically pumped his hand with a firm grasp.

"Likewise. You must be the guy my sister dumped coffee on a couple of weeks ago."

He smiled sheepishly.

"About two weeks, and yeah that was me, although I really think I should claim responsibility for that one. I wasn't looking where I was going."

Sloane raised an eyebrow at him.

"Really?" She turned to her mother. "Do you have the stuff somewhere? What is it, anyway? If it's just old junk I might throw it out. You save too much."

"There are three or four boxes for you in the library. You can go in and grab them whenever you're ready. Mostly just old pictures that I thought you'd like and a box with your yearbooks and some things from your room."

"Fine. So, what's new with you, Moira? Still conquering the world one cookie at a time? Katie was really mad at you for what you said to her, you know."

"What did I say to her?"

"That you weren't going to organize a bachelorette party and that you wanted her to do it. If you don't want to be involved in the wedding, you should have said something to me, you know."

Moira looked as though Sloane had slapped her in the face. "I never said that I didn't want to be a part of your wedding! And when Katie called me the other day, I was very busy, and she was really quite insulting."

"Oh yeah, how?"

"She likened my job to the girl guides and laughed at me on the phone. I don't need that shit from her."

Jack had sensed that this was a sore spot and put his hand on Moira's shoulder for support. She was grateful to know that someone was on her side.

"I wish you two would stop your bickering. Sloane, your friend Katie is not the best character to be trusting with opinions about your own sister. Why don't you just let it be? Moira, tell us the news about the store. You think if today goes well you'll let Jaye run things more often, so you can have some time off?" Angela was trying to make peace by changing the subject.

"I really don't think so, Mom." Moira sighed, sinking into a lawn chair and giving Jack's hand a slight squeeze as he sat down beside her. "Business is going too well. I have to keep the stock up almost daily with some of the items. Jaye and I were just talking the other day about hiring on someone to work the counter. Also," she turned to Jack, "I was thinking about doing a whole new webpage. The bland one we have now is seriously out of date, and I'd like to expand the cake side of things to a broader area."

Jack smiled broadly at her. "I'll help!" he said, as eagerly as a child. "C'mon, Moira, it's what I do. I'd love to design you a new webpage, if you'll let me."

"I'd love that," she said.

No one could deny the fireworks going on between them. It was obvious that they had become more connected than either of them had let on, and it made Angela and Siobhan so happy to finally see Moira smiling so genuinely.

"Of course, you'll have to see the one we have now. It's not much, but it has brought in some business. Can you show me some of your work?"

Jack turned to Angela. "Do you have a computer?"

"In the library."

"You have a library in this house?"

Siobhan laughed. "Actually, it's just a room at the back of the main floor where we put all the bookshelves and the computer. We like to call it the library because it sounds so grand. Only the manor houses back in Ireland had something like that."

"Speaking of Ireland, weren't you going to tell us something once Sloane got here, some big secret?"

"What secret?" Sloane asked.

"It's no big deal. Actually, it's not really a secret at all, it's just one of those things that we don't really talk about. But if you want to ask questions, I'll answer them. Like your Jack said, there's no point hanging on to all these old issues, just say it out loud and be done with it. Quite smart, actually."

"So, what do you want to know?" Angela asked.

"First of all, what was the reference to lending money all about? You had no problem lending me money to start up," Moira stated.

By now Sloane had also taken a seat on one of the lawn chairs and was alternating between glaring at Moira and shooting questioning looks at her mother and grandmother.

"I'll field this one, dear, if you don't mind," Siobhan said, shifting herself in her chair. "First you should know a little bit about what happened when I married your grandfather. We were very young, only eighteen when we got married. His family were farmers and he inherited a lot of land when his father died of a heart attack. Land was very important back then. I was the oldest girl of four, and my parents were happy to have me off their hands, especially into a family with land and some money. Now I would be able to take care of them and of my sisters. You have to understand, that was a big deal back then. Marry into a family with land and an income, especially in a house with just daughters. We weren't expected to work, we were expected to marry well. I didn't have too many prospects, so when Morgan came along, we were practically pushed together by my parents. He was a good man, worked hard, took care of me. We were really happy at first. I became a woman in my own right and there was a certain respect that came with that, and I liked it. It took me three years to discover that Morgan was a gambler. He started gambling with his uncles on weekends at the track or in back rooms at the pub, but what they wanted was the land. By the time I was twenty-one, my husband had lost his birth right to his uncles, and we were forced to work for the farm that we had owned." A sad, wry smile came over her.

"My sisters married too, over the next few years, all of them good matches, better than mine, and I stayed away from them, too proud to admit to what had become of my young marriage and my life. Then I had Angela." The dryness of her expression softened at this.

"Oh what a joy to have a baby, but her birth was a hard one, and the midwife had to send for the doctor, who was drunk and butchered me so that I could never have any other children." She paused as Angela reached out and squeezed her hand.

"It was a hard time for us, and Morgan dealt with it by drinking for long hours and betting away the few precious wages his uncles paid him. We managed as best as we could. My sisters would come by for visits at first, to see Angela and to bring me news of our parents, but they stopped as the years rolled on, too embarrassed to see that I had taken in laundry and sewing to make ends meet in our small house and to keep Angela and ourselves fed."

Again she paused, but the girls and Jack were rapt, eyes wide open, listening to a tale of their history that had never been told before. Angela was smiling at her mother, her eyes wet with unshed tears.

"I was sixteen when we lost the house," she supplied. "I remember it so clearly, Dad coming in so late at night, the terrible row you had in the kitchen. We had two weeks to get out and find somewhere to live."

Siobhan reached out for her daughter's hand. "I always hated that I had to put you through that."

"It doesn't matter, it wasn't your fault. I never blamed you," Angela said lovingly.

"I never blamed me either," Siobhan shot back with a laugh.

"So how did you manage to come here?" Moira wanted to know.

"I borrowed the money from my sister Caitlin. She only gave it because by that time, what with her doing so well, we were a bit of an embarrassment to her family. I think she just wanted to be shot of us. I hated being beholden to her, though. She sent me a telegram once a month for a year to remind me of keeping up with our financial obligation to her. It took that long to pay her back, and with Morgan working at the factory, gambling on the weekends with the new chaps he met and dealing with my anger and frustration toward him, he fell to a heart attack before the year was over. Angela was fine, though. She graduated high school, went to college and got her teacher's certificate. I always managed to pull in some money, so we kept afloat."

"When did you meet Dad?" Sloane asked Angela. She was suddenly looking very young. This was a lot to take in for her, having never really had to deal directly with big challenges.

"I met him right out of university, when I got my first job teaching. He was the landscaper who was hired to plant new gardens in the school where I worked. We fell in love almost immediately. He was also from Ireland, which gave us plenty to talk about."

"I'm confused. I don't remember why he left. Dad wasn't a gambler too, was he?" Sloane asked. Moira was quiet. She already knew the answer to this question, but wanted to let her mother explain. Jack kept his tongue also, just happy to be here for Moira and amazed at the courage and determination of this family.

"No, he wasn't a gambler. He was a drunk."

Sloane gasped. "He can't have been. Wouldn't I have remembered something??"

"He wasn't a violent drunk. Nothing like the terrible and stereotypical tales you hear about the Irish and how they can't hold their drink and beat their wives. He was just a sad drunk. He missed Ireland so much, always talking about going back there. He would drink quietly to forget about it. He was never mean or physical, just sad. By the time you girls started getting older, he stopped drinking so much at home and started drinking out in the bars, where he would meet up with other sad drunk Irishmen. It was when he started bringing them home that I began to worry seriously. We had bought this house early in our marriage, when two salaries were more than enough to sustain us, but as the years went on, your father's share of wages went more to the pubs than to the house. It was hard going. I was trying to keep this place together and raise you girls on less and less money and then feed the vagrants he brought home before kicking them out again. At the lowest point, I would wake up in the morning to make breakfast for you girls and find one or two strange, bedraggled men passed out in the living room or the kitchen. It was no picnic for me. They smelled. A lot of the time they had wet themselves. The longer it went on, the stranger and older and smellier the men got. Finally, I told him that he couldn't bring home any more men, and I wanted him to get help for the drinking. It was no environment to raise you girls in. That night he didn't come home. I got divorce papers a year later."

"It's not a great family legacy, I'll give you that," Siobhan stated.

"It's not a bad one, either," Jack piped up. "Who wouldn't want to belong to a family of such strong women?"

Angela gave him an admiring look. "Your mother raised you right," she said.

"My mother died when I was fifteen. Car accident," Jack told her.

"Well then, raised by a good man, that's even more

impressive. You tell your father I said that."

Jack nodded to her, smiling. Moira was amazed. Here in the peace and tranquility of her mother's beloved garden, which she now realized probably reminded her of happier days with her father, all the walls were falling down.

"I'm surprised at both of you," Sloane stated.

"Why?" asked Angela.

"Neither of you said a word against rushing into marriage when Martin and I got engaged. It didn't do either of you any favours."

"Martin is a good man, which was apparent right from the get go. I have no problem with him, no reservations. He's a good man, Sweetie, and you'll be just fine."

She smiled at this, placated by their kind words.

"Besides," put in Siobhan, "both of you are so much older now than your mother and I were when we wed. You've both had time to figure yourselves out first. That's something I never really did, and I'm not too sure your mother did either. I think that we raised you strong. Or at least, Angela did."

"Thank you, Mother. Though I always felt bad that I hid so much from you both. And that you had to do so much, Moira. I was never really any good at asking for help when I needed it. Probably why you're so much like your Nana, a real force in your own right."

Moira grinned at her and wiped away an errant tear that had slid down her face. It was the biggest compliment she had ever received.

Sloane was looking as confused as before. She seemed to be mulling over the revelations with some trouble.

"I don't see why you should be thanking Moira. What did she do? She wasn't much older than me, and I hardly remember any of this."

"Maybe you should go get those boxes I set out for you and have a look. Might jog your memory," Angela said gently.

Moira harrumphed. "It won't make much of a difference," she said. "Sloane still won't get it. But it doesn't matter. I gave up trying to understand her ages ago. We're just too different."

"What's that supposed to mean?" Sloane demanded.

"Nothing."

"No, I want to know. If we're airing all this out, hang your laundry with Mom's and Nana's."

"It means, dear sister, that you have no idea of any of this for a reason. You are so consumed with your own life that you've never seen what the rest of us have done to give it to you. Mom was always working to keep the house, Nana was working to help her from the moment she moved in here after Dad left, and I was the one who kept you from knowing there was anything hard about it."

"Who says I needed your protection anyway? Maybe I couldn't deal with it because none of you ever gave me the chance."

Angela, Siobhan and Jack looked surprised—a few exchanges and the tone of the day had become volatile. They each opened their mouths to jump in and rescue the situation, but the girls were having none of it. Sensing the need to interject, Sloane stayed them with a flick of her hand.

"Don't!" she said. "You're always trying to stop us from fighting. I'm sick of you always acting like you're better than me, Moira. Just because you've got your own business and your own apartment, you think you're something special. I have a degree too, you know. I went to college and studied like you did. Maybe I haven't jumped into my own business and put such a clamp on my life, but I think it bugs you that I'm not married to my work and have a social life. I think it has always bugged you that I don't need to be such a control freak and that I have friends and go out. You've always been jealous of me, and that's why you've always been so hard on me."

"Fine, you want to air the laundry, here you go: you don't even know how good you have it. You went to school in great little outfits because Mom worked her ass off not to lose this house, and I did the laundry and the shopping and made sure things here weren't going to fall apart. You had clean clothes and meals because the rest of us provided it for you. You have no job, even with your degree, and have no idea what it is to deal with accountants and taxes and suppliers who keep dicking you around just because you're a woman. You don't have any battles to fight and you never have, because we fought them for you ... I fought for you."

"You never said you were still having trouble with that supplier, dear," Angela said, trying to interject a break in the fight.

"Yeah, he keeps shorting me and overcharging."

"See!" said Sloane triumphantly. "Even now you're just swallowed up in your work. I think you thrive on conflict. If you're not fighting with someone, you're just not happy."

"You wouldn't understand," Moira shot back at her. "Running a business is very different from organizing a social calendar. It takes attention to detail and cultivation of working relationships."

"Oh, pull your head out of your ass, Moira. You shouldn't have to overanalyze every aspect of this. It's a simple solution. Fire that asshole and get a new supplier. Even I can see that."

"Maybe you should stay out of this," Moira snapped at her.

"Maybe *you* should grow some balls," Sloane flipped back at her. The other three were silent: *this* exchange was not one they wanted to jump into. Even Angela, the peacemaker, seemed unusually mute, perhaps overly cautious after her conversation with Moira in the garden.

"Let me add that to my 'to do' list. I think there's some space between picking up my dry-cleaning and pulling my head out of my ass."

Sloane stood up and stomped out of the backyard, muttering about picking up her boxes and getting back home. Moira looked at the other three.

"What?"

Jack raised his hands, palms towards Moira in an "I'm staying out of this" gesture, and Angela shrugged her shoulders. She looked at Siobhan, who was mutinous in her chair.

"What, Nana?"

"She's got a point. Tell this guy where to shove it and get a new supplier. That's business, babe. If he won't meet your needs, find someone who will."

Moira sank into her chair. "I know you're right. I just didn't want to hear it from Sloane."

"Why you two don't get along is beside me. I've never understood it," Angela said.

"I'm sorry, everyone. I really didn't want to fight after everything you just told us. We just can't seem to help it, lately."

"I'm sorry too. Maybe I shouldn't have suggested you air things out. Not the greatest way to be introduced to family," said Jack.

"Oh dear boy, don't you worry. This family has seen far worse fights than that. It was barely on the Richter scale. The girls will put it right eventually. Not to worry," Siobhan put in.

"Thank you, Siobhan. Moira, perhaps we should go?" He rose and stretched out his hand to Moira.

"I won't hear of it," said Angela. "You'll stay to lunch first. In fact, I'll go and start on it now." She disappeared into the house. Siobhan motioned for Moira to help her, and they followed suit, into the kitchen for a cup of tea and some sandwiches to wash down the sour taste left from the exchanges on the deck.

Chapter Twenty-One

The inside conversation was far more polite and relaxed. The women questioned Jack a little on his job, and he happily explained the details of what he did and how much he enjoyed it. The firm he worked for was great, small enough that everyone knew everyone else, big enough that they had been landing more and more prestigious clients in the past two years. Jack's own reputation was starting to grow as more clients requested him personally. He was engaging, animated as he talked of designing graphics and webmercials.

Angela set out a plate with some sandwiches on the table and added a second plate with soda bread, grapes and fat golden and orange chunks of cheese. There was a jug of cool water and a pot of piping tea in its cozy. Moira grabbed a stack of plates from the cupboard. She looked around the room.

"You don't suppose Sloane really left, do you?" she asked.

"No, her purse is still on the counter," Siobhan pointed out. "Try the library, your mother put out some boxes of things for her in there to take to her new house."

"Go get her," Angela instructed, barely looking up from ministering to Jack, arranging a plate for him piled high with food.

Moira stood up and walked down the narrow hall from the kitchen to the small but bright room in the back. Sloane was sitting on the floor, legs crossed, surrounded by three medium-sized boxes and with a sheaf of photos in her hand, as well as several loosely piled on the floor beside her. She wasn't staring at the picture, though. She was staring at the back.

"Lunch, Sloane," Moira said and turned to leave.

"Wait. Do you remember this?" She held up a photo of Moira holding the back of a bright pink bicycle while Sloane sat triumphantly on the seat. "It says: Moira teaching Sloane to ride her bike, 1989. Do you remember it?"

"Sure I do ... "

"What about this one," she interjected before Moira could finish her thought. Now she held up a picture of Moira reading to Sloane. "And this one?" A photo of Sloane's sixth birthday, Moira carrying in the birthday cake. "You're in all of these. All of them."

"I know." Moira shrugged.

"Why? Where was Mom? Where was Nana?"

"Earning a living. You were only five when Dad left, I was almost nine. I remember how sad you were, and how mom was scared that we would have to sell the house. So I stepped in a bit. You know this though, I've told you before."

Sloane frowned, leafing through a few more pictures, flipping her wrist to check the inscription on the back each time.

"How come I don't remember most of this? And don't tell me it's because I was spoiled."

Moira sighed and sat down on the floor next to her. "You were so busy all the time. You had a crowd of friends around you from the first moment you stepped into the kindergarten door. I stayed out of it mostly, except when we were at home. I never had your capacity for making friends, and I was never interested in keeping up with you in that department, so I made the most of the time we had together at home. It made Mom so happy that we were so close and that I could do so much for you when she was so busy, so she and Nana took a lot of pictures of us. You were so bright and quick and beautiful when you were little, still are. Always the life of the party and the one people flocked

234

around, including Mom. I was kind of jealous of you, I guess."

"You were jealous of *me?*"

Moira didn't answer. She just got up and walked out of the room, back to the kitchen. She sat down next to Jack and squeezed his knee, smiling at him. He rubbed her shoulders and pushed his heaping plate of food between them. Sloane came in and sat down across from them, taking a plate for herself and loading it up with the fare before her. Her face was working overtime, not just the motions of her jaw as she chewed thoughtfully on a sandwich, but Sloane, like all of the Ryan women, seemed to wear her deliberations in her expressions. It became a sort of game, everyone eating a quiet lunch, seemingly wrapped up in the good food, but really trying to work out when Sloane would finish processing whatever it was she was contemplating and speak to them about it. If there had been a fly on the wall, it would have become dizzy watching as the ladies and even Jack's eyes darted from Sloane's face and back to the others at the table, like a tennis match, back and forth. Jack felt like he should have been uncomfortable in this setting. His mind was saying that he was intruding on a huge personal moment for these women, but his heart was soaring that Moira should let him in like this, so easily. There was no doubt now that he had indeed fallen for her, and hard. He began to wrack his brain, eager to defend her should her sister go on the offensive again. It was Siobhan, finally, who broke the silence.

"Well, that clinches it," she said loudly. "Once this wedding is over I'm going on a diet. I've never eaten so much as I have in the last few weeks. This old chair is going to break under the strain."

"You don't need a diet, Nana," Moira told her. "You're just gorgeous."

Siobhan patted her silvery thinning hair. "Why thank you, dear. I never said I wasn't that, but gorgeous isn't going to do me any good when my giant ass can't get around."

They laughed.

"I can't thank you enough for the tour and for letting me latch onto your family time today," Jack began, talking to Angela. "I don't know when I've had so much fun."

"Well, if you think family spats and sad histories are fun, you should come around more often," she chuckled back at him. "But thank you, you're welcome anytime. Did you say that you're going to see your father later today?"

"Yes. That is, we were going to pay him a visit later." He winked at Moira.

"I would like to give you something from the garden for him, if you don't mind. Don't leave until I do that."

Jack was seriously touched. "Thank you. That would be lovely," he said.

Finally, Sloane looked up.

"Moira, do you think we could spend some time together, later this week?"

"Sure, just let me know when."

"Okay, I'll do that." She stood up. "I have to go. Thank you for the pictures and stuff, Mom. Jack, it was a pleasure to meet you."

Jack stood up. "Do you want a hand with anything? I'd be glad to help you take your boxes out to your car."

"Thank you, that would be very nice."

They left the room and returned a minute later, Jack carrying a large box under each arm, Sloane with the third. They went out, and Moira watched as Jack helped Sloane place them in the trunk of her car, then stood talking for a few minutes. Siobhan noticed as well.

"You were right. That's quite the man you've found yourself."

"I know," she said absently, still watching them talk.

"You better hang on to that one."

"I think I will."

Moira tore her gaze from the window and started to clean up. Angela immediately got up to help her, but Moira shook her head. "Let me, Mom. I can do this, you take a break."

"Okay, if you want. I'll get Jack and take him out to the garden for some flowers." She opened the kitchen door that led to the mudroom and, invariably, the backyard and grabbed a pair of gloves from the small shelf and some shears that were hanging from a hook under it. Then she went out the door and headed Jack off as he came back up the steps, walking him around to the back garden.

Moira was putting away the leftover food and tidying up the dishes. Siobhan was watching her with interest.

"How long did you say you two have been seeing one another?"

"Not long, about two weeks. It feels like much longer, though."

"And you're already sleeping with him? Not that I blame you, he's very handsome."

Moira looked aghast. "How did you know that? Does Mom know?"

"Of course not! But I could tell. You keep touching one another. And it's in the way you look at each other, the way he looks at you when you're not paying attention. I'd say that young man out there was completely smitten."

"And you think it's all too soon?" Moira ran water in the sink for dishes.

Siobhan hooted. "Who, me?! Lord knows I'm no-one to cast stones in that direction. Haven't I just told you that both your mother and I, and Sloane for that matter, ran towards our marriages full steam? Stop worrying, Moira dear. Fast found love seems to run in this family." She raised an eyebrow at her, "You do love him, don't you?"

"Yes, I really think I do."

"Don't give me that 'think' crap. You either do or you don't. Love is a feeling, not contemplation."

"I love him."

"Good."

Moira finished washing the dishes as Siobhan wheeled her chair carefully around the table, wiping the crumbs and tea stains from the light wood. By the time Jack and Angela came in from the backyard, the kitchen

237

was sparkling. Moira opened the mudroom door all the way when she heard their voices. Angela was rooting around in a closet in the back room, and Jack was holding a plant in his bare hands, cupping them to keep the dirt from escaping onto the floor.

"I know I've got one back here, I always have extras," Angela was saying, her bum sticking out as she bent over to root around the floor of the closet.

"Aha! Here we go." She came up with a clay pot in her hands and gingerly took the plant from Jack, placing it lovingly in the pot and, reaching into an open bag on one of the shelves, she sprinkled a few granules of something onto the soil.

"This will be just lovely," she said. Then, having just noticed her daughter, "Moira, aren't your violets beautiful? There is a late bloomer under the hedge at the back corner of the garden." She turned back to Jack. "Now, they'll need watering later today, but only a little. If your Dad has a windowsill in his room, that's where they should live. He can give them a little water late in the day, everyday, or," she noticed his face going momentarily dark, "one of his nurses can. It's no big deal, it's a small plant, so they won't need much, but they will smell just lovely for at least another week or two." She looked triumphant, a smudge of dirt on the side of her face from where she had wiped away an errant hair or a bug. Jack was standing with the plant in his hands again, although this time contained in the pot, and looking seriously close to tears.

"Thank you," he said to Angela, and impulsively leaned in and hugged her. Then passing Moira the plant, he crossed to behind her and planted a kiss on Siobhan's cheek. "Thank you for the wonderful morning. And the company." He turned back to Angela. "And the plant. I'll tell my Dad it was a gift especially from you."

"Oh no, dear boy. Those are Moira's violets. She plants those and adds a few every year. I just babysit them for her."

"Bye Mom, Nana," Moira said, leaning in to hug

them as well and slipping her shoes back on her feet.

"Bye dears. Enjoy the rest of your day," Angela said as Siobhan waved at them from her chair, blowing kisses and winking.

***

Moira and Jack settled happily into the car and sped off down the quaint little street.

"Do you mind if we go to my place? I really should change my clothes," he asked her.

"Nope, not at all. Did you enjoy yourself? We're a little crazy."

"Maybe that's why I liked it so much. You're family is great."

"If you don't mind a fight every ten minutes," she said.

"Hey, that's going to happen. At least you get it all out, not let it fester forever. That's more than most women would do. I've always thought women have the greatest memories when it comes to holding grudges and fighting."

"Not us. Get it out, loudly and messily, and then move on. That's how we operate."

"Probably much more healthy than the alternative," he agreed as they pulled up to his building. They got out and headed in, Jack opening the door to his apartment to let Moira go first.

"I'll just be a few minutes," he said, heading into the bedroom. Moira lingered in the living room for a moment, and then, noting the time, opened the door to the bedroom and walked in to sit on Jack's bed. Jack was standing in front of his closet in his boxers, searching for a clean shirt that wasn't a work shirt, and holding a pair of jeans in his left hand. He turned to her.

"Yes?"

Moira was playful. "When did you want to go back and visit your dad?"

He dropped the jeans on the floor and turned to face

239

her. "Not till later this afternoon. I thought we could take a walk, unless you had other plans ... "

"I was just thinking, it's only a little after one, and we have some time ... but if you want to take a walk, I could do that."

"Can I tell you something?"

"Of course."

He took a few more steps towards her, so that now his knees were touching hers where her legs hung over the side of the bed.

"I don't really want to take a walk."

Moira stood up, her voice husky as she answered him.

"Me neither," she said.

"I want ... "

"Yes, Jack?"

"To take a shower. Whoooo! I stink." He howled with laughter as Moira swatted him on the behind.

"You're a stinker," she said. "There's a difference."

Jack went over to the bathroom and stepped in, turning on the light and then the water in his shower. He tugged suggestively at the waistband to his shorts. "Why don't you join me?"

"You think I won't?" she asked him.

"I don't know, shy baker girl. You might get nervous when you see me do this." He turned his back to her, taking his shorts off completely, his bare bum whiter than the rest of him, which made Moira laugh. She crossed the room and came over to where he was reaching his hand in past the shower curtain to test the water temperature.

"Listen whitey, I'm not so shy." And with that she pulled her shirt over her head and dropped it to the floor, soon to be followed by her bra and jeans. Jack gave her a slow, up and down appreciative look, wolf whistling at her.

"Now that's more like it. But I believe you forgot something." He gently hooked his fingers into the waist of her panties and eased them down her legs, kissing her thighs as she stepped her feet out, one at a time.

Moira dropped a hand down and covered herself a little. This was very different from being naked in a dark room late at night. She was suddenly feeling as shy as Jack had alluded to seconds ago.

Jack took her hand and swept back the shower curtain with the other one. They stepped in, the water hot, but not unbearable and immediately found each other's lips, their naked bodies pressed together and water cascading down their backs. Moira's mouth was warm and soft to Jack and he kissed her with more intention and passion then he could ever remember having with another woman. Her soft tongue ran lightly over his bottom lip, causing him to react in a most obvious way. Their kisses so intense, Moira lost the feeling of the water; the heat and the steam rising up just vanished, as there was nothing to feel but their lips, every inch of skin where it touched and the hard palpitations of her heart beating against her chest. Jack's hands reached up and threaded through her now soaked hair, pulling it off her face, and he pulled back from the kiss, staring into her eyes ... her amazing emerald eyes.

"I have to say something," he whispered.

She nodded at him.

Jack leaned in, his hands still in her hair, as if holding on to her would give him the courage to say something enormous.

"I love you, Moira," he mouthed at her earlobe. "I am in love with you."

"Oh Jack," she murmured back, kissing him on the neck, the throat. "I love you too. I didn't want to scare you, so soon. I didn't want to scare myself. I love you so much."

Their mouths found each other again as the revelation of their feelings swept over them, and they laughed at themselves in their fervency and desire, the buoyancy of their feelings bubbling up like a mixture of baking soda and vinegar, causing an explosion of energy and excitement. They grabbed at the soaps and shampoo in the shower and delighted in washing each other's bodies and hair, each connection of hand to skin a new affirmation and exploration of one another and their declaration. They rinsed each other in awe as the dwindling suds revealed their bodies to each other again. Jack turned off the water and stepped out first, holding out a large towel for Moira, who stepped out and wrapped herself in it and in his arms. Jack shifted the towel so that it wrapped around them both, pressing against her once again, reveling in the feel of her delicate skin next to his. Tracing his finger tips gently across her collar bone, her shoulder, he felt giddy that this beautiful woman was so completely his. He wanted to hold her, protect her, and show her off to the world. So many emotions flowed through him that he found it hard to keep still, wanting to touch every inch of her. Moira too was feeling overwhelmed by the intensity of moment. She could scarcely believe that Jack was in love with her: meek little Moira who always fell first for the wrong man, always spoke the words first with little or no return, who had started to believe that this kind of connection just could not be possible. They shuffled and made their way back into the bedroom, where the towel was discarded on the floor, and they fell onto the bed together, still exploring one another and continuing to gaze into each other's eyes as they made love. They moved achingly slow, savouring the sensations and moving as if time stood still for only them, prolonging the final culmination of the act for as long as possible, not wanting to end this glorious possession. Every so often, Jack would pause, literally holding still within her and reach up to her face, caressing her cheek, tracing the lines of her lips, making her quiver and smile as it tickled her, delighting in the twinkle of her illustrious eyes and, when she could stand it no longer, she would bite at the tip of his finger, pressing herself against him, clasping him to her, until finally they could hold out no longer, and the explosions of passion broke over them in waves, making them each cry out, whispering each other's name over and over through the embraces of their lips.

It was Moira who moved first, afterward. She rose up on her elbow and kissed Jack on the forehead lightly.

"We should get dressed," she said.

"Do we have to?"

"Afraid so. And I think I need to get a drink of water."

"Definitely, but let me." Jack rose and didn't bother to don anything, heading off to the kitchen, where she heard the tap running. He came back in and handed her a glass of cool water, sipping at his own.

"You are so beautiful," he told her.

Moira smiled a thank you to him. She was trying hard not to protest. It would only bother Jack if she argued this point with him, though it was hard not to *feel* beautiful when he made love to her like that. She looked around the room for a minute.

"They're on the bathroom floor." Jack laughed, realizing that she was searching for her clothes. "Do you want me to get them for you?"

"No, I can do that," she said and, playing at Jack's game, she rose from the bed without covering up with a sheet or the now crumpled towel, an action that had certainly been a part of every other sexual episode in her life, and went into the bathroom to scoop her clothes from the floor. She also grabbed Jack's shorts and tossed them at him. He was sitting up, still sipping at his water and watching her walk naked around his apartment.

"Oh my goodness!" Moira said suddenly as she pulled her clothes on. "It's after three!"

"No need to thank me, anything to please my lady," Jack said playfully. "But I guess that means we should get going."

"You think?"

"Unfortunately. Don't stress, though. Time well spent." He began to dress now, too. "Want to go straight to the hospice or get a bite first?"

"Hospice," Moira said, actually looking forward to spending time with Kevin now that she knew his nature.

"Right-o. Whatever the lady wants, the lady gets," said Jack, finishing the last of his buttons and sweeping the now fully dressed Moira into his arms. "Let's go."

Chapter Twenty-Two

Hastily grabbing an apple each from the kitchen and the potted violets from Angela's house, they once again locked doors and climbed into Jack's car.

"Do you want to check in with Jaye?" Jack asked her as they headed downtown towards the bridge and The Cakery.

"No, I'm sure she's doing just fine today. Besides, she'd only get mad if I came in on my first day off."

"Right. Onwards and upwards, then." Jack swung the car onto the bridge and made a left turn on the other side, following the river upstream and towards the hospice. They passed by other offices like Jack's on the way; large modern buildings with highly manicured and landscaped lawns. It was a part of town that had only been developed over the last seven or eight years, and it showed. All of the buildings were impersonal looking cement blocks, designed for maximum durability and ergonomic layout. Perhaps that was why Jack had been somewhat relieved to find that the hospice was a converted old mansion. It was over a century old, and although it had received all of the upgrades and modern conveniences one could ask for, its outward and old charm had not been touched by modern thinking builders. One got the impression as you drove down the winding drive that you had left Canada all together and driven straight onto an old plantation straight out of *Gone with the Wind*. Moira seemed to be appreciating this too, he noted, for as they wound their way around the parking lot, her eyes never left the grandeur of the front of the hospice for a second. Jack parked the car and came around to get her door.

"Pretty, isn't it?" he said to her as she climbed out and straightened her shirt.

"It's beautiful. I didn't notice last night."

"Well, it was darker, and we had other things on our minds," Jack said quietly. He took her hand, and they walked together into the front entrance. This time there was no trepidation from either of them. This visit wasn't for Jack to prove a point or honour a dying man's wish, and Moira had no qualms today about seeing a dying man. She simply wanted a visit with Jack and his dad. Inside on a weekday, there was a bustle everywhere. Jack had rarely visited outside his own working hours, and so had no idea, really, of how things were here on a weekday. Nurses and nurse's aides walked briskly through the corridors, sometimes carrying mysterious looking trays with white coverlets on them. Occasionally, a doctor would emerge from a room, his brow furrowed and wiping glasses on his shirt. There were few family members here, if any. No one who did not look official was roaming in the hallway except himself and Moira. They popped into Kevin's room, and Jack bent over the bed to whisper softly in his slumbering ears.

"Dad? Dad? Are you asleep?"

Kevin didn't move; he was so still that, for a moment, Jack feared the worse. Finally, his chest shifted slightly, and he opened his mouth.

"No ... I'm dead."

Jack cracked a smile, but Moira laughed right out loud, causing Kevin to wrench open his eyes.

"Oh, it's you two. I thought my doc was here and I was playing a little joke on him. Keeps falling for it, third time in a week." He tried to laugh, but all that came out was a soft wheeze. He turned to Moira. "How are you, dear? So nice of you to come back and see me again."

"My pleasure," Moira said, and she laid down the pot of violets on the bedside table. "These are for you. From my mother's garden," she added.

Kevin looked at Jack for confirmation. "Moira's mother has the most stunning garden you've ever seen, Dad. You would love it."

"Mmmm. I take it you've seen it, then?"

"Only just this morning."

Kevin processed this for a moment.

"It's not the weekend yet, surely?"

"No, we took a day off," Jack told him.

Kevin regarded the two casting their little looks at each other, their mannerisms, and their body language, and closed his eyes again, drawing in a deep breath.

"So, you thought about what I said, huh?" he stated. It really wasn't a question. There was no doubt that they had rounded a corner together. He opened his eyes again and grinned at the two of them.

"Okay, then. What shall we do this afternoon? I rather fancy seeing some new scenery. This room gets a little *boring* after a while. Why don't you two wheel me down to the sun room and we'll have a nice chat?"

Moira moved the violets to the windowsill so they would have some light, and Jack went out in search of a nurse to help him disengage his father from the medical trappings of his bed.

They spent the afternoon talking in the sun-filled room at the back of the hospice overlooking the river while telling each other stories from their lives. Only twice did Jack bolt up in alarm when, as he laughed at a story told by Moira, Kevin seemed to lose the ability to breathe completely. But both times he was waved back to his seat by his father, with halting reassurances that it was nothing to get alarmed over.

"It's in my chest now, you see. All of the organs are shutting down. I expect the heart will go next. That small attack gave me an arrhythmia. Doc says it's been interrupting my sleep, even though I don't wake up from it. Probably the stuff they give me for pain at night. In a way it's a relief." He turned to Jack and kept his eyes held. "I'll see your mother soon."

247

Oddly, it did not make Jack want to cry, to hear this. Nor did it seem to make him angry, as it might have done a short time ago. Instead, seeing how calm and assured his father was, he was comforted to know that death was simply an opportunity to him now, a means to reunite with his beloved wife, and obviously now that he was sure of Jack's relationship with Moira, there was little to keep him in this world. Even though the words and their intentions were sad, there was an odd, though not unsettling peace about them. Kevin was relaxed, seemed to be struggling less to talk compared with their previous visit, and the stories flowed between the three until finally it was time to move Kevin back to his room for his night meds to be administered. They promised to come and visit with him every evening from now on, with the exception of any pre-wedding commitments Moira had to Sloane.

***

Holding hands once more, Moira and Jack reluctantly left the hospice and headed back across town. They were both thinking that, since tomorrow was another work day, there would be a real need for sleep tonight in their own places, though they were loath to leave one another. Jack walked Moira up the stairs to her apartment.

"I guess this should be goodnight," he stated glumly.

"Yeah. Today was so wonderful. It's really easy to forget we live in the real world, where work awaits us both in the morning."

"I gotta get some sleep, though."

"Me too. I'm sure there'll be lots to catch up on tomorrow morning. Usually I fill in the supplies as the day goes on. I doubt Jaye could have done that while manning the store."

Jack smiled and planted a soft kiss on her cheek, then one on her lips.

"Don't worry about it until morning. I'll come get you after work tomorrow. We'll get some dinner and then go and see Dad, okay?"

"That sounds perfect."

They shared another long kiss, trying to put all the meaning into the connection of their lips that had come to them in the course of the day. It seemed to last a lifetime. Finally they broke apart, and Jack ran lightly down the stairs, humming to himself as Moira let herself in the door.

She made herself a light snack and settled down to watch some TV, but there was nothing on to hold her attention. Her mind was racing with the activities of the day. Finally, she understood why it was that her mother had come here so many years ago. She also understood why it was that her grandmother had such strong opinions about lending money, especially to family. She remembered now, how strongly she had pushed Moira to take the loan four years ago, and how she had often balked at her attempts to repay it. She could have done in one year what Siobhan made her do in two, but the wonderful woman had been adamant that she was firmly standing on her own feet in the shop before she began handing over large sums of money. No matter now, it had been good to find out where she came from, what kind of a background followed the women of the family. It shouldn't really have surprised her then, when the phone rang just as she was planning to go to bed, and Sloane's voice came floating down through the line.

"Hi, Moira. Um, I just wondered what you're doing tomorrow." She sounded timid, quiet, somewhat like she had in the library at the house that afternoon while surrounded by the pictures and memorabilia.

"Working, of course. It'll probably take me an entire day to catch up from missing today. Why?"

"Do you mind if I come and see you? At the shop, I mean."

"I don't mind, if that's what you want. But you'll have to come and sit in the kitchen and talk while I work, I really won't be able to stop a whole lot."

"That's fine. Thanks."

"Everything okay? You sound strange, and ... aren't

you usually out with the girls this time of night?" She glanced at her clock. "It's only ten-thirty."

"I decided not to join them tonight. Martin and I have been going through all of the stuff Mom left for me and having a bit of a talk."

Moira decided not to press it. "Okay, well, I'm going to bed so I can be up early. I'll have the back door open, so come anytime after 8:00, if you're up."

"I'll be there." She paused. "Thanks, Moira."

Surprised, but too tired to contemplate it, Moira hung up the phone and collapsed into her bed. She was asleep before she had time to consider what it could be that her sister wanted to talk to her about.

Chapter Twenty-Three

Friday morning dawned a little darker and cooler than the preceding few weeks had been. It felt like the temperature was in stasis, unwilling to commit to an actual change, but sitting on the cusp, as if waiting for some event or date to tip it into full-scale Fall. Moira didn't mind. She had a feeling there would be a great deal of bread to catch up on today, and early morning cool temperatures were the best time for preparing anything that required long lengths in the ovens, the heat of day not being a drastic contributor to changing the climate in her kitchen. She would just crack the back door open a hair before loading up her ovens with sweet and doughy smelling breads. Throwing her hair up in an elastic, and donning a pair of heavily washed jeans and a flattering golden yellow t-shirt, she skipped breakfast in her apartment and headed straight down to the store. Letting herself in, she first took a walk through the front, inspecting the stores of goodies and receiving a shock when she found that most of the display coolers had been cleaned out. There was almost nothing in them at all. This had to be a mistake. There was no way Jaye could have gone through so much stock in just one day. Thinking that she must have stored some back in the larger walk-ins in the kitchen, Moira dashed in to search for the trays of comestibles that she assumed would be awaiting her in pretty rows. There were none. Starting to feel frantic, she checked the cash tapes from close. Incredibly, it seemed as though Jaye *had* actually nearly sold out the store. Her search now started for a note of some kind from her friend, something to explain this phenomenon, but there seemed to be none. Now that was really unusual. Jaye almost always left a little note of some kind for Moira, something to let her know what stock was in urgent need of replacing, and what would not be urgent, but would need attention soon. Sometimes she just left a note to be silly, but there was almost always something.

Nothing. Nothing to indicate what could have cleaned them out so thoroughly, what needed re-doing, or how Jaye had coped. Not even a note to ask her how her day had gone with Jack. Stymied, Moira slumped back into the kitchen and started a large pot of coffee, then let herself into the cooler and started taking out large bowls of dough, plain, un-iced slab cakes and any other items she could find that would enable her to start prepping to replace her stores for the day.

She was bent over one of the lower shelves when she felt a hand on her back.

"Aaaaarghhhh!" Moira yelped, straightening up and whipping around to see who it was.

Jaye stood in front of her in the doorway with a sheepish smile on her face.

"Surprise," was all she said.

"What the hell do you mean, surprise? You scared the crap outta me, everything is gone, and not a word left from you to explain it."

Jaye's sunny face didn't break for a moment.

"You're not mad?" she asked, incredulously.

"Well, no, but I mean … you must have been non-stop!"

"Kinda. We had a really large group in yesterday around noon from some office saying that they had heard we were the best shop in town. I wound up selling out of almost everything within the hour. I pulled out whatever we had left in the back to get me through the afternoon and popped in some of the bread we had rising from late the other night, but by the time I was getting ready to close, another wave came in, a lot of the same people from the lunch trade, and they swooped up everything to take it home with them. I was amazed. I'm going to put up a sign saying we're opening at noon today, so we can catch up."

Moira had to catch her breath. It was more than she had hoped for when she had first opened the store. Now, not only were they getting a fairly steady trade from the town, but they were finally attracting some of the business from the large offices across the river, like Jack's. She wondered momentarily if this sudden surge in business had anything to do with him talking her up at work. Well, it sure was a good sign that all those folks had come back in the evening after having already sampled her work at lunch. They must like it.

"I was hoping to beat you in this morning, get started before you came down. I wasn't sure if you'd have company last night again or not." Jaye was definitely giving her friend a sly look.

"Nope. We had a great time yesterday, but we both needed to get to work in fresh clothes today. Besides, I wanted to get an early start, and now I'm really glad I did."

Happily busy, they bustled around the kitchen for a while, burning through one pot of coffee in less than thirty minutes between the two of them and Jaye starting a second when Moira again let out a yelp.

"What's the matter?" asked Jaye, her hands covered in the glimmering brown residue of cinnamon as she rolled out gingerbread cookies onto the marble slab.

"We're out of icing sugar ... again."

Muttering to herself, she picked up the phone.

Jaye watched in awe as her normally non-confrontational friend unceremoniously located and fired her supplier.

"Do me a favour," she said as she hung up the phone, "go up to the bulk food store and buy a whole bunch of icing sugar, and tell Marina to call me about becoming our official supplier. I don't want to deal with that asshole," she glared at the phone, "ever again."

Jaye clicked her heels and gave her a mock salute.

"Yessir," she said and grabbed some cash from the till and headed out the door. Moira threw herself back into portioning out dough for the bread molds. She was engrossed in her work, so she didn't hear Sloane when she let herself in the back door.

"Wow, this place gets hot. It's only 9:45."

"Yeah, we're not exactly glamorous today. I'm sorry, I forgot you were coming. I have a bit of a situation on my hands. Can we do this later tonight?" At that, Moira looked up to regard her sister and was stunned to see that she looked nothing like her normal self. There were slight bags under her eyes, which were not made up. In fact, she looked as young and lost as she had yesterday in the garden, listening to the tales of her mother and grandmother, only more so, because now she had none of the effort behind her clothes and hair that she had been donning since high school.

"What's wrong?" she asked immediately.

Sloane sank into the chair that was kept in the corner of the kitchen, then immediately got up and made motions toward the coffee pot. "May I?"

"Of course. You can refill me too, if you don't mind."

Sloane grabbed Moira's mug from the counter and pulled another one from the tray near the sinks. She took her time making up the coffee cups, and Moira decided not to rush her. Instead, she finished filling the bread trays and slid them into the oven, gave a brisk wipe off of all the flour on the surface, and then pulled a large colourful bowl of strawberries towards her and began hulling them.

"Where's Jaye?" Sloane asked as she set down the coffee before her sister and once again took up the chair.

"She had to run out to the bulk food store. You were right about how I handle that supplier, though. I fired him this morning."

"Really? Well, that's good, right?"

"Yeah, it is." Moira looked up from her work and smiled at her sister. "Maybe I should have asked you for your advice earlier."

"You might not have wanted to hear it."

"I didn't want to hear it yesterday either," she said with a laugh. "But you were right, and I appreciate it."

"Thanks."

"So what's on your mind? You were awfully quiet yesterday, and you sound really ... " Moira searched for the right word to describe how she was feeling, "lost."

"I guess you could call it that. I've been thinking a lot lately. Maybe I should have thanked you more and not been so ... I don't know, indifferent."

Though she was taken slightly aback, Moira was trying not to react too much. She wanted to wait and see first where this was going to go.

"And you realized all this from a few photographs?" she asked, though not harshly.

"Sort of. I mean, I was really surprised to see you in so many of them, and then on the way home I started thinking about the important things in my life and where you were for them. Like when you drove me to get my driver's license, or when you helped me pick out that dress I wore to the junior prom at school. It was almost always you. I just didn't really *think* about it. And I'm sorry for that."

"It's okay."

"No, it's not. You're always so irritated with me these days and I just feel so ... out of sorts. So it's not okay. But I hope we can make it better."

"No need. I don't think we should dwell on it. What did Martin think about all this?"

"He—hey, how did you know I talked to him?"

"C'mon Sloane, you two are about to get married, it's only natural that you would tell him everything. Otherwise I would think that there was something missing between you."

"Okay, I talked to him. Actually, we talked for a good portion of the night last night, and he said that I've been really tough on you, especially around my friends. He also thinks you may be right about Katie having a problem."

"Of course she has a problem, she's a drunk," burst

out Jaye as she came in through the back door laden down with bags. She hefted them onto the counter. "I could tell that right away. Hi, Sloane."

"Hi, Jaye. Need a hand with any of that?"

"Um, sure." She raised an eyebrow at Moira, who shrugged. "Just take all those bags of icing sugar and dump them in here." She opened a large drawer, which had a huge white plastic bin in it. "This one is for the icing sugar. I'll get the other stuff dealt with."

Sloane tore open the four large bags of icing sugar and poured them into the bin, coughing a little as a fine cloud of delicate white dust sprang up around her.

"So, you're just figuring it out, about Katie?" Moira asked.

"Yeah, I—I mean, Martin and I were talking about it last night, you know, after we talked about that other stuff, and he said that he had noticed her with a flask sometimes adding booze to her coffee or juice or whatever. I hadn't really noticed."

"No? I noticed her doing it at that last fitting, and at the mall, and the night she called me she was definitely drunk. In fact, if you think about it, every story that you tell me about her has to do with her being hammered."

Sloane looked as if she were chewing on the inside of her lip.

"I hadn't really thought about it."

"You should," said Jaye. "She's about to stand up with you at your wedding soon. You don't want her doing something embarrassing."

"Jaye, I'm sure Katie wouldn't embarrass Sloane."

"I don't know. If she's as bad as all that, do you really want to leave it to chance?"

Sloane seemed to be having a hard time with this line of rationale.

"You don't think she'll do something awful, do you?"

"I don't know, truthfully. She sure doesn't like me much right now," Moira told her.

"Well, that's not all her fault, you were kinda mean

to her last time we were all out."

"Me? She was downright bitchy."

"Okay, well, I don't want to fight on this anyway. It's not really why I came here."

"Why did you come here?" Moira had finished taking the tops off the berries and was now rinsing them in the sink. She looked at her sister, slightly exasperated. "I mean, I have work to do. We ran out of almost everything yesterday, and we'll have to open late as it is. If you just want to chat, really, we can do it later."

"I'm trying to tell you that I feel bad about how things have been between us." Sloane pouted.

"Great, so you feel bad. I'm happy to hear it, but I don't know what you want to hear from me. I'm fine. I'm not mad at you, okay?"

"I guess. But don't you have anything else to say?"

"Not really."

"Aren't you sorry too?"

Now Moira rounded on her, brandishing the knife she was using to cut up the strawberries into little pieces.

"Me, sorry! For what? For helping you through all that stuff when you were younger? For never getting a thank you? For putting up with the insults of your drunken friend? No, Sloane, I'm not sorry for that."

Sloane stood up. "Not for that, for this. Every time I try to talk to you lately you get so … cold. I don't know how to fix things with you if you're going to be like that. I'm trying here, Moira."

Moira softened a little. Jaye was pretending to get on with mixing large quantities of sugar cookie dough and lifting the trays of the now golden and gorgeous bread from the ovens. She dared not catch Moira's eye; this was for the sisters to work out by themselves.

"I know, I guess it's just habit now. I feel like I need a wall up sometimes."

"I thought Jack was helping you get past all that a bit."

"Like Martin is helping you?"

"I guess so."

Moira smiled at the thought of handsome Jack gently encouraging her family to open up with one another yesterday. She noticed at mention of Martin, Sloane was smiling as well.

"You really love Martin, don't you?"

"Duh."

"I like him a lot. I never should have said that you were his problem. I'm sorry for that, Sloane."

"Thank you."

"You're welcome. Now, can we just start over?"

"Done. Whatcha making?"

"This will be strawberry mousse cakes. Then I have to make more babycakes. Then probably more cinna-crisps. There's a lot to do. Want to help? If you're not busy today, that is?"

"Can I?"

"Of course. Why don't you grab those icing bags over there and start spooning some of this icing in." And she reached into the pull-out refrigerated drawer and took out several bowls of icing in various colours, from pale pastels to bold and bright, almost neon hues.

Jaye, who had largely stayed out of the conversation, was now finished loading up the tray with cookies ready to be baked. She seemed happy to just keep ferrying things in and out of the ovens as they needed. Between the three of them, it took two more hours to load up the displays in the front, while making sure that there would still be stock left over for the rest of the day.

Chapter Twenty-Four

Sloane had kept her seat and spent most of the late morning icing cupcakes or dusting cinnamon sugar over the crisps, or whatever it was they needed an extra pair of hands for. Moira was loath to stay closed past noon, so at twelve sharp, they opened the doors. Within fifteen minutes, they were full of customers. Sloane helped Jaye out front, making sure that everyone was being helped while Moira kept up pace in the kitchens. If she thought that the day before was bound to be a one-off, she was totally wrong. By mid-afternoon, despite Moira's efforts to keep up with demand, they found themselves once again running low. Moira put in a call to the bulk food store and, after a brief conversation with the manager (who wasn't expecting to hear from her until after close) arranged to have a bunch of supplies delivered to the back entrance by one of their stock boys.

Sloane was actually a huge asset to them; she was charming and easy with the customers and, despite not having appeared to take a huge interest in her sister's business, seemed to know an awful lot about what was for sale in the shop. The extra pair of hands was indispensable. By the end of the day, all three ladies were tired and sore.

"God, Moira, I had no idea you were so busy in here. Things are really taking off for you, aren't they?" Sloane exclaimed by the time the last customer had left and the ladies were enjoying some coffee while they cleaned up and took stock.

"Yup, it's really going well." She turned to Jaye.

"You were right; we are going to need extra full time help, if we're going to keep up with this, especially if Jack is going to redo our website for us. I don't know how on earth we'll manage with just two of us." She turned back to Sloane again.

"Thanks for your help today. We really needed it, and you did great."

"You're welcome. I had fun here. You know, I'm not working right now, so if you really need someone, I can always come in and work after I get back from the honeymoon."

"You sure this kind of work wouldn't be beneath you? I thought you were going to try and do something with your degree."

"It's not beneath me, and I thought I might put off getting an office job for a while. Of course, if you'd rather hire someone who's not family, I'd understand."

Moira looked at Jaye, who shrugged.

"Okay, we'd love to have you, but you have to treat this like a real job, okay. I can't have you taking off to go to lunch with your girlfriends. You saw what it can get like in here."

"Of course it's not like this everyday, but when it is ... whammo!" Jaye added.

"Have a little faith in me, okay." She pouted. "I can work. I can take it seriously. I know how much this place means to you."

"Okay, it's a deal. Today's Friday, so be here at 8:30 Monday morning, okay?"

"Yes, boss," Sloane said, grinning. She was about to leave when she turned back. "Oh, and by the way."

"Yeah."

"You don't have to worry about putting up anyone for the wedding. Martin and I figured it out."

"Oh ... I had almost forgotten about that. That's great; I really didn't know where I was going to put them."

"Yeah, Martin thought that would be a problem. Bye then girls, today was fun."

And she disappeared out the door.

Jaye was just finishing wiping down tables and counters in the front. She walked over and slung an arm around her friend.

"Where is the Sloane we know, and what happened to her?" She was half joking.

"I dunno, but I think I like this side of her."

"Me too, she's much easier to get along with." They giggled a little. "Ah! Your man cometh."

Out the window they could see Jack getting out of his car.

"Got any special plans tonight?" Jaye asked, wiggling her hips suggestively.

Moira swatted her on the bum. "Yes, as a matter of fact, we're going to spend some more time with his dad. I think he's not long for this world."

"Oh, sorry."

"Not to worry. I actually like spending time there, Kevin is a really gentle soul. He makes you feel like he's known you forever."

"Sounds nice, too bad he's so sick."

"I know. I wish I could have known him longer."

"Well, you're getting to know him now. That's pretty big of Jack to include you like that."

"Actually, it was Kevin's idea."

Jack knocked on the glass front window, and Moira went to let him in. He greeted her with a kiss and then said hello to Jaye.

"I don't know what you ladies are doing, but half the staff in my office had your take away boxes sitting on their desks today."

"Hmm, yes, I was going to ask you about that. Any chance you've been talking us up at work?"

"Who, me?" Jack asked, but his twinkling eyes betrayed him. "Ready to go?"

"Absolutely. Jaye, you still okay with locking up?"

"Yeah, go, go, and get out of here."

So Jack and Moira left as Jaye waved to them from

the window. She watched them drive down the street and turn around to head back to the bridge to the business side of town, shaking her head. When they were out of sight, she picked up the phone and called her own boyfriend. It was good to have someone to go home to.

***

Ironically, Moira and Jack didn't spend much time with Kevin that night. He was slipping quickly, and his moments of lucid conversation were becoming fewer and farther between. It was apparent that he knew they were there; occasionally he would open an eye and smile at the young couple, sometimes he would reach up and take the hand of one of them. They stayed for an hour. Moira watered the violets, and Jack tidied a few of the photos and books. Vicky popped in to check on Kevin and told Jack that he really wasn't even eating anymore. They had kept the feeding tube out at his request, but he could hardly manage more then a small drink or spoonful of broth during the day. Mainly, it was the IV that was giving him his nutrition. Jack shook his head sadly, but was reassured that this would not be the case for much longer. Like an old watercolour painting, Kevin was simply starting to fade away.

Moira smoothed Kevin's wrinkled brow and planted a soft kiss on his forehead, to which he mumbled briefly, before they left for the night. They went to Jack's apartment, where Moira made them a light dinner and Jack opened a bottle of wine from his stores. They talked about the store, they talked about work. They kept themselves distracted with conversations about things that they could control and did not refer to the gentle man slipping away from the world. Jack asked Moira to stay the night, but she declined, still having a business to run the next day and, with the amount of sales she had been making lately, it was really important to be in the kitchen early.

"Okay, that makes sense. Don't worry, I'm not trying to pressure you or anything like that."

"Of course I know that! But I do have to be in really early."

"Do you need help?"

"Why Jack, are you thinking of taking on a second job?" she teased him.

"Not at all, but if you're going to be so busy, wouldn't you like a second pair of hands?"

"I'd love them, especially if they're yours. Throw some stuff in a bag and come with me."

Jack didn't wait to be asked twice. He threw a few old clothes in a dark brown carry-all along with his toothbrush and deodorant. Then he escorted his lovely lady out of the apartment and to the car.

By now the sun was just hovering on the horizon, and the myriad of clouds that had been permanent fixtures of the sky for the last few days had burnt a deep purple, looking at once both angry and bruised.

"Think we're going to get rain again?" Moira mused to Jack as they neared her place.

"Mmmm, I hope so." He brushed her hair from her cheek and winked at her.

They let themselves into the apartment and collapsed into Moira's soft bed, falling asleep quickly, their arms wrapped around one another, their bodies pressed against one another.

***

Moira and Jack awoke feeling silly, both of them with a serious case of the giggles. They bumped into one another as they bounded around throwing on clothes, brushing their teeth, pausing for deep kisses and long lingering caresses. Jack went into Moira's kitchen and made them both a quick egg scramble and toast, which they ate straight from the frying pan, balancing large golden clusters of fluffy egg on forks. They went downstairs right at 8:30, just in time for Jaye to join them. She said nothing about Jack's presence, but when he was busy putting on the coffee, she nodded at her friend and mouthed a quick *oh yeah* at her, causing Moira's giggles to erupt once again. The three of them darted around the kitchen together, laughing, tossing the odd handful of flour or powdered sugar at each other, then finally opened up for business at 10:00 to a lineup of at least eight people standing outside. Among the shoppers were the skeleton and her identically dressed plump friend, and none other than Jack's boss, Evan.

Jack smiled sheepishly as Evan came in the store.

"Gee whiz, Jack, I just gave you a promotion. Don't tell me you're still not earning enough?"

"Yeah, but I thought I'd just give Moira a hand for the day." He held up a finger and darted his head around the corner to the kitchen and beckoned to Moira, who was kneading bread dough on the marble top.

"Can you come out for a minute?" he asked her.

"Sure, one sec." She wiped off her floury hands on her apron and joined Jack at the front counter.

"Evan, this brilliant woman is Moira Ryan. Moira, my boss, Evan Derbis."

She extended a still slightly white hand to him. "Great to meet you," she said.

"Likewise. You know, my wife and I have been coming here for a few months. She really loves your marble rye bread. But it was Jack here who persuaded me to try some of your sweeter stuff. He was right. Your strawberry mousse cakes are the best thing I've had in ages."

"Well, thank you. I don't know what to say. Why don't you take your wife some of my twelve grain brown bread, with my compliments? If she likes the rye, she'll really enjoy this one too. I've just added it to the repertoire."

"That's very kind of you. I'd like to ask you to do something for me, though. It's my wife's birthday in about three and a half weeks. Would you make her cake? There will be about fifty or so people at the party, and I've already asked Jack to invite you to come along."

Jack slapped his forehead.

"Oops, I forgot." He reached out and took Moira's

hand. "Moira, would you be so kind as to accompany me to a party next month? I'd be so grateful."

"I'd be delighted," Moira said to him, and then turning to Evan, added, "I'd be delighted to do her cake, too. Just let me know what flavor and design, and I'll bring it with me."

"Well, that's just great!" Evan beamed. "I'll drop off some specifications next week, if that's okay. I want to get some ideas from my wife first."

"Perfect. Or you can just email me with them," Moira said, handing him a business card from the stack beside the till.

"Will do," Evan told her as she slipped back into the kitchen to continue working. "Wow, Jack, she's just beautiful. How on earth did you wind up conning her into dating you?"

"I have no idea! I'm just happy she still wants me sticking around. Now, what else can I get for you?"

Evan took his time selecting various items from the assortment available while Jaye continued to serve the other customers. Finally, Jack laid out all his choices for Jaye to ring them up, letting her know quietly that Moira had offered the loaf of bread as a gift. Jaye gave Evan a bright smile as she was introduced by Jack, shaking his hand energetically and thrusting a large cookie into his hand, with her own compliments, of course.

By the end of the day, the stock was still kept up, and the three were tired, but satisfied. They decided that once Moira and Jack had checked in on Kevin, they would meet Jaye and her boyfriend at La Cantina for dinner together. Moira put in a quick call to her mother's house before they left, just to check in.

"Hello?" It was Sloane who answered the phone. Moira could hear several voices in the background.

"Hi Sloane ... what are you doing there?"

"I decided that I really didn't want a stagette night out after all. I mean, Martin's not really having a stag night, just a night of cards at the house with his cousins and a few friends, so the girls and I decided to come here and hang out and watch movies and stuff with Mom and Nana. Want to join us? I was about to call you soon, anyway."

"I would, but I'm going to the hospice with Jack to see his dad and then out to dinner with Jaye and her man. Do you want me to reschedule? I mean, is this like a wedding party kind of thing?"

"Well, I could be a bitch and say yes, but I know you said Jack's dad isn't well, and that's more important. Go, have a good time. We'll be just fine here."

"Okay then."

"Oh, did you want Mom or anything?"

"No, just checking in, really."

"'Kay, no problem. We're good, go have a good time. Say hi to Jack."

"Okay then. See you later."

"Byeeee!" She trilled, and then hung up the phone.

Moira put her phone back in its cradle. "Sloane says hi," she told Jack.

"Oh, that was nice. You okay?"

"Yeah. She's having her girls' night out at the house tonight."

"Do you want to cancel dinner? I haven't called my man yet," Jaye offered.

"No, no. She said it's fine. She's being really ... nice lately."

"I know, I picked up on that too. Weird. You think she's feeling bad about that fight the other night? Or nervous about the wedding?"

"Whatever it is, I'm not going to question it. It's too nice to have a decent conversation with her."

"Shall we, then?" Jack asked, holding out his arm for her.

"We shall," she said, looping her own arm through his and heading out the door.

Chapter Twenty-Five

Kevin was awake when they arrived at his door. His features crackled into a smile when he saw them coming in to the room. He had none of the wires and tubes left on him except for the IV.

"Dad, where's the heart monitor?"

"Gone, they took it off this morning." He seemed highly proud. "I don't want it anymore. I'm sure they'll figure out when I die, they don't need an absence of a beep beep sound to let them know."

His breathing patterns had changed yet again. There was a deep *Hunhhh* sound coming from his chest and mouth now as he tried to get out the sentence. His eyes had deep black circles around them; his mouth was dried and cracked. The rest of his face appeared almost swollen, bumpy, and had a pale yellow tinge to it, as if someone had opened up the side of his face and thrust in lumps of congealed butter. Nothing though, not one of these physical changes could mar the sparkle in his gaze and the calm of his demeanor. Moira was sure that throughout history there had been world leaders, spiritual figureheads and even kings who had not remained nearly so calm in the face of mortality.

"I'm glad to see you both. It does my heart good to see you looking so happy." Kevin forced a weak smile. "Tell me, Moira, have you thought anymore about our conversation? I'd hate to think you were spending all this time with my son and still didn't believe in love."

Moira shook her head with a smile.

"I've thought about it. You made a lot of sense, I guess it was just hard for me to let go of some of the hurts in my life and still see Jack for himself."

"Well then, you and he have something in common. Jack has had trouble letting go too, but I hope that it's becoming easier for him."

"It is, Dad," Jack put in. "Now, are you sure you don't want the heart monitor on, considering that small heart attack? And didn't you tell me you had developed an arrhythmia? It's not really *treatment*, is it? I know it would make me feel better." He was trying to make his voice sound light, take the seriousness from the situation, but Kevin put his hand out and held his son, his face moving in thoughtful motions, searching for the right way to say what he must.

"My Jack. Let us now drop the pretenses. I've only been hanging on to see you happy, so that I can take it with me when I go, and your mother will know you're going to be okay. It hasn't been me at all getting treatments all this time, it's been you. And now you have Moira." He turned to her with a look of pure love and serenity. "You have each other. I can go now. I've stopped holding on."

With those words, Kevin gave Jack's hand a feeble squeeze and drifted back to sleep. Jack stood stunned, motionless. A distinct understanding came over both him and Moira in that moment. With a nod to Jack, Moira quietly slipped outside to make a phone call, and Jack called Vicky into the room.

Within ten minutes, Moira had gotten Jaye on the phone and managed to cancel their dinner plans, and Jack had gotten his father and his few possessions of books and photos moved to a slightly larger room with a second bed in it. He met Moira in the hall and walked her down to the new room—the last room. It was far more cheerful and peaceful than his original room on the ward. There were lovely lamps set on dark wood tables in the corners of the room, an oversized chair full of pillows, and a second bed against the wall, right beside where Kevin's had been wheeled. Vicky offered to bring them in some tea, which they gratefully accepted, and then the two snuggled up together in the chair reading through some of Kevin's favourite books and poetry. Some they read out loud, to each other and to the sleeping ears in the bed, and some they read quietly to themselves. They stayed all night, and all through Sunday, attending Kevin when he stirred, but mostly just watching him and keeping him company.

***

In years to come, when Jack looked back on that Sunday evening that his father finally passed away, he did not remember it as a sequence of events or a series of breakdowns in an old and ravaged body. The things that stayed with him and gave grace to the last living moments of the only father he had ever known were fleeting, A twitch of the weathered old hand in his. The smell of violets that had been placed on the windowsill a few nights previous, a gift from Moira. The tears in her eyes, the taste of salt in his mouth when his own tears fell unattended down his face. The sound of the same orderly who had annoyed him only weeks before shuffling into the room and then out again, silently. The slow descent of breathing, the hollowness of his father's face and chest.

These were the stuff of his memories, the legacy of his father's last moments on this earth, but they did not make him sad. He was grateful that he had been a part of it all, that the relationship, which had been strained at best of times, had finally come full circle and had reached a plateau of utmost peace and love. No, it would not be the slow replay of a series of events that made Jack think of his father, but the smell of violets, Yeats on the bookshelf, and the green eyes of his mother in the photograph at his bedside, reflected in the eyes of Moira, sitting quietly by his side and allowing it all to sink peacefully into the night.

Chapter Twenty-Six

Monday morning was a blur to both Moira and Jack. They moved on autopilot. The speed with which Kevin's life had ended had left them feeling drained and tired. Moira closed the shop, placing a black outlined notice in the window that claimed a death in the family, and she and Jaye moved quietly around in the kitchen making food while Jack used the phone in Moira's apartment upstairs to call work and make the last of the arrangements for the funeral, which would take place the next day, since the details had been worked out ages ago. The two women downstairs gave him his space, allowing him to come down when he was ready.

"You were really right there when it happened?" Jaye quietly asked her friend, her hands deep in bread dough.

"Yeah, but it wasn't really sad, it was so peaceful. It was like he just decided to let go, and fell into a really deep sleep."

"Wasn't it weird?"

"No, not really. The staff there was so kind. They brought us in some food from time to time, but just let us stay with him. Sometimes we slept a little, but mostly we just talked and read and held his hand. I just wish I had gotten to know him better, he seemed like a really amazing person."

"When's the funeral?"

"Tomorrow. Kevin was so organized. He's had this planned for weeks, maybe months. We'll stay closed until Wednesday."

"Of course." Jaye was more reserved than Moira had ever seen her before. "I admire you. I don't think I could have done that, sit with a man as he dies. You really have an amazing connection with Jack, don't you? I mean, you two just seem to ... fit."

"It's strange, I thought everything was going so fast, but now it feels like I've known him forever."

Jaye came over and hugged her friend. "It's good to see you like this. I'm happy for you both that you found each other."

Jack came into the kitchen just then and smiled at the women locked in a floury embrace.

"It's all set," he said. "I just spoke with the funeral director. Apparently Dad told them a month ago that this was coming soon. We're ready to go for tomorrow. The hospice has already released his body."

Moira let go of Jaye and put her arms around Jack now.

"Anything I can do?"

He kissed her on the nose. "I need to go home and change, have a shower. I'd really like you to stay with me, if you don't mind."

"Of course not, we're just filling time here, really. Let me grab a few things from upstairs and we'll go, okay?"

"Sure."

Moira left, and they heard her feet moving lightly up the stairs, and then back and forth above them. Jaye tentatively spoke.

"Jack?"

"Yes, Jaye."

"I'm really sorry for your loss. God, that sounds so rehearsed, but I do mean it. I'm so sorry."

"It's okay. It's kind of a relief to know he's not in pain anymore."

"Um, I called Moira's mum this morning, I hope you don't mind."

"No, thank you."

Jaye gave him an awkward hug, and then stepped

back again.

"Listen, uh, Moira's mum wanted you to know, if you need a space for it after the funeral, she's more than happy to let you bring people back to her house. An apartment really isn't built for it, you know."

Jack frowned for a moment, looking slightly confused. "Do you think I need to do that?"

"Sure, people do it all the time. A chance to pay their respects without hanging around a funeral home, feeling all formal. That's what we're making bread for—if you want it, that is. We'll put out some food and stuff. You don't have to worry about organizing it."

"That's so kind. Please tell her I'd be happy to accept."

Jaye went back to work sectioning out loaves as Moira re-joined them in the kitchen. She gave Moira a slight nod, to let her know that things were fine and the plans were in place, and then hugged them both goodbye as they left and walked in the dark and heavy looking morning out to the car, then drove away.

***

In the apartment, Jack showered and changed while Moira made them some lunch. It was good that they had come back, since the phone rang constantly with last minute arrangements, calls from the local florist wanting to know where to send flowers, co-workers of Jack's and finally Angela, calling to confirm that they would host a lunch in Kevin's honour the following afternoon. Moira sifted through the box they had brought from the hospice and put Kevin's books and pictures in places of honour in Jack's apartment. By evening, when the sky looked as though it was fit to burst into storm at any moment, they finally lay down on Jack's bed. Moira pointed to the window.

"Even the sky looks like it wants to cry," she said quietly, but Jack had already fallen asleep, fully clothed on the bed. Moira snuggled into his body and drew a shaky breath, saying a silent goodbye and thank you to the man who had been taken away so quickly.

***

The morning of the funeral was unusually bright, no hint of the rain that threatened on the horizon the night before. Moira and Jack lay on the bed, still fully clothed, hands clasped and staring with wonder at the sight of the sun poking through the few remaining leaves on the tree outside of his bedroom window. They moved as if in slow motion, first with small cat-like stretches, and then finally off of the bed and around the apartment, making coffee, gathering papers and cups laid strewn throughout the rooms from the last few days. Although they barely uttered a word out loud, it was as though their communication had evolved on its own, each motion had an interpretation, each blink asked a question, and each smile answered. Eventually, the inevitabilities of the day broke upon them, and the spell of the long night dissolved into the reality of the day. As the phone shrieked from its cradle and Moira made to answer it, Jack gently caressed her elbow for the briefest of moments before heading off to the bathroom to shower.

"Hello?"

"What time, honey?" Sloane was being remarkably calm.

"Eleven. Thanks, Sloane."

"Sure. See you then."

Through all of the fighting, through all of the demands of the wedding and the layered years of guilt, jealousy and frustration, Sloane gave her just what she needed this one time. Peace. Understanding.

By the time Jack emerged from the shower, Moira had already changed into the clothes that she planned to wear and had brought with her the night before. A black non-descript dress with a bright yellow sash tied around her waist.

At eleven o'clock, the doors of the funeral home were opened, and Jack tightly held Moira's hand in his, marking out her place at his side. He hadn't expected much of a crowd, not really. Most of his relatives were already gone on or lived too far away to make the trek on such short notice, but the sight of the staff of the hospice making their way up the stairs was an unexpected and pleasant one. He shook their hands, he accepted their words of regret.

By the time at least ten of them had filed in, Jack had stopped looking at their faces. He merely saw a myriad of blurred dark colours swish past him, droning a melodic whisper of condolence. Finally he felt the light tug of Moira's hand steering him towards the front, where the resting figure of his father laid in a box in a room, looked down on by his beloved picture of his wife, which Moira had brought in and clutching his book of Yeats. *He looks happy,* Jack thought, and he sat to await his turn to say goodbye.

One of the staff of the home stood at a small podium at the front of the room.

"Welcome, friends. We have come here today not to mourn, but to celebrate the life of a great man, Mr. Kevin Wallace.

"Kevin was a gentle and kind soul. Most of you may remember him from the last months of his life, and think of him as a man in a bed, bound to his illness, but I encourage you to think upon a different Kevin. He was a husband, a father and a friend. I met with Kevin several times in the last months of his life. What a blessing he considered it to have time to prepare, time to plan and time to say goodbye to those he loved. I would like to read for you some words of his choosing."

He cleared his throat and opened a book that lay on the podium.

"This is 'The Everlasting Voice', by William Butler Yeats."

O sweet everlasting Voices, be still;
Go to the guards of the heavenly fold

And bid them wander obeying your will,
Flame under flame, till Time be no more;
Have you not heard that our hearts are old,
That you call in birds, in wind on the hill,
In shaken boughs, in tide on the shore?
O sweet everlasting Voices, be still.

He paused once more, giving a slight cough and adjusting his glasses before replacing his book. "We don't come here today with anything other than pure spirit, and a need to acknowledge the life of a man who has touched our own lives in his own way. We come here to support Jack, Kevin's son, as he suffers through the loss of a parent. We come to say our final goodbyes to our friend. We come to know that there is a part of life that goes on after death. Kevin has left that best part of himself with all of you. I would now like to invite two people to speak to you about the man that they knew and loved." He lifted his chin, as if to physically indicate the arrival of someone.

Sure enough, from a few rows behind Jack, a man stood and made his way to the podium. As he nudged his way gently past the people in the room, his eyes locked for a moment on Jack's, and then on the casket.

"Good morning everyone, my name is Brian Teller. I doubt that any of you here today would remember me, but I was one of Kevin's first employees at the gas station, and, I hope, a good friend for many years after I moved on."

He looked down at where Jack and Moira sat, smiling at them. Jack's mind was reeling. He barely remembered the men who had worked for his father all those years ago when the station was just getting started. Nothing about this man seemed familiar. He gave Moira a quizzical look and a small shrug. Then it dawned on him, the man in the hospice going over papers with his father just a week or so ago—*is that all it was??*—who had seemed so friendly, so pleased to meet him. This was the same man. He offered a slight smile and listened to his story with awe.

"When I was seventeen, I tried to rob Kevin. I was young and stupid and, like most seventeen year olds, ignorant of the consequences of my actions and their effect on those around me. I wanted to run away, and I needed money, so I walked in to that little station and told Kevin to hand over the contents of the till while I held my fingers in my pocket to look like I had a weapon." He paused and gave a sad smile. "I'm not proud that I did this, but I'm not sorry either. Because meeting Kevin was one of the best things in my life. He didn't seem scared, he just asked me why. Kevin had this way of staring at you that made you think he could really *see* you. I walked out of there two hours later without the cash grab I had been going for, but a job instead. He said to me, 'Why take my money and run, knowing that it will run out sooner or later? Why run from whatever is making you so unhappy, knowing that you'll have to deal with it sooner or later? Why not stay, work for me and get yourself a way up, not a way out?' So I did.

"I worked at Kevin's station for two years while I finished high school. He helped me to understand some of my classes better, and eventually helped me get into college. All the while he wrote to me, and I to him. He bragged to me about his son, and opened my eyes to possibilities that I would never have realized if I had just taken cash that day and taken off. He even came to my graduation from college and finally from law school, and helped me get my first post in a good firm in Chicago, where an old friend of his worked."

Brian looked straight at Jack.

"Kevin was my teacher, and my friend. Now I am trying to give back like he did. I work with a lot of youth in trouble, and my favourite clients are the ones who are so like I was, a little scared, a little lost, and full of all the potential of the world. The lessons that he gave to me in that little station down the road are the ones that will stick with me for the rest of my life, and I will always be thankful that I knew him."

Brian left the podium and met Jack as he stood up to take his turn at the front of the room. He pressed a piece of paper into Jack's hand, hugged him warmly, and made his way back to his seat.

Jack finally stood now, facing the assemblage and nervously twitching the inside seam of his pocket. He glanced at Moira, who nodded at him and smiled slightly through her wet cheeks. As his eyes made their way through the faces before him, he noticed Evan, Rebecca, and a few others from his office, several unfamiliar faces and, in the back, Sloane, Martin, Angela, and Siobhan in her wheelchair. His face snapped back to Moira, and he spoke.

"My father is the greatest man I know. There were a lot of years when I would never have said that. When my mother died, we began a ritual of pushing each other away that took ages to repair. We all have our own ways of coping with loss, but something happened to my dad. He found a way of being still and sound that I have yet to discover, that all of us would be so lucky to find. By the time they told him he was sick, he was the most completely whole person I knew. Maybe that's why his outlook was so good, even when the news from the doctors continued not to be. The sicker he got, the more he seemed able to connect with the people around him. I was jealous of his ability to do that, often to the point of frustration and anger, but he never wavered in his optimism. I truly believe that his great love for my mother was what saw him through these last few months. I will miss him terribly, as I miss her, but I'm glad they are finally together again." He turned his head slightly to towards the coffin on his left and uttered a deep shaking breath. "Goodbye, Dad."

Five more members of the staff joined the man at the front, gently closed the casket and hoisted it up onto their shoulders, making their way down past the pews with Jack and Moira walking stony faced behind them. Kevin's only musical request was that they play a song that had come out some years after his beloved wife had died, but one that he was sure that she would have loved, that repre-

sented what they had together and how they dealt with the
hand that fate had played out for them. So, as the proces-
sion made its way down the aisle, the soft sounds of Beth
Nielsen Chapman filtered through the speakers singing
"Sand and Water". Jack didn't even check his tears as the
words filled him with grief and love.

>*All alone I didn't like the feeling*
>*All alone I sat and cried*
>*All alone I had to find some meaning*
>*In the center of the pain I felt inside*
>
>*All alone I came into this world*
>*All alone I will someday die*
>*Solid stone is just sand and water, baby*
>*Sand and water, and a million years gone by*
>
>*I will see you in the light of a thousand suns*
>*I will hear you in the sound of the waves*
>*I will know you when I come, as we all will come*
>*Through the doors beyond the grave*
>
>*All alone I heal this heart of sorrow*
>*All alone I raise this child*
>*Flesh and bone, he's just*
>*Bursting towards tomorrow*
>*And his laughter fills my world and wears your smile*
>
>*I will see you in the light of a thousand suns*
>*I will hear you in the sound of the waves*
>*I will know you when I come, as we all will come*
>*Through the doors beyond the grave*
>
>*All alone I came into this world*
>*All alone I will someday die*
>*Solid stone is just sand and water, baby*
>*Sand and water and a million years gone by*

Chapter Twenty-Seven

At the cemetery, the small group of people huddled around as Jack leaned over and plucked a single flower from the arrangement on the coffin and watched as it was slowly lowered into the ground.

Finally, Jack faced the group that had joined him and announced that there would be a light lunch provided at Angela and Siobhan's house on Marksam if they would all care to join them.

Evan and Rebecca and a few of the other office members that had come all gathered together in one car and waited for Angela and her family to pull out and lead the way. Several of the staff from the hospice followed in their cars, but Jack hung back with Moira. They stood together, holding hands, Jack twisting the flower in his free hand and staring at the fresh ground in front of him. "It was beautiful," Moira said to him.

"Exactly what he would have wanted," Jack agreed.

Then Jack pointed to the headstone next to Kevin's fresh grave. "That's my mother," he told her, quietly.

Moira took a few steps over to the side and sat down beside the headstone that had the picture of an angel on it.

Lucy Helen Wallace
1956-1993
Beloved wife and mother
She has found her wings and gone home too soon.

Moira ran her hand over the top and down the side of the smooth pale grey stone. It really was unfair that she had been taken the way she was, torn from her family and from her only child.

"It's nice to meet you," she whispered.

Moira stood and wiped the dirt from her dress and, taking Jack's hand, walked away from the stone and the fresh dirt in a mound and back to his car. Jack held open her door but before she could get in, he held her tight and buried his face in her lovely, dark hair.

"Thank you for being with me."

He kissed her and helped her in, tucking the front of her dress away from the doorframe. Then they too left for the house.

All along the sides of the road by the beautiful house there were cars. If Jack had thought that this would not be called for, he had been sorely wrong. Inside had gathered almost everyone that had been at the funeral, including Brian, the man whom Kevin had mentored and who had told such a shocking yet stirring story at the funeral. He was standing in a corner holding a cup of tea and, presumably, talking law with Martin while Sloane flitted around with a plate of sandwiches in one hand and a stack of napkins in the other. Vicky was holding court with Siobhan and a group of staff from the hospice, telling stories of how Kevin liked to tease and joke with them, how he referred to his IV's and tubes as "modern day bondage" and of the time that he had left a handwritten sign on his privates that said "empty me" when she had come in the middle of the night to check on a catheter he had in. Jack was pleased to see the others nodding in agreement over Kevin's cheerful and playful disposition while wiping away tears of mirth from their cheeks.

Jack went to find Evan and thank him personally for taking the time to come while Moira headed into her mother's bright kitchen to offer her help, and to thank her for arranging all of this for Jack. She was blown away by the sight of the kitchen. There were large bowls on the table filled with potato salad, green salad and macaroni. There were at least three large plates heaped with sliced sandwiches of various fillings, a large tray with veggies and dip and an assortment of juices, wines and tea and coffee laid out.

"You've been busy," she said to her mother, who was placing a stack of plates on the end of the table.

"Just a trifle, hand me those cups there, dear," she said, pointing to the stack on the counter behind her with a pinky finger.

"Jack really appreciates this."

"Good. Gives me something to do, since your sister hired a caterer to do the wedding. Besides, people need food to grieve. It's how nature works. Gives them something to do with their hands."

Moira peeked back into the other room and noticed that people did indeed seem at ease with a plate of food in front of them. Trust her mother to understand that. Jack was shaking hands with Martin as Sloane introduced them. The people from his work were starting to leave. Brian, the man who had spoken before Jack at the funeral, was saying something that made Jack's nose wrinkle up. Moira left the kitchen and went to see if everything was alright.

" ... before I leave," he was saying. Jack was nodding his head.

"Is everything okay, Jack?" she asked him.

"Yes, it's fine. Brian has to leave to get back to Chicago soon, but he wants to go over some stuff with me first. Is there somewhere we can go to talk alone?"

"Sure, you can use the library. Let me show you." She led the way through the remaining people to the room at the back of the house. She made to leave, once she had shown them in through the door, but Jack held her hand and motioned for her to stay.

"Well," Brian cleared his throat. "I just have a few things, really. But first, I just want to tell you that I meant every word that I said today. I really admired your father, Jack. He was like a second father to me. If you ever need anything, don't hesitate to ask. That's why I gave you my contact information earlier. I want to keep in touch with you as your father did with me."

"That's very kind," Jack said, unsure of how to properly appreciate such a gesture at this point.

Brian lifted his briefcase onto the desk by the large window, popped it open and pulled out a folder with the name "Kevin Wallace" written across the top. He handed Jack some of the papers.

"These are your records, as per your dad's will. All the proceeds from the sale of his house and his business will be transferred to you by the end of the week. It just takes a few days to release the funds from the trust he had set up. If you take a look at the bottom of page two ... " he waited while Jack flipped it over, "you'll notice that you are about to become a fairly wealthy man. Kev did well when he sold that place."

Jack's eyes bulged at the figure staring up from the bottom of the assets page. In a few short days, he would be a millionaire. He could hardly cope with the idea.

If Brian noticed this, he made no mention, nor did Moira, who was trying hard not to peek so as to give Jack some privacy in the moment.

"Next, a portion of the trust has been activated to tend to the grave sights of both your parents. I assume you have no problem with that?" Jack shook his head no.

"Finally, here is the key to the storage unit where your father kept the rest of his books and a few of the pieces of furniture from his residence. This passes to you now, and you can do what you choose with it. That's all." He handed Jack the key and a few more papers, then put the rest of the folder away and snapped the briefcase shut again. Then he gave Jack a slightly awkward hug and turned the door handle.

"Jack, it was a pleasure to finally meet you, and you Moira. Please stay in touch."

They watched him walk back down the narrow hall to the kitchen, where he thanked Angela for her hospitality and left through the kitchen side door, then headed out to the main rooms again to thank those who had come out.

Chapter Twenty-Eight

"What's up for you tomorrow now?" Siobhan asked later, when the guests had left and none but Moira's family, Martin and Jack still remained. They were all seated in the kitchen, picking from the rest of the food for their dinner.

"Back to work," Jack said with a small shrug.

"Me too," said Moira.

Sloane was being remarkably quiet. She was sitting poking a plate full of potato salad with her fork, but not eating any. Martin was helping Angela gather dishes to be washed.

"I really should get some sleep," Jack said as he stood to stretch. "Angela, thank you again for lending me your house. I truly appreciate it."

"Nonsense," she intoned. "Just make sure you make a habit of coming back."

"Of course I will. You'll be sick of me in no time," he said. Siobhan chuckled and winked at Moira.

"So we'll see you on Friday, then." It was a command, not a question.

"Um, sure."

"For the rehearsal dinner, silly. I assume you're Moira's guest," Siobhan said.

"Actually, I hadn't officially asked him yet," said Moira. "But I'd really love you to be here with me. If you're okay with that."

"Yeah, if your sister doesn't mind." He looked at Sloane.

"Well, she needed a date anyway. We just assumed you were coming, didn't we Martin?" Sloane said. Martin nodded at him.

"Then that's settled." Siobhan dusted her hands off. "Now, go get some sleep."

They made the rounds, hugging everyone, and then clambered off into the car once again. When Jack pulled up outside the store, he put his arm on Moira for a minute before she could get out.

"I'm going to go home tonight. I need a couple of days to deal with this stuff," he said, pointing at the papers. "I'll call you tomorrow night."

"Okay." Moira was slightly disappointed that she wasn't going to see him right away, but decided to say nothing. Instead, she kissed him back when he pulled her in close to him and held him tightly for a moment.

"I love you," he said as she got out of the car.

"Me too."

She waved to him as he drove away and finally let herself in the back door and climbed the stairs to her little apartment, where she fell into a deep sleep almost immediately.

***

By the time Friday rolled around, Moira had only spoken to Jack twice on the phone. He sounded at once so tired and so harried that she chose to just go along and keep her nose to her own work instead of stressing over their relationship. The old her would have thought of a million reasons why Jack was so detached—lost interest, another woman, retreating into himself again now that he had lost the other parent—but the new her was more trusting and knew that whatever reason he had for keeping his distance was a good one, and that he would tell her when the time was right. Besides, the store was as busy as ever after, having been closed for two days for the funeral, and she barely had time to dwell on it. Not to mention the rapidly approaching wedding and the trickling arrival of long distance relatives of Martin's. The plan was for her to spend the night at her mother's house with Sloane after the dinner so that they could get ready for the wedding together in the morning. As she closed up the shop for the day and chatted with Jaye about the interviews they were setting up next weekend for some full-time counter help, Jack came bursting in the front door, looking a lot more like his old self.

"Hi!" she said, laughing as he crossed the shop in three easy strides and swept her up in a huge hug, planting kisses on her cheeks.

"I missed you this week, but just wait until I tell you my news," he said. "Hi, Jaye."

"Hello there, stranger. You look much better."

"I feel wonderful. Moira, what time do we have to be at your mother's house?"

She glanced at her watch. "Umm, in about three and a half minutes. We took a little longer than I expected closing up here tonight. Why?"

"I want to talk to you first. Do you have everything you need?"

"Nope, I have to go upstairs and get my bag for tonight. Come with me, we can talk while I get it."

He agreed and followed her out as she locked up while she went. Jaye went on her way, and the couple went up to the apartment.

As Moira rooted around in her bathroom, tossing deodorant and a toothbrush in a toiletries bag with a few other essential items, Jack sat on the bed, bouncing with enthusiasm.

"I'm sorry I haven't really talked to you since, well, you know. But you won't believe what's happened," he told her.

"What?"

"Well, I had just started to work on this project at work, for a high school that was fundraising for a new gym, and it occurred to me, I don't really need all the money my

289

father left me. It's too much for me. Then something Brian said at the funeral, about how my dad helped him to turn his life around, and how he now helps teenagers in trouble, it all just clicked."

He reached into his jacket pocket and pulled out a piece of folded paper.

"This is what I've been doing," he said, unfolding it for her to see. "I've been on the phone with the principal, the school board and Brian for the last three days and have finally arranged for it to be started."

Moira looked at the paper in Jack's hand. It was an architect's rendition of a large school gymnasium. On the front outside of the building in gleaming silver letters were the words "Kevin Wallace Memorial Gymnasium". She was at a loss for words. It was beautiful. Jack was so full of pride, he was fairly bursting.

"They're going to break ground next week. Brian's law firm is kicking in about half the cost as their personal donation. You wouldn't believe how it's all come together."

"Oh Jack, this is amazing! What a tremendous way to honour your father. I'm so happy for you!"

She bowled him over on the bed with a hug, whereupon Jack peppered her with kisses.

"I've missed you so much. Thanks for letting me have the space to sort through all this."

"I've missed you too," she said as their kisses grew deeper and more intense. Suddenly Moira sat up, just as his hand began to creep under her shirt.

"What?" Jack asked.

"We have to go. I almost forgot."

"Rats, just as I was starting to have fun. Okay, let's go."

They got up, and Moira straightened out her shirt as Jack playfully pinched her bottom. She threw her toiletries bag into a larger overnight bag that she had on the floor near the door of the bedroom, and they left.

The spirits were high at the Ryan residence. Sloane was in her best form, with all the attention focused on her.

She looked sweet and lovely in a white summer dress with pale pink flowers on it. Martin was beaming beside her in a crisp blue shirt and navy blue pants. Introductions were made back and forth between the two families, and Moira kept giggling as Siobhan was pretending to be deaf again, roaring out her hellos and asking for people's names over and over again. Everyone talked over everyone else, and Martin's father, a jovial man with a face like a boiled tomato, boomed over all the other voices to announce that he would like to make a speech.

"When our Martin came home and told us that he was going to marry this little spitfire after just having known her for a few months, my wife broke down into tears."

Martin's tiny, perfectly coiffed mother on his side gave him a swat with her napkin. "BILL!" she said, indignantly.

"Now, Adele, it's true!" he belted out. "We thought it was a big huge mistake. Crazy kids barely knew each other. The Mrs. and I here were together for six years before we got married, but kids today don't know how to wait for anything." He paused, evidently waiting for some laughter, but was met with some stunned, and slightly embarrassed looks.

"Anyway," he continued, "well, he brought home this lovely girl, and we couldn't have been more wrong. Sloane, we're proud that you're going to be a part of the family, and we hope that your marriage will be long and fruitful. Congratulations, kids!" Then he briefly raised his glass and downed it in one to the sound of "cheers" and "here here" from the other assembled guests. Then he leaned down and planted a wet kiss on Sloane's cheek with a loud smack. She grinned at him.

"We got the kids a little gift," he said, his voice now taking on a different tone. "I hope you like it." And he thrust an envelope into Sloane's hand. She opened it slowly, pulling Martin down by the sleeve beside her.

They stared together, neither saying a word. Finally, Martin spoke.

"It's a cruise. They've upgraded our honeymoon tickets to a first class cruise! Thanks Dad, Mom." Martin was clearly blown away.

"That's not even the best part!" Bill boomed again. "We're going too! We got the cabin right next door to you."

"Isn't that a hoot?" his mother gushed, and they rushed in to hug Sloane and Martin before they could utter one word on the subject.

Moira and Jack looked at each other and laughed. Whatever she thought of Sloane, or their fights and disagreements, one thing was for sure: she was going to have a handful with the new in-laws, and for that Moira didn't envy her even one little bit. They spent most of the night laughing, as Martin's friends and family told stories of him as a gawky child, and even produced pictures, and Angela stood to welcome Martin into her family, but broke into such tears that she was barely understood. Jack was loath to say goodnight, but left to get some sleep with a promise to see Moira at the wedding the next day.

Chapter Twenty-Nine

Sloane's wedding couldn't have gone more perfectly. Moira had decided that the hated bridesmaid's dresses were funny after all, Siobhan had abandoned the idea of the orange wig and looked simply lovely in her dark green suit with the white blouse, and Angela was stunning. Even Katie seemed to be sober and behaving herself, twittering around with Michelle as they waited for Sloane to make her appearance. When she did, she fairly took their breath away. The wedding dress, which had been kept largely a secret by Sloane and Lara the seamstress, was the most elegant creation they had ever seen. It was a heavy oyster satin with a deep V for the neckline and a plunging V in the back. The dress hung on her as if it had been custom made to hug her curves gently and gracefully before falling away from her hips, as if the very fabric were sighing. It fell ever so beautifully to her feet, floating around her as if just hovering over the ground. Her golden hair had been gathered by sparkling clips into loose curls piled on her head and falling in soft tendrils around her face. She wore sheer makeup, and light pink gloss on her lips, so that her face was bright, fresh and shining with a radiant glow. Sloane looked like a dream, and for the first time, Moira truly appreciated how lovely her sister was without a single feeling of jealousy.

She approached the waiting women slowly, making the most of her grand entrance.

"Well, Mom. Do I look okay?"

"I've never seen you look so well in your life," Angela told her.

"Nor I," Moira agreed.

"Martin's gonna shit himself," Siobhan put in.

"Let's hope not." Moira chuckled. Then she handed her sister her bouquet, and they made their way out to the waiting cars.

There were three cars to take them to the church for the wedding: one for Angela and Siobhan, with a wheelchair lift; Katie and Michelle to go in Katie's sports car; and finally an old fashioned Rolls Royce for Sloane and Moira to bring up the rear. They sat carefully in the back, Sloane trying not to crease her dress.

"I'm really happy for you," Moira told her. "Honestly. Martin's great."

"I'm nervous," Sloane confessed. "All that stuff you said about me needing people to take care of me, what if I can't take care of Martin? What if you were right, and I can't do it? I've never taken care of anyone. I don't want him to get fed up with me like you did."

Moira started to laugh, and once she got started, it was hard to stop.

"It's not funny, Moira!" Sloane said to her.

"No, you're right," she agreed, still laughing. "It's not funny. But I just can't believe that you of all people are having reservations because of something I said. You never listen to me! Besides, it's like you said, you're going to take care of each other. I've seen you together; you're going to be just fine."

"Really?"

"Of course you are. Martin loves you so much, anyone can see that."

"Kind of like how you are with Jack."

"Hmm?"

"I was watching you guys last night. You're so comfortable with each other. And he is always watching you with that smile on his face. And touching you. It's so obvious."

Moira blushed a little. "Is this how you felt when you first got together with Martin?"

"What, like giddy and silly and happy and with butterflies and just wanting to be with him every second of
every day?"

"Yeah, like that."

"I still feel like that. Isn't it wonderful?!"

"It's fantastic."

Now Sloane started to chuckle a little.

"What's so funny?" Moira asked her.

"This. We're finally having a conversation like normal sisters, and I'm about to get married!"

They looked at one another and burst out laughing.

"Kinda bad timing, isn't it?" Moira spluttered.

"I'm only getting married, not dropping off the face
of the earth. Besides, I thought you were going to let me
work at your store for a while? I'll still see you all the time."

"You were serious? Don't get me wrong, I'd love the
help, but you really think you can work for me?"

"I figure it's time for the shoe to be on the other
foot," Sloane said. The car stopped, and they embraced and
quickly wiped their eyes before getting out.

"Ready?" Moira asked her.

"Bleedin' right I am," she said, putting on Siobhan's
feisty accent and demeanour. And they linked arms and
marched up to the church doors, together.

They opened the doors just in time to see Jack wheel
Siobhan down the aisle to her place at the front. He winked
at Moira briefly as he caught her eye. Then Katie and Michelle were escorted by two of Martin's cousins. Finally,
Moira walked unaccompanied to the front and smiled as she
noticed that Martin was looking nervous. They turned to
face the back as the assemblage rose to see Angela escorting
her daughter down the aisle. Martin made no attempt to
hide the tears that sprang to his face at the sight of her
and, as they joined the group at the front, he planted a kiss
on Angela's cheek and whispered "Thank you" to her before
taking Sloane's hand and turning to the front.

***

Back at the house, under a huge white tent, they partied all night. The wedding cake was brought out by Moira with help from Wayne to oohs and ahhs from the group. It was a four-tiered cake in snow white icing and fairly covered in icing roses. It was one of the most beautiful cakes Moira had ever made, and as she adjusted its place on the table, she looked up to see her sister mouthing "I love you" to her, making her feel proud and wonderful. It wasn't until after midnight that she finally allowed Jack to take her home, where he stayed with her, laughing over the antics of Siobhan wheeling around the dance floor, the sight of her mother dancing with Martin's loud and boisterous father, and the many, many slow dances they had shared that night. They snuggled together on her couch, talking about the wedding and sharing a large slab of the cake and a bottle of champagne that Sloane and Martin had insisted they take with them, then finally collapsed together in Moira's bed, each marveling at how far they had come in such a short time, and how grateful they were to have found one another.

***

Sunday morning was crisp and clean, the bright blue sky deceptively inviting looking despite the now cool temperatures. When the family gathered together with Martin and Jack on the back porch overlooking the garden for brunch, they were all donning heavy cable knit sweaters or jackets. Not cool enough to be moved back into the house, mind. The last allure of the garden was simply too tempting to resist, with the leaves surrounding it just starting to turn, and the plants looking weathered and tired and bending over in their beds. However downtrodden the plants appeared, the spirits of the little party couldn't be higher. A cleaning crew had arrived and left already, taking with it all the evidence of the wedding, and the rental place had picked up the tent. Everyone was feeling brisk and happy from the celebrations of the night before, and Angela had managed to put together a rather fabulous feast for them on the wooden patio table. She was just about to add some champagne to the orange juice, when a slight wince from Sloane stopped her.

"What's the ma-matter, dear? Not in the mo-mood for mimosas?" Angela chuckled at her own joke.

"Weeeell, it's only 11 o'clock in the morning, right Martin? A little early, wouldn't you say?"

"I GET IT!" Siobhan howled, as Sloane blushed furiously. "By jaysus I get it! Sloane, what did you drink last night?"

"Um, sparkling grape juice," she replied, as Martin stood behind her and put his hands on her shoulders.

"I KNEW IT!" Siobhan was triumphant.

Moira and Jack exchanged looks with one another, but Angela still seemed to be trying to cop on to what was going on. Finally, slow recognition spread across her face. For a moment, everyone seemed frozen as the realization claimed them. It was Martin who broke the ice.

"How do you fancy becoming an Auntie, Moira?" he beamed at her as Angela and Siobhan started to cry.

"Auntie Moira has a nice ring to it," she said back to him.

Angela immediately went to hug her daughter and her new son. Siobhan wheeled her chair over as well, and the four of them crowded around each other in jubilation.

"I'm sorry we didn't say anything sooner. Call me old fashioned, but I wanted to wait until after my wedding to announce my pregnancy. Besides, it's only a month. Early days. But I'm sorry I've been so moody lately. Now you know why." She kissed her new husband, who was bending down with his hands wrapped around her shoulders. "We're just so excited."

They drifted off into a conversation about whether it was still a good idea to take the cruise or whether they should go somewhere else, and how they would break the news to Martin's family, as Martin explained that they already had the go-ahead from the doctor to travel. Jack leaned in to Moira, who was wearing a happy smile on her face.

"Auntie Moira, huh?"

"I like it, it fits me," she said to him.

He grinned back at her. She was so beautiful.

"How about Uncle Jack?"

"That sounds just wonderful," she exclaimed, planting a kiss on him and throwing her arms around his neck her, eyes dancing with laughter and joy.

"Are you kidding?" Siobhan said loudly. She was watching them from her side of the table. "That sounds fan-bloody-tastic."

www.ingramcontent.com/pod-product-compliance
Lightning Source LLC
Chambersburg PA
CBHW071900020726
47502CB00003B/839